Beneath These Walls

Shade Owens

ISBN: 978-1-990775-39-0

Published by Red Raven Publishing

Edited by Maggie Morris
https://www.indieeditor.ca

WARNING

Before you start reading, please be warned that this book contains the following:

- Domestic violence and abuse (physical, emotional, and psychological)
- Death/description of a dead body
- Swearing

PROLOGUE

At first, I'm convinced my house blew up from underneath me. The blast was so explosive that all sound has fled the room.

That is, until a pesky high-pitched sound sizzles in my ears, and I blink hard, trying to make sense of everything.

Then, I see it.

Blood.

It's everywhere—on my dining room floor, inside my trembling palms, and all over the gun.

But . . . how?

It wasn't supposed to end like this.

My legs give out from under me, and I drop to my knees. Slowly, I lose focus of my surroundings, and my kitchen cabinets warp into an abstract blur of whites and browns.

Despite the darkness closing in on me, I feel at peace . . . safe, for the first time in as long as I can remember.

Maybe this is exactly how everything was meant to end.

CHAPTER 1

The road ahead is long and seemingly never-ending.

One more hour.

My eyes flicker to my rearview mirror and at the only thing that has kept me alive this long—my boys.

Lucas plays on his iPad, the screen's reflection causing his ocean-blue eyes to gleam brighter than usual. A pair of cracked pink headphones sits over his ears as he bobs his head, moving along with the music of his game that sounds like the hum of insects from here.

The headphones used to be mine, but with how much he kept asking to borrow them, I decided to give them up.

My ex-husband, James, always gave me a hard time about it. Something about how Lucas isn't gay and shouldn't be wearing pink headphones.

They're headphones, for crying out loud.

I shudder at the thought of James and peer through the mucky rear window that looks as though it hasn't been washed in years.

He isn't following you, Alice. You did it right this time.

Lucas lets out a squeal and pumps a fist in the air, causing tingles to spread up my arms and into my white-knuckled hands around the steering wheel.

I want to tell him to keep it down, but how can I explain that to a seven-year-old?

We're running away from Dad, and Mom has a ton of anxiety right now. So can you please not make any sound? At all? Just keep quiet and don't move, either, because you might give me a heart attack.

I can't do that to him.

He has no idea what's going on. Well, maybe he does. Sometimes I don't give him enough credit. But right now, he looks happy, and the last thing I want to do is make this whole experience scary for him.

My job is to shield him from the darkness.

From James's darkness.

My gaze shifts to Grayson, my eldest. He sits with his head pressed against the back passenger window of my old Honda CR-V, gazing out into the cornfields as if he's lost everything in his life.

In a sense, he has.

His friends, his home.

At fourteen years old, his face has started to mature, and a dark peach fuzz clings to his upper lip. His hair, brown locks as dark as his father's, sits above his eyebrows as if intended to be used as a sun visor.

He's quiet, and the scowl on his face reminds me of James. A cold look that makes you wonder what's lingering beneath the surface.

Grayson isn't James. He's soft and caring.

I swallow hard.

So was James at one point.

I look away from Grayson, feeling guilty for comparing him to the monster of a man I married. I don't mean to, but the resemblance is uncanny. How am I *not* supposed to be reminded of James?

No, Grayson won't turn out like James because James isn't in the picture anymore. He's no longer an influence.

You can't combat genes.

I grit my teeth, feeling awful for having such thoughts. I shoot a quick glance back up at Grayson. His eyes roll toward me, but only for a second. With tight lips and flat-lidded eyes, he looks annoyed. Either that, or depressed.

I can't blame him.

He didn't want to leave.

We'd finally found ourselves a home, away from James, where we managed to stay for six months and live a relatively normal life.

Well, my boys did.

I spent the bit of money I had scavenging for used security cameras at the thrift store to install outside the house.

Thankfully, my neighbor Gary offered to help, saving me a hefty installation cost that a local electrician wanted to charge.

Deep down, I think my neighbor knew about my past. There was a sadness in his eyes every time he looked at me—pity, maybe, as if he wanted to save me.

But I'd already done that—I'd saved myself, and my boys. For a while, at least. There was always a chance that James would find us again. And I couldn't keep living like that.

Now, we've escaped for good.

CHAPTER 2

BEFORE

I tiptoe my way down the stairs, careful not to wake Lucas. After an hour of bedtime stories, he's finally out.

Grayson finishes his nighttime routine by brushing his teeth and turning off his tablet. He flashes me a smile, wraps his arms around me, and says, "Goodnight, Mom."

I bend forward to kiss the top of his head and rake my fingers through his hair. "Night, sweetheart. Sleep tight."

He walks away in his Spider-Man pajamas and hops up the stairs two steps at a time. I click my fingers and give him a stern look, warning him to keep quiet to avoid waking his baby brother.

He grimaces apologetically at me and climbs the rest of the staircase without a sound.

The moment he's gone, I step into the kitchen and start cleaning up supper's cold leftovers. Meat loaf, boiled carrots, and sliced cucumber. I've never been much of a cook—something James is inclined to mention every time we eat—but I get us by.

I crack open plastic containers and start shoving the cold food inside, suppressing the urge to slam things.

James was supposed to be home at five.

It's now seven thirty.

I know exactly how this will play out—he'll come home and sense my irritation, then turn it around on me and say that I'm not understanding the fact that he's the one who pays all the bills. That if he doesn't give his company his all, it'll crash, and we'll be left with no money.

He acts like he's the CEO of some multimillion-dollar

industry.

Sure, he's the owner of a small business that is doing exceptionally well, and I'm proud of him for that. However, being the owner gives him the ability to set his own hours and choose who he hires. Doesn't it? Why can't he hire someone to stay late so he doesn't have to?

It's probably not that simple. He oversees everything.

I gulp in a deep breath, trying to set aside my anger.

Maybe he's right.

Maybe I should be more appreciative that he's the sole provider for our family.

You both agreed to this. You both wanted this for Lucas, at least until he's old enough to go to daycare.

James promised he wouldn't be one of those dads—the kind that is never home and never makes it to events, like a child's soccer game. Despite his promise, James has missed his fair share of events since Lucas was born six months ago.

It's almost as though he doesn't want to be home.

I breathe in again, trying to push these thoughts away.

The worst part is that I can't stand stereotypical gender roles—I never wanted to be a stay-at-home mom responsible for all the cooking, cleaning, and child-raising. I wanted to run my own business, too. Be my own boss.

But James makes good money—way more than I made as a shelf stocker at a local grocery store. Maybe if I hadn't gotten knocked up at nineteen years old, things would be different.

I rinse a plate, trying to rid my mind of these thoughts. I wouldn't want a life without Grayson. He's my world, and so is Lucas.

When I turn to set the leftover containers in the fridge, the front door cracks open.

I shoot a glance at the oven's clock—7:49.

The anger returns.

Don't let it show, Alice. He's probably already had a long day, and you know how James has gotten when he's tired lately. He's become an asshole.

James has always been a bit of a grump. Back when he used to drink, alcohol exacerbated his anger tenfold. His drinking got so out of hand that it led to us breaking up. He'd gotten into a drunken rage one night and raised a fist at me before punching a hole in the wall.

But there had been a glimmer in his drunken eyes—a look that told me he *wanted* to hit me.

That had been the final straw.

We'd split for two years after that.

Two awful years of me raising Grayson by myself and James coming around now and then, begging for forgiveness only to lash out at me when I refused.

Then, he went quiet for six months, and when he returned, he was different.

He was sober.

And somehow, we reconnected, and things only got better from there. So much better that we got married when Grayson turned four.

But now that we have another child, it's as though he's regressing and going back to his old ways. To being an angry prick.

I can't live through that again.

I won't.

He walks in with heavy strides and tosses his overpriced Italian lambswool jacket on the sofa. I hate that thing—the price was preposterous, but James insisted it would help him land more clients. Something about looking the part.

What kinds of client is he even trying to attract?

Every time I ask him how business is going, he says it's going great. But I don't know anything about it. All I know is that he works from a rented space downtown with a group of five other employees and that they're going to achieve big things.

Really big things.

I wish he'd talk to me about what these *things* are. Maybe I have ideas, too.

But he says it'll go over my head. It's all about Java and coding that my brain wouldn't understand.

I glare at his stupid lambswool jacket, wishing he'd stop leaving it lying around like that.

I do my best to keep this place clean, and the last thing I need is for James to add to the clutter. When he catches me eyeballing the jacket, he sighs like an annoyed teenager and scoops it up.

I should say hi—hug him, even, but I can't bring myself to do it. I'm mad. I wish he'd put more effort into caring for our boys and me rather than thinking a paycheck is a replacement for his love.

It isn't.

"Hey, honey," he says, his voice grainy.

"Hey," I say back.

Make eye contact, for crying out loud. Put some effort into it, or he'll get even crankier.

I attempt a feeble smile, but nothing happens.

So instead, I return to what I was doing and finish cleaning the dishes. Rather than offer to help, James walks into the kitchen with a confident gait as if he just raked in millions of dollars in sales at the office, pries the fridge door open, and sticks his perfectly gelled head inside.

His beard is immaculately trimmed, and despite spending a whole day in the office, he smells good. Typically, I'd find this attractive. But right now, everything about him irks me.

"Where's supper?" he asks.

I clench my teeth, fighting the urge to tell him I'm not his housemaid or his mom and that supper isn't something I *have* to make for him.

"Top right shelf," I say coldly.

He reaches in, ignoring my tone of voice, and pulls out the leftover containers I placed there a few minutes ago.

He cracks them open, and his brown eyes roll up at me, a hint of a scowl threatening to darken his eyes even more. "This is all that's left?"

I can't hold back my anger any longer. "If it's not enough, make yourself something else."

He chucks the container on the counter, and I flinch. "Damn it, Alice. Why are you acting like this again? Why do you have to be so angry when I get home? For fuck's sake, I bust my ass all day to make sure my family has everything they need."

Here it is. His speech.

I cross my arms, consciously stopping my eyes from rolling.

"You have any idea how much money we could soon have if everything goes according to plan?" he says. "We need the money, Alice."

"I'm not upset about you working long hours, James. I get it. I know how business works, especially in the beginning."

I hold myself back from adding, *I know how this works since you've started and failed three businesses since we've met.*

Instead, I continue, "I'm pissed off that you can't take one minute out of your day to shoot me a text to let me know you'll be home late. I never know when you'll be home. Grayson is constantly asking for you, wondering where you are."

He scowls at me. "Don't bring Grayson into this."

"You're a dad," I say. "Grayson *is* a part of this, whether you like it or not."

Cool air slips out of the fridge's open door.

He scoffs and lets out a forced laugh. "Play the victim. Act like I'm a bad dad. Whatever. I'm working to keep us alive, and I come home exhausted and hungry. It's not like you do anything during the day. You sit on your ass and watch Lucas. So I don't get why making me a meal is so damn hard for you. And look at this place—"

He points to a pile of dirty laundry sitting on the sofa and then at some of Lucas's toys on the floor.

I grit my teeth, holding back a slew of hateful words I want to unleash.

How could he be so callous?

"I deserve a good wife," he says. "And my sons deserve a good mom."

The hatred in his eyes is unmistakable.

I want to scream at him and cry at the same time. How could he say such hurtful words to me? Make me feel so little?

He must sense my hurt.

Bowing his head, he sighs. "I'm sorry. I shouldn't have said that. I'm just really tired. You know I don't mean it."

I swallow hard, trying to push the pain out of my throat.

"Listen," he says, more softly this time. "We agreed you'd be staying home to take care of things around here, right? Isn't this what we agreed to?"

He's not wrong. We did agree to this.

"What more do you want from me, Alice? I'm trying, here. I'm really trying, but it's like it's not enough for you. You think I'm a horrible husband and father."

Once again, I'm left feeling like a pile of steaming garbage as I do every time we get into a fight about this subject. By the end of it, I'm a whiny wife who does nothing but complain.

Maybe James is right.

I'm not holding up my end of the deal, and I'm making him feel bad for the way he's managing his end.

I can't expect him to work overtime *and* for him to always be there for us. We knew there would be sacrifices to make.

This isn't forever. Once Lucas is old enough, maybe you can look at starting an online business like you've always wanted. That way, you can alleviate some of the financial stress off James.

James takes a step toward me. "Are we okay?"

I nod.

He wraps his arms around me, pulling me into his muscular chest, and kisses the top of my head. A bold, clean smell emanates from him as he holds me tight. I appreciate the warm embrace. He makes me feel safe and somehow has a way of dissipating my anger.

"How can I make things easier for you?" he asks.

I shrug. There's nothing I can ask of him. Nothing realistic, at least. It's not like he can reduce his hours and spend more time with us.

We need the money.

And his business seems to be doing well right now. Well, enough for him to buy himself an eight-hundred-dollar jacket.

Maybe if things keep going well, we can get a nanny or someone to help out so I can go back to work.

"Nothing I can think of," I say.

When I look up at him, he cups my face with his strong hands and smiles, little crinkles forming at the corners of his eyes. That's the James I miss—the James I want by my side. Why isn't he around anymore? I catch little glimpses of him here and there, only to have him taken away from me seconds later.

Slowly, he leans forward, his lips pressing into mine.

I breathe out against his face, calm and assured. When he pulls back, a strange scent enters my nose. It's the strong smell of his favorite peppermint gum. It's so overpowering that you'd think he chewed an entire pack before stepping through the door.

But there's another aroma concealed behind all that peppermint.

It's faint, but I recognize it.

Alcohol.

CHAPTER 3

Lucas's eyes nearly bulge out of his head. His jaw hangs slack as he takes it all in. The look on his face makes me smile, but my smile immediately vanishes when I look up at Grayson.

If *this* doesn't have him wowed, how will he ever come around?

"So are we, like, rich now, or something?" Grayson asks.

"No, not rich," I tell him.

And it isn't a lie.

Sure, we're standing at the doorstep of a two-million-dollar Victorian house, but I don't have more than a grand to my name, which I somehow have to stretch out until all the legal paperwork is done.

This is yours, Alice.

"Do you guys remember what I told you in the car on our way here?" I ask.

Grayson takes a step back, the tip of his hockey ball cap aimed up at the frighteningly large house. His gaze is fixed on the small black windows of the attic as if he's waiting for some cryptic figure to materialize.

Isn't that what these houses are known for?

Ghosts? Angry spirits?

It's a beautiful house with its blue and white paneling, custom molding, slick black roof, and countless trimmed hedges surrounding the property.

But the house is very large and very old.

I stare at the iron lettering next to the door—1472.

1472 Thorn Lake Drive.

My new home.

When neither of them answers me, I repeat the question. "Well? I only explained it about five times."

"Something about an old man dying," Grayson says.

I shoot him a warning look. "That old man was your uncle, Victor."

"Yeah, and I never met him," Grayson says.

It's not his fault. I've never talked about Victor. I thought he'd been dead this whole time. After he returned from a covert mission in the military, no one ever heard from him again.

He was never reported as dead or missing, either.

So where had he gone? Here, apparently.

Lucas ignores us and hops down the large front steps before venturing off into the front yard.

"Don't go too far," I warn him.

Head bowed, eyes on his tablet, he walks in circles and keeps playing his game.

"I don't get why we had to come here." A flash of resentment glints in Grayson's eyes. "Why couldn't we go live with Grandma and Grandpa?"

"I've already told you," I say through clenched teeth. When I'm certain Lucas isn't around to hear me, I add, "Do you really want them getting hurt?"

Grayson goes quiet. He knows exactly what I'm talking about—involving my parents puts them at risk. And Grayson knows this firsthand. James threatened his life when he thought Grayson wasn't around to hear it.

I reach for Grayson's shoulder and give him a tender squeeze. "Why don't we give this place a chance?"

Without looking up at me, Grayson says, "Did Dad find us? Is that why we left again?"

When he finally looks up, our eyes lock.

He's fourteen. Not six. Just tell him the truth.

Although I never told Grayson, James *did* find us. Or at least, our state. But it was only a matter of time before he found our exact location.

And then, by some miracle, I received the call about

Victor's estate.

Everything aligned so perfectly. Almost too perfectly. I'm still fighting off my paranoia—the thought that James is responsible for all of this and that it's a whole setup.

Grayson is still staring at me, his pleading eyes waiting for me to explain to him how close we came to being found again.

"He did," I tell him honestly. "Not our exact address, but our state."

He averts his gaze momentarily, watching a fly swirl around the front door handle.

"Are we gonna keep living like this?" he asks. "Running all the time? Why won't the cops do anything?"

"They've done what they can," I say, even though I believe they could have done a hell of a lot more. "He was arrested, and charges were pressed that night." I pause, trying to push aside memories of that horrific night . . . the night he almost killed me.

Grayson's eyes flicker toward the scar above my right eyebrow.

He remembers.

And although he doesn't talk about it, I'm sure the memory still haunts him.

How couldn't it? James beat me to a pulp, and when Grayson ran downstairs to try to protect me, James threw a beer bottle at his head and told him if he got involved, he'd kill me.

All I could do was stare at Grayson pleadingly, begging him to call the police. I must have looked terrifying with a beet-red face and bulging bloodshot eyes as James squeezed my neck so tightly that if I didn't die of oxygen deprivation, a crushed throat would do me in.

Thankfully, Grayson ran back upstairs and used my cell phone to call the police.

I clear my throat, suddenly feeling as if the oxygen around me is thinning.

"I can't promise we'll be here long-term," I say. "But I think I did things right this time. That's why I had our names changed."

He nods. "Collins. Why'd you choose that?"

It's not like it's my maiden name. The choice was random.

I shrug. "I like the name. Emma Collins. Grayson Collins. Lucas Collins. Sounds nice, doesn't it?"

Grayson pops a brow at me. "I mean, I guess."

He doesn't know why I chose the name *Emma*, but he doesn't have to.

Lucas lets out a chuckle in the distance. He's playing next to some cedar shrubs, well within view.

"Promise me you'll keep an eye out for your brother," I say. "I know I've been drilling it into the both of you for the last two days, but you can't use my real name. Not ever. And I need you to make sure Lucas doesn't forget."

"Emma," Grayson says.

I nod. "Alice is gone. Understood?"

He rolls his eyes at me. "Mom, you literally told us, like, over a hundred times now."

"I'm not sure you realize how important this is," I say.

He shifts his weight onto one leg and crosses his arms. "I *do* understand."

"That goes for you, too. Grayson Remington is gone. You're Grayson Collins."

"Why didn't you change our first names, too?" he asks.

It's a valid question. But they're kids. I can't expect them to remember to go by different names. Besides, Grayson and Lucas are popular names. It's not like it will raise any suspicions.

"Makes it easier for you both," I say.

When I glance past Grayson again, Lucas is gone.

He was just there.

"Lucas?" I shout out, hurrying down the wooden stairs.

Grayson stands behind me, watching.

"Lucas?" My voice quivers this time.

My pace quickens as I start racing across the front lawn. Where is he? He was *right here*.

Grayson runs down the stairs and starts circling the

house around the back. "Maybe he went this way."

I nod, wiggling a finger toward the backyard. "Good idea. Check there. I'll check the front."

James found him and stole him from you, like you stole his kids from him.

I shake these thoughts away.

No way would James have found us so soon.

He followed you.

No way.

"Lucas!" I hurry to the front of the yard and to the edge of the sidewalk.

To my surprise, Lucas is sitting on a metal bench next to a lamppost. He sits with his head bowed and his eyes focused on his game full of flashing vivid colors.

"Lucas!" I hiss.

His head snaps up.

"Hi, Mom," he says sweetly. "I made a friend."

I scowl at him. "You know the rules. Always stay in my line of sight. Why didn't you listen?"

"But—"

"Give me the tablet," I say.

He frowns. "Mom!"

"No," I say sternly. "You got so involved in your game that you weren't paying attention to your surroundings. It's time for a break."

Still frowning, he hands me the tablet.

As I reach for it, I spot a figure in my periphery. I snatch the tablet and turn sideways to spot a man in a long black trench coat and a yellow hat that looks too big for his head.

He's pale—vampire pale, as if the sun hasn't touched his skin in decades.

His gray sunken eyes focus on Lucas before slowly rolling toward me.

Why is he staring like that?

Awkward, I wave a hand to say hi, but he doesn't wave back. He's staring, and it's making me more uncomfortable by the second.

"Come on," I tell Lucas, unable to take my eyes off this man. "Let's go inside."

With a dramatic pout, he begrudgingly slides off the bench.

"Did you find him?" Grayson shouts, running our way.

We round the hedges, and I wave at Grayson as if to say, *All good.*

When he catches up to me, he winces at the man across the street. "Why is he staring like that?"

"Get inside," I urge them, believing that any second now, this man is going to come charging full speed.

It's an irrational thought—he's very old and frail looking. But that doesn't mean he couldn't overpower me.

For a moment, I feel completely helpless as I did countless times in James's grasp. I hate this sense of vulnerability, of being a mouse in a world of cats.

"He's still staring," Grayson says, walking backward.

He looks like he's about to tell the man to get lost—Grayson is a bit fearless like that—so I point ahead and tell him to keep moving.

I don't realize my hands are shaking until we've reached the front door, and I fidget with my new key.

"Here," Grayson says, grabbing it from me.

He inserts it into the keyhole and unlocks the door with a click.

The door creaks open, allowing a cool breeze to sweep out, bringing along with it the scent of something fruity. Possibly old candle wax. Or lemon cleaner.

"Come on," I say, urging them inside.

I don't bother going back to the car for our bags.

Instead, I slam the door behind us and lock the deadbolt.

CHAPTER 4

Rapid footsteps echo throughout the house as Lucas runs in every direction, admiring the cathedral ceilings, the curved wooden staircase gleaming beneath a chandelier, and the massive paintings that hang on almost every wall.

He stops for a second, mouth agape, and points up at one of the golden-framed paintings that looks to be of this very house. Around it, however, is farmland rather than hedges and a perfectly trimmed yard.

"Is that this house?" Lucas asks.

I step closer. "Looks like."

"Before we had neighbors," he says.

I nod, admiring the artwork, as well as Lucas's attention to detail.

In awe, I continue my way through the house. A huge living room with a cherrywood fireplace and a massive flat-screen TV has Grayson sneaking closer.

"There's a TV?" he asks.

I nod absentmindedly, my focus drawn by the intricate moldings and high-end furniture.

I had no idea what to expect coming here. Victor's lawyer and executor, Mr. Yonuk, was the one to inform me that my uncle had passed, and that as per his will, I was to be given all assets, including his fully furnished house.

But I never expected *this*.

Leather sofas, an oversized kitchen with brand new appliances, and that TV that is easily over seventy inches.

It almost feels wrong.

Along with all this came prepaid utilities for a year, saving me a costly bill at the end of each month until I receive the inheritance money.

Mr. Yonuk warned me that, despite the prepayment set up by Victor, it was my responsibility to have the accounts transferred under my name; otherwise, I would be committing fraud.

"Come on," I say. "Let's go find our rooms. Lucas!"

My voice carries through the large house, and Lucas comes running from around a corner.

"We're going upstairs," I say, gesturing for him to follow.

As we climb the wooden staircase, only a single step creaks. The rest of the staircase is absurdly solid, like it was built to last millennium.

Lucas runs his finger along the staircase's wooden spindles as if counting them one by one.

The upstairs looks a lot like the downstairs—made almost entirely of wood except for the walls. Elegant mahogany doors run down both sides of the hallway.

According to Victor's lawyer, there should be four bedrooms on this floor, along with two bathrooms—one ensuite and one shared.

"Stay close," I tell them.

Grayson looks at me as if I've gone off the deep end.

I get it.

The house is empty, and there's no one here. But how can we be certain? What if this is all a plot orchestrated by James to get us alone in some remote area?

You're being paranoid. This is very much real.

However, the timing of it all seems almost too perfect.

Stop overthinking. Be grateful.

I open the door nearest to me.

A storage room.

Behind the next door is a smaller drab bedroom. The bed is covered in gray sheets and surrounded by wooden posts that look more like prison walls than decor. There's nothing exciting or vibrant about the room—nothing that would attract a child to want to sleep in here—but Lucas steps in with popped eyes and makes an *ooh* sound out of his small mouth.

I leave the door open in case he wants to go in, then move on to the next room.

Average-sized. Again, nothing special. Although I'd be lying if I said I wasn't taken aback by the impeccable cleanliness. According to Mr. Yonuk, Victor died several months ago. Shouldn't there be dust? Spiders? Dead flies?

Or maybe the house was so well taken care of that barely any dust has collected in the heating ducts. Who knows?

Next, the bathroom.

Although the house itself is old, everything inside looks modern. Victor must have spent part of his fortune having everything gutted and reinstalled.

Marble tiles, gold fixtures, a glass-door shower that looks like it was installed yesterday.

The man may have lived in isolation, but he knew a thing or two about interior decor.

More than me, anyway.

When we reach the master bedroom, I'm taken aback by its luxurious beauty.

The four-post mahogany bed rests atop a red-and-gold rug. Golden drapes cover a large window. A chandelier hangs in the center of the room, its bulbs faux candles.

Lucas appears next to me. "Can this be my room?"

Before I can answer, he lets out an excited squeal and runs straight for the bed.

"Lucas," I hiss.

Although the floors look spotless, I imagine the sheets are rather dusty. I'm afraid if he jumps on them, a cloud of gray will erupt upward. But the moment he jumps on, the scent of fresh laundry slips into my nose.

How did Victor manage to keep this place so clean? And why would the bedding still smell so fresh after all this time?

He'd been savvy enough to prepay utility bills for me.

He might have also hired a cleaner to come in after his passing. It would explain how everything sparkles and smells like lemon.

Lucas giggles on the bed, flopping from side to side over a comforter that looks more expensive than my car.

Smiling, I join him by sitting at the edge of the bed. It's like a big puffy cloud, and I fight my desire to lie down.

If I do, I'm afraid I might not get back up.

"This is my room," I say. "You two can decide which rooms you want—"

"I want the first room we saw," Lucas says, like he already made up his mind.

I smile at his decisiveness. "How come? Is the bed comfier than this one?"

"No," he says, his voice chipper. "I made new friends in there."

CHAPTER 5

I stiffen and turn to look at Lucas, trying to stay calm despite feeling like someone is playing a drum kit inside my chest.

"Friends?" I ask.

He flashes me a gap-toothed grin. "Yeah!"

Then, he raises two little figurines that look to have been sewn out of potato bags.

I breathe out slowly. So he isn't seeing ghosts. That's a relief.

Neither of his little figurines has a face, which is a bit eerie. But both fit in his fists with their legs dangling out the bottom and their arms resting at the top.

The one in his left hand has blond hair down to its shoulders, while the one on the right has short brown hair and is a bit larger.

"These are your *friends*?" I ask him.

He nods. "Haven't thought of names yet, but I'll figure it out."

They look ancient, like something kids might have played with in the Middle Ages. Despite this, they don't look dirty, so I don't take them from him.

"Anything else you found in there?" I ask.

"Nope, just this. Even under the bed was really clean. Like, way cleaner than under my bed at home." He lets out a giggle, and I can't help but smile.

I turn to Grayson. "You okay with the second room?"

He shrugs like he doesn't have a choice in the matter. He does, but if he wants to be a good big brother, there's no choice.

I'm relieved when he adds, "I'm fine with whatever."

At least I don't have to get in the middle of a fight. Not that Grayson fights with Lucas very often. The age gap definitely helps.

"Those things are creepy," Grayson points out.

Lucas pouts. "They are not."

"They are," Grayson says. He glances at me for backup, and I give him a quick purse of the lips as if to say, *They're little dolls. They won't hurt anyone.*

Grayson rolls his eyes and leaves the room.

I don't bother going into the attic; I've never liked them. If James were here—the old James that I fell in love with—he'd be the first to go into the attic, the basement, and any crawl space to make sure we were all safe and that no intruders were hiding.

He was always paranoid like that.

Something he passed onto me, apparently.

I turn to Lucas. "How about pizza for supper?"

His lips stretch into a bubbly smile. "Yum."

I jerk my head sideways. "Let's head back downstairs."

When we return to the main floor, Grayson is sitting on the leather sofa in front of the television. It's powered on with a blue screen, casting a bright glow across his face.

"Do we have Wi-Fi?" he asks.

I shake my head. Mr. Yonuk was clear about that—Victor hadn't been one for using the Internet. He'd been very mistrustful about the world in general and preferred to remain in isolation.

Seemingly bummed out, Grayson places the remote next to him on the couch and leans back.

"I'll have it installed tomorrow," I tell him.

He isn't the only one who needs it. If I want to keep us alive by bringing food to our table, I need to get my business running. Either that, or I'll have to find a job somewhere in town.

Getting all of this done isn't what has me stressed. I'm worried the utility companies are going to give me a hard time given my lack of credit history under my new name. But Mr. Yonuk assured me that so long as I provide them with Victor's death certificate and my ID, everything should be fine.

The timing couldn't be more perfect. I received my new ID last week.

I still can't believe I pulled this off. I smile at the thought, feeling like I accomplished the impossible. I'd been wanting to change my name for a while, and when I received that call from Mr. Yonuk, it catapulted everything else.

If some random lawyer could track me down, it was just a question of time before James had our exact address.

The restraining order wouldn't stop him.

Within a month, I'd changed my name from Alice Remington to Emma Collins and informed Mr. Yanuk of the change.

So while Grayson and Lucas were at school, entirely unaware that their lives would soon be changed again, I spent a week running from one office to the next, filling out forms to have my name changed everywhere—Social Security, the Department of Motor Vehicles, and a bunch of other places that still have my head spinning.

On top of all that, I got in touch with Thorn Lake Elementary and Thorn Lake High to register Grayson and Lucas.

It took a lot of coffee and determination, but I'm here. We're here, and we're safe now.

You did this, Alice. You made this happen.

It's Emma, now.

A metallic ringing fills the house.

"I'll get it," Grayson says.

I blink hard, returning to the present.

"Hm?" I mumble. "Get what?"

Grayson lunges to his feet and rushes toward the front door.

"Grayson!" I call after him.

He reaches for the deadbolt, and I grab his arm in a

panic.

He looks at me as if I've lost my mind. "What're you doing? Pizza's here."

The pizza.

That's right—I ordered as soon as I came back downstairs. Although I didn't want to pay money for takeout, this is to celebrate our new home. That, and the fridge is completely empty. I'll explore Thorn Lake tomorrow once the boys are at school.

I disengage the lock and pull the door ajar.

On the front porch stands a young boy no older than eighteen with his red, pimple-infested face and crooked ball cap. He barely smiles, and rather than look at me, he leans sideways, inspecting the inside of my house.

It's rude, but he's only a kid, I remind myself.

"Um, hi. Um, your . . . pizza." He raises the extra-large cardboard box, which will be enough for supper tonight and tomorrow. It's far from ideal, but after driving for over thirty-three hours, I'm not in the mood to run out to do groceries.

"How much?" I ask.

"Twenty-five," he says.

Twenty-five dollars?! Pizzas used to cost ten when I was a kid.

I stick a finger in the air, instructing him to wait a moment, and hurry to my purse on the kitchen island's white marble countertop.

When I return, he's still looking all around, mouth agape as if he's never seen a place like this before.

Grayson, still standing at the doorframe, raises a brow at him, no doubt feeling the same way as me.

"Can I help you with something?" I ask the pizza boy.

"Oh, uh, sorry," he says. "I've heard so much about this place. Biggest house in Thorn Lake, ya know? Everyone knows it. But no one ever saw who lived inside of it. That, plus the stories."

"Stories?" I ask.

He shakes his head, and his ball cap shifts slightly

over his hair. "Probably only rumors," he says. "But cops started finding these weird notes around town about the old man who lived here. Apparently, the messages said he did really bad things."

"What bad things?" I ask.

He shrugs. "Different stuff. One of the notes said he skinned rabbits in his basement for fun, and another said he sexually abused women of the town."

I swallow hard, completely flummoxed.

I think back to the Victor Huxley I remember from my childhood. He'd always been such a gentle soul. There's no way he did such terrible things.

How would you know? You haven't seen him in over twenty years.

Speechless, I hand the boy his twenty-five dollars.

He grabs it, pausing momentarily to look at the change in his palm.

I get it—he's waiting for a tip.

"I'm sorry," I say. "It's all I have right now."

He purses his lips, then lifts both eyebrows at my new multimillion-dollar home as if he doesn't believe me.

I don't blame him—I wouldn't believe me, either.

But right now, every dollar counts, and twenty-five for a pizza is already going overboard.

When I don't tip him, he shoves the cash into a little pouch around his waist and nudges his chin toward Grayson. "You going to Thorn Lake High?"

Grayson glances sideways at me, then says, "Y-yeah. Why? You go there?"

For the first time, the kid smiles. "Yeah, man, I do. You'll be real popular. Everyone's been talking about who will be living here. So they'll have a bunch of questions for you."

Grayson doesn't look thrilled about it. He's never enjoyed being the center of attention. He likes to keep to himself and hang out with only a few friends at a time.

"Well, there isn't much to tell," I say. "Thank you for the pizza, and Grayson will see you at school tomorrow."

The boy waves and stands on the tips of his toes,

peeking one last time over my shoulder as I close the door.

"You think those stories are true?" Grayson asks as I lock the deadbolt and hand him the pizza.

I don't want to believe them, but the truth is, I didn't know Victor very well. Sure, he was an amazing uncle when I was a child, but that's as far as our relationship ever flourished.

I still don't understand why he left me his house.

Why not give it to my biological dad? Or to my aunt? Why me?

"Pizza!" Lucas shouts.

He runs into the kitchen, his legs kicking behind him as his socks slip on the polished hardwood floor.

"Don't eat it all tonight," I tell him. "We'll finish the rest tomorrow."

Grinning, he hurries to the box and pulls out a slice with hot, gooey cheese.

"What about breakfast?" Lucas asks, a glob of cheese escaping from the corner of his mouth.

"For breakfast?" I say. "No, you can have a peanut butter sandwich."

He nods, making *mmm* sounds as he chews on his slice.

When we finish eating, I place the leftover box inside the remarkably clean fridge.

"Help me bring our bags in, and we can start putting stuff in our rooms," I say.

I move to the front door and slap several light switches until the front of the house lights up. When we step out, I can't help but stare at my car.

The frame is dark gray with rust accumulating on the side doors. Worse, there's a dent over the rear fender—the result of someone backing into me in a parking lot.

I don't mind the damage.

What bothers me is how these flaws make this car easily identifiable. If James were to see it on the road, he'd instantly know it was mine despite the new license plate.

Unfortunately, I don't have the money to get a new car right now.

He isn't out here. You have time.

I open the trunk and pull out our bags—duffel bags, backpacks, and a few reusable grocery bags stuffed with dried goods.

Grayson grabs the heavy bags like a gentleman, and I smile up at him, but he doesn't see me.

Once the bags are all inside, I move my car to the back of the house and return, swatting away mosquitoes in the darkness. Crickets hum all around me, and swarms of flies circle exterior lights attached to the house's side paneling.

Every little sound that isn't a cricket draws my attention.

A dog barking in the distance.

A high-pitched chirp.

The snapping of a small branch.

Although irrational, I can't help but imagine James hiding somewhere in a bush, his dark eyes filled with a vengeful rage.

He'd come at me, fingers curled and mouth agape, prepared to strangle the life out of me.

I can't stand this feeling.

This vulnerability.

I quicken my pace, wanting to get inside.

Tonight, I'll lock all the doors and windows.

But tomorrow, I'm buying a gun.

CHAPTER 6

Air brakes cry down Thorn Street as Lucas's bus comes to a complete stop. I kiss him on the head and wish him good luck on his first day.

As he climbs the stairs, a little more timid than usual, Grayson's bus pulls up next.

It's hard to say goodbye to them, but I have so much to do today.

Lucas walks into the bus, sits down, and waves at me from one of the front windows. Grayson isn't as sweet about it. He throws his chin out at me, turns around, and disappears somewhere inside.

That high-pitched sound returns as both buses leave with my kids, toward what I hope will be a good experience for them.

The second they're gone, I hurry inside, snatch my keys, lock the doors, and make my way to my car parked at the back of the house.

Condensation from the cool morning dew coats its windows, which is to be expected in mid-October. The heat is leaving us, and winter's coming sooner than I'm prepared for.

Who's going to plow this massive driveway?

I don't have the money for a snowblower right now. I'll have to hire someone, which will also be very expensive, but hopefully, they'll accept payment at the end of the season. But there's still time . . . time for me to get my business off the ground and rake in a bit of cash.

I start the car, my engine rumbling softly, and pull out

my phone to load my GPS.

The nearest gun shop is ten minutes from here, but they only open at 9:00 a.m.

I googled Thorn Lake more times than I can count before uprooting our lives and moving here. There's a local grocery store down by the lake. It wouldn't hurt to grab a few things while I wait for the gun store to open.

I pull out of my overly long driveway and onto Thorn Street—a long road with barely any houses. In front of ours is a small bungalow that has had its lights on since we got here. But between each neighbor is at least several hundred yards.

It's quiet. Too quiet, as if no one around here works or ever leaves their home.

When you first enter Thorn Lake, there are numerous streets of newly developed houses. I assume this is where most kids live. Thorn Street, however, looks like something pulled right out of a museum. The greenery is meticulously trimmed and maintained.

Mr. Yonuk mentioned something about a landscaper—an older retired gentleman who enjoyed keeping Thorn Street clean and *vibrantly green.*

I don't remember his name.

But I do remember the part about his services also being prepaid for a year.

Passing an oversized dew-covered lawn, I grip my steering wheel and mutter, "Thanks, Uncle Victor. For everything."

I don't know if he can hear me, or sense me, or whatever. I've never been much of a spiritual person, but sometimes, I can't help but wonder what lies beyond the physical world.

If radio waves can travel unseen for miles upon miles, is it so far-fetched to believe that living beings, or some form of shapeless intelligence, can do the same?

More importantly, why the hell am I thinking about this at 8 a.m. on a Monday?

Something dark suddenly rushes across the road, and

I slam on my brakes, my tires squealing. The sound screams down the quiet road, likely waking anyone still in bed.

On the left curb is a black squirrel with a bushy tail. It chews on something, perks up, then dashes headfirst into a cedar bush.

I glare at where the little creature sat only seconds ago, trying to calm my heart.

Moving at a sluggish pace, I resume my drive and pass through a small town full of white and pale-blue houses that appear to have been built on a slope. Everything is old, possibly centuries old. But the houses aren't what capture my attention—it's what lies beyond the houses.

A massive lake that spreads so far I can't see the end of it. On the coastline are several fishing boats with metal bits gleaming under the morning sun.

A few men walk along the docks, likely preparing their fishing equipment for a day of work.

I descend a long road that snakes around white-paneled homes until I reach a large building that looks like an old warehouse.

On the front, above its large double doors, hangs a sign that reads, Thorn Lake Grocer.

It looks a lot like the picture I saw on Google Maps with its boat anchors and fishing nets acting as decor.

I park my car in the small parking lot. Three other cars are parked, including a police cruiser sitting at the opposite end of the lot. The lack of liveliness doesn't come as a surprise. Thorn Lake has a total population of two thousand people. Half of those come from the new development neighborhood. I imagine this grocery store is rarely ever busy.

I turn off my engine and step out onto the gravel lot. The scent of fish and wet earth immediately hits my nose. It's not a bad smell, but it's unmistakable. A smell the locals have no doubt gotten so accustomed to they no longer notice it.

As I march my way toward the main entrance, an older

man steps out with a paper bag stuffed to the top. He hugs it like he's afraid to lose it, but when he sees me approach, the fear on his face disappears, and he offers me a curious yet warm smile.

I smile back, unaccustomed to this level of friendliness from a stranger.

His eyes linger on me a bit longer than I'd like, but his gaze seems harmless.

I set foot inside Thorn Lake Grocer, admiring its quaintness. It's nothing like a commercial grocery store with bright fluorescent lights, top hits blasting on the radio, and people scurrying around in such a rush that anger gets the best of them.

Another shopper strolls leisurely across the produce section before picking up a red fruit, inspecting it, and placing it back.

Trying to kill time, I match this woman's pace and stroll through one aisle at a time. Many local products fill the shelves—some with labels obviously printed at home.

It's different and creates a sense of entering a whole new realm, but I enjoy it.

After gathering a few essentials—milk, eggs, fresh bread, cereal, and some meat—I push my cart toward the cash registers at the front.

There are only three in total, which is nothing like what I'm used to, where over a dozen cashiers are available, excluding a whole section for self-checkout.

A young girl stands behind the register.

When I approach, she smiles sweetly at me and says, "Good morning."

"Good morning," I say back.

I place my items down one at a time, when something draws my attention. It's more of a feeling than anything—the feeling of someone watching me.

I've never understood how we can sense someone's eyes on us. But the feeling is usually accurate.

I glance up quickly to spot a man with a brown suede jacket and chestnut-brown hair that sits in very short waves on his head, with a single strand dangling above his eyebrow. Intentional or bedhead? Either way, it suits him.

A dark stubble covers the bottom half of his face, and when he catches my eyes, he nods curtly and continues searching—*like he was really even searching*—for something on one of the display shelves near the front of the store.

He's tall, lean but not bulky, and easily my age—in his thirties—and handsome.

Okay, *very handsome.* The kind of guy women swoon over. And although I should be flattered that he was looking at me, my heart is suddenly racing, and I find myself clenching my teeth.

All I want is to get out of here, away from him.

He didn't do anything. He was only looking at you.

I race to empty my cart, and the girl behind the register keeps up with my pace. "Found everything you were looking for?"

"Y-yeah," I say, my eyes darting back up at the man.

He's gone.

Where did he go?

And why does it feel like this place is closing in on me? Like the lights are too bright? Like this girl is talking from the other end of a long tunnel?

"Ma'am?"

I blink hard.

"Cash or card?" she asks.

Her septum ring looks shinier than it should.

"Are you okay?" she asks.

I nod fast and reach for my wallet in my purse, hiding my trembling hands from the cashier's view.

"Debit, please," I say.

She observes me like she's trying to assess whether she should proceed with payment or get me a chair to sit on.

"I'm fine," I say quickly.

She helps me pack my two paper bags, and I thank her before rushing out through the front doors. I toss my bags in the trunk, the gallon of milk dropping to one side and sloshing around in its container.

After I pry my door open and drop down into my seat, I immediately lock my doors and tug at my collar. The sensation is constricting, as if it's going to suffocate me.

Why the hell am I feeling like this?

Pins and needles spread down my arms, and I lean my seat back, breathing in deeply.

Calm down, Alice. You're fine. Nothing happened.

Is this what it's like to experience a panic attack?

I've never had one before.

I think I'm going to die.

He isn't James.

I'm not sure why that little voice just spoke.

The man looked nothing like James. Why would I even think that? Okay, well, his height and his dark hair, although James's hair was practically black. Not chestnut brown.

And that's where the similarities end.

He was handsome.

And he was looking at you.

That's when I realize—it wasn't the man's physical appearance that subconsciously reminded me of James.

It was the way he looked at me.

The way he watched me.

If he wanted to, he could easily follow me home and overpower me. Or, get in my car, and order me to drive to some remote location before killing me and dumping my body.

You're being paranoid.

Even though I *know* I'm probably letting my imagination run wild, these thoughts didn't materialize out of nowhere. James threatened to kill me more than once. And the last day I saw him, I knew he had every intention of one day taking my life.

His threats were real.

So real, in fact, that it isn't so far-fetched to think he'd hire someone to hunt me down and do the dirty work for him.

My eyes flicker toward the clock on my dashboard—9:04 a.m.

And this feeling—this sense of vulnerability—is exactly why I'm going to buy a gun.

CHAPTER 7

BEFORE

Things should have gotten better by now.

After our fight a few weeks ago, I promised to be more understanding, and James offered to be more supportive.

Yet nothing has changed.

He still comes home smelling like peppermint masking an underlying note of alcohol.

I've been debating confronting him, but I know exactly how it'll play out—he'll brush it off, make excuses, and then lash out and accuse me of being an overbearing wife.

But I can't keep living like this.

Like I'm walking on eggshells.

When he stomps his way inside, barely looking at me, I keep my distance until his boots are off. He's always cranky when he gets home—especially these last few months—and I don't want to exacerbate things.

When he enters the kitchen, I force a smile. "Cream of mushroom chicken is on the stovetop."

His eyes flicker toward the lidded pot, but he doesn't thank me. I clamp my jaw, repressing my anger as best I can.

You don't even deserve to have meals cooked for you, you ungrateful asshole.

I feel bad even thinking of my husband this way. But that's exactly what he's become—an asshole. I understand that having a baby is stressful, but it's no reason to treat me like garbage.

He rummages through the kitchen cupboards, clanging dishes as he pulls out his go-to plate—a plain circular plate he likes to use exclusively while expecting me to clean it for him every time.

It doesn't match the rest of our black and stone-gray dishware, but he insists that this one is his favorite, and he's not parting with it. He also insists that no one else use it.

I don't always understand James's strange compulsions or obsessions, but I've learned to accept them.

He pulls out a fork, inspects it under the light, then goes on to wash it.

"That just came out of the dishwasher," I say.

I would know—I spent the last hour cleaning this kitchen from top to bottom.

"It has a spot," he says gruffly.

Then maybe you should clean your own dishes if you need them to be so perfect.

I bite my tongue.

"Do you need anything from me?" I ask.

He doesn't answer. Instead, he grabs his food and makes his way to the dining room table.

I had wanted tonight to be civil. I'd wanted to sit down and have an open discussion about why he's been smelling like alcohol after work. But with how he's treating me, I can't bring myself to stay calm.

If I stay here, I may end up shouting at him.

So instead, I say, "I'm going to get some air," and go to the front door.

He doesn't say anything.

In the distance, his chair creaks, and he plops himself down.

I shouldn't be doing this.

I really shouldn't be.

But I want proof.

Quietly, I snatch his truck's keys, slip on my shoes, and make my way outside.

There's a chance I'll get caught, but if that happens, I already have a plan in place—I'll tell him I lost one of my credit cards and I'm looking for it.

Moving quickly, I sneak into his truck through the driver's side, and I start searching every nook and cranny.

The gap in his door.

The console.

The glove box.

This is ridiculous. If he's drinking, he isn't stupid enough to leave booze in the car. Be an adult and talk to him.

But I want to *catch* him.

I want to raise a bottle of whatever he's been drinking and tell him that if he doesn't stop, we're done.

Because unless I have proof, he'll deny it until his face turns blue. I know James. He's a good liar, and he's exceptionally charismatic and well spoken, which makes any battle against him difficult.

Rarely do I come out victorious.

"Alice?"

My heart almost climbs up through my throat and onto his black leather seat.

How did I not see him approaching?

"What are you looking for?" he asks.

He's trying to stay calm, but the dark anger in his eyes makes me weigh my next words very carefully.

"My credit card," I say. "I can't find it, and the last time I had it was when we went to the store in your truck."

"You don't sit in the driver's seat," he says. "I do."

His words come across as a threat, like he's warning me to stay away from his things. James already doesn't like anyone going near his fancy truck—a black souped-up Ram that his parents helped him buy several years ago. It was the last bit of money they gave him before they cut him off and told him he needed to earn his own living.

He threw a fit and said his business wasn't off the ground yet. I remember thinking he was acting like such a man-child. It was unattractive, to say the least.

I'd never approved of his parents giving him money. Sure, it helped pay the bills, but for the most part, he used it to fund his businesses, promising them a return on their investment. They must have realized after so many failed attempts that James didn't have it in him to launch a successful business.

After a bout of depression and countless fights, he finally put all his energy into being an entrepreneur and took charge of his business, surprising not only me but also his family when the money started coming in.

For his success, I'm genuinely proud of him.

I only wish he'd involve me more. I could do bookkeeping or even administrative stuff from home.

"You ignoring me?" he asks.

I'm instantly pulled back to reality, where I'm standing between his driver's door and his leather seat.

"Give me my keys," he says.

It comes out sounding like more of an order than a request. But he's always been like that when it comes to his truck.

It's his, and only his.

He can drive my beat-up CR-V, but under no circumstance am I allowed to touch his *baby*.

"You gonna help me look?" I ask.

I'm pushing it, especially knowing full well that my credit card is tucked in my pocket. If I'm smart about it, I'll pull it out at the last minute and say I found it, which may lessen his suspicion over me searching his truck.

I hand him the keys, and he snatches them angrily. "Next time, ask me, and I'll help you."

"Why are you so upset?" I ask. "I'm not driving your truck. I'm looking for my card."

"It's my truck," he says. "How would you like it if I went through your belongings?"

A laugh slips out of my mouth. "Seriously? You do all the time, James. I don't say anything. We're married. We're supposed to share things."

"Not everything," he says. "I don't want to turn into one of those couples that has a shared bank account, either. Individuality is important."

While I understand where he's coming from, he's going about it all wrong. He's tense and watches me with an irate scowl, which means he has something to hide.

And that something is his alcohol.

"Your truck stinks," I lie.

He pulls away from the door, looking at me as if I punched him in the throat.

"There's a smell," I say. "Like alcohol."

He lashes out. "Are you for real right now? Did you come out here to *smell* my truck?"

I should have kept my mouth shut and brought up the smell of alcohol another time.

Way to go, Alice. You just made things a hundred times worse.

"Forget it," I say. "Can I look on the other side for my card?"

"Not until you tell me what this is about," he says. "You're accusing me of something, and you don't have the balls to say it." He's angry now. Pissed. Because this is what he does when he's caught in a lie. He gets so angry that I back down.

Part of me wants to back down and explain to him that I wasn't accusing him of anything—only stating a fact. But the other part of me . . . the one that's grown tired of how he treats me and how I have to tiptoe around him constantly when he's in a bad mood . . . that part wants to lash out, too, and tell him that I know about the drinking.

I stand there, staring at him coldly as I contemplate which side to unleash.

"What?" he snaps.

I flinch, but the fear only lasts for a moment. Next, anger sets in, and I give him a hard shove. "You lied to me! You said you'd never touch alcohol again! And now you're back to drinking!"

My throat swells, and tears prick my eyes.

"How could you do this, James? We have two kids together. And here you are, spending your nights—"

"So you were snooping through my shit? Trying to find booze?" His jaw pops, and little blue veins squiggle on his forehead.

He's angrier than I am, but I don't care.

"No," I say, pulling in a quivering breath. "I came out here looking for my card because I didn't want to be anywhere near you. Not like this." I throw an arm out at him. "I can't stand this version of you, James. So stay the hell away from me and the boys. Do you hear me? Unless you clean your shit up, stay away from us."

He breathes out hard, his nostrils as wide as his lips, his dark eyes looking almost black. "If you weren't so goddamn expensive, I wouldn't have to resort to cheap shit like alcohol."

The weight of his words hits me like a jab to the gut.

Cheap shit?

What is he talking about?

James has a history of drug use, but he was clean before we even met. At least, he said he was.

I fight off the burst of anxiety building inside of me. "What are you saying? That you're using again?"

He laughs so loudly that his voice carries down the street, and a kid on a bike glances sideways at us.

"I would if I could," he says spitefully. "With your whining and the boys always needing all my attention, it's too much. I can't handle it. But I also can't afford it. Not with how much you guys cost me."

Were these words supposed to reassure me?

They did the opposite.

Not only does he blame us for his substance abuse, but now he's admitting to wanting stronger drugs but not having the financial means to obtain them. What will happen when his business continues to expand? When he starts raking in even more money?

"So you're a drunk, instead?" I say.

He smashes a fist into his truck, right next to my thigh. I tense, my fists clenching into little balls.

He breathes so hard, in, and out . . . in, and out.

Would he hit me?

It's hard to say. I never imagined James could be physically abusive, but that look in his eyes tells me he wants to take a swing. It's the same look he had all those years ago.

But we're outside, with people walking their dogs.

He won't do it.

At least not here.

"I'm not a drunk," he says. "I had a rough week. That's all."

I'm not buying it.

I peel away from the truck—away from his reach—and stiffen my stance. My legs are a bit wobbly, but I refuse to let him see this.

I clench my teeth to prevent them from chattering.

"If you're back to being your drunken self, this is the end. Do you hear me? You either stop right now before it gets out of hand, or I'm filing for divorce."

I expect him to form another dent in his truck, but to my surprise, his anger dissipates instantly, only to be replaced by perplexity.

"I'm putting Grayson to bed now," I say. "Don't you dare come say goodnight to him like this."

He parts his lips but doesn't move. Instead, he stands there, staring at the ground, while I go inside and slam the door behind me.

CHAPTER 8

The older man behind the counter smiles at me like he's known me his entire life.

"Hello there, miss."

He smiles, the corners of his lips nearly reaching his fuzzy white sideburns. "How can I help you today?"

I look around me, overwhelmed by all the large guns stored on display stands. They appear to be missing pieces, as if someone dismantled them and left only the frame, and every single one of them is locked up with a thick cable.

Everywhere I look is a weapon of some kind—crossbows, rifles, shotguns.

"I—I'm looking to buy a gun," I say.

With that smile still plastered to his face, he extends his open palms as if to say, *Well, you've come to the right place.*

"You into huntin'?" he asks.

I shake my head, and his lips part, making a soft sticky sound.

"Ah, I see."

The look on his face tells me he understands I'm here for only one thing—protection.

"We've got all kinds of different handguns for sale," he says, his gaze lingering on me.

I nod. A handgun—that's what I want.

He walks over to the plexiglass counter separating me from a bunch of different handguns resting on their sides. "Well, we got—"

"What do you recommend?" I cut him off.

I don't want to hear about all the different *calipers* or whatever. I don't know much about guns other than the fact that I've never wanted one in the house.

Until now.

"Well, my go-to for self-defense is the Glock 19," he says, tapping his finger over a medium-sized black gun.

We lock eyes for a moment.

I can't help but wonder what he thinks of me. Does he assume someone is after me? Or does he think I'm some helpless single woman wanting to feel safe in her own home?

It doesn't matter.

I'm here for one thing—to protect my boys and myself.

"It takes 9 mm bullets," he says. "Cheapest and easiest to buy. The gun is the most reliable. Nothing fancy, but it's easy to use and gets the job done. But . . ." He pauses. "You ever shot before?"

I shake my head.

His big index finger slides across the glass. "Then I'd recommend the Glock G44."

"What's the difference?" I ask.

"The difference is .22 caliber rounds," he says, as if this is supposed to tell me anything.

I must be making a face; he leans forward, resting his elbows on the plexiglass counter. "Now, I apologize miss, as my intention ain't to be sexist in the least. But most women—well, first-timers—prefer a small compact gun like this one. That's not to say women can't shoot the biggest gun I have in here. I'm just lettin' you know what is easier in smaller hands. And the G44 has smaller bullets and is more compact, making it easier to fire a shot, and there's less kickback."

I part my lips, but before I can say anything, he unlocks a small metal mechanism, slips out a cable, and opens the plexiglass display. He removes yet another wire from around the gun, then hands it to me. It's cold, and it's surprisingly light. I always thought a handgun would be heavy.

I look over at the Glock 19, which doesn't look all that much bigger except for the barrel, which is longer.

"You know how to shoot?" he asks.

I blink, and I'm relieved when I don't have to say anything for him to smile knowingly and shake his head. "Don't worry. I'll give you a basic how-to before you buy. Well, that's *if* you decide to buy." He gently takes the gun out of my hand.

"How much?" I ask.

"Four hundred and fifty," he says.

My eyes bulge involuntarily. I knew a gun would be expensive, and deep down, I probably also knew it would be around this mark. But I'm worried about making a big purchase like this when I barely have anything left in my bank account.

This is a priority. Nothing else will matter if you're dead.

"You from around here?" he asks.

I nod.

"Whereabouts?"

I hesitate to tell him, but the man seems like he wants to help me. Not cause any trouble.

"Just moved onto Thorn Street," I tell him.

His eyes go big. "That mansion? Victor Huxley's house?"

I nod again.

"Everyone's been wondering who would move there. I can definitely understand why you'd want to get a gun."

What the hell is that supposed to mean?

Is that house a target or something?

I must have made a face. He lets out a chuckle and says, "The place isn't haunted or anything. I'm just saying it's the biggest house in all of Thorn Lake. Some people like big houses, but me, personally, I think if anyone is going to want to break in somewhere, it's gonna be the richest house on the block."

"Not necessarily," I argue.

He cocks a white bushy brow.

"Rich people tend to have high-security systems in place," I say.

Not that I'm rich. But with how he's wording things, he's insinuating that the house makes me look rich.

He purses his lips, nodding slowly, then taps his temple. "That's true, I suppose. You got a security system, then?"

That's none of your business.

"Not yet," I say, before throwing a lie at him. "But it's getting installed later today."

He puffs out his chest and smiles like a proud father. "Sounds like you know what you're doin', miss. Good on ya."

The truth is, I don't have enough money to buy a gun *and* get a security system. I'm surprised that Victor didn't already have one set up.

I scan a white name tag on the man's chest.

Jones.

"Are there a lot of break-ins in Thorn Lake, Jones?"

He shakes his head. "Not that I'm aware of. This town's as safe as they come. I mean, you get the standard teenager that likes to pull pranks on us older folk, but I've never seen anything serious around here.

"So do you think me installing that security system today is a little extreme?"

He ponders this for a moment, then leans in. "Normally, I'd say yes, but since you're living in that big old house . . . I don't know." He looks around like he's trying to make sure no one is listening. "Rumor has it that notes were found around town about Victor. That he was a bit of a psycho."

Just as the pizza guy said.

"So I don't know," Jones continues with a shrug. "If someone wants revenge, they might take it out on his house." He lets out a big sigh. "I'm sorry. I wish I had a better answer for you. At the end of the day, it's always better to be safe than sorry, right? And me, well, I'm a big advocate for guns, as you can see."

His big warm smile returns.

"So I think you're doing the right thing by getting yourself a gun."

I want to smile back at him, but I'm getting a bit queasy. This is the second time someone has talked about Victor being an awful person. Will I become a target living in his old house? Will my sons be targeted at school?

We were supposed to be running toward safety, not danger.

What if coming here was a horrible mistake?

"Miss?"

I look up at Jones.

"You disappeared for a second," he says.

"S-sorry," I say. "I'll take the gun, please. And whatever ammo I need for it. And I'll need you to—"

He smiles, and creases form around his eyes. "Don't you worry about learnin' how to use it. I'll show you."

I appreciate his kindness, though I'm too stressed out to express my gratitude.

He places the gun back into the display area and reaches under the counter only to reemerge with a brand-new box that reads Glock G44. Then, he reaches behind him and grabs another box, only this one is made of plain brown cardboard with bold font that reads 22 LR on it.

He pauses. "Do you want any sort of box?"

"Box?" I ask, staring at the two boxes he already pulled out.

"Safety box. A safe or cabinet."

"Oh," I say, taken aback. I got so carried away with buying a gun that I forgot about safe storage. If I lived alone, I'd leave my gun in a drawer. But I have two kids, which means I need to take every precaution. "Y-yes, absolutely."

"Got kids?" he asks.

I hesitate, feeling like a bad mom for bringing a gun into my house with children.

No, you're doing this to protect them.

I nod.

"Then I'd recommend the P-42 Locker," he says. "Just came out last month."

He points overhead at a small black box with a shiny circle right at the center.

"Fingerprint technology," he says. "Don't have to worry about your kids getting hold of the key."

I should ask him the price, but I can't put a price on my children's lives.

"I'll take it," I say.

He rings me through, then places my new deadly weapon inside a brown paper bag that has no markings or any advertisement for his shop.

I'm happy about the discretion.

"I'll leave this right here," he says, bending down. When he gets back up with an achy grunt, he grabs a paper sign with a stringy rope from beside his cash register and limps his way over to the front door. He hangs the sign on a small silver hook, the text facing outside, and locks the door.

Probably some sign that reads, Be Back in Fifteen Minutes.

Is that all it takes to teach a person how to kill someone?

Fifteen minutes?

"This way," he says. He takes a few steps before turning his head toward the back of the shop. "Be back in a few, Wyatt."

"Sure thing, Jones," comes a response.

There was someone else in here all along?

I don't have time to spot the other employee.

"Right this way," Jones says, showing me through what looks to be an office door. "You'll be a pro shooter in no time."

CHAPTER 9

I walk out of Jones's unusually small training room only slightly more confident in my ability to use a gun. He set up paper targets on his walls and a human-sized dummy in the corner.

I didn't get to actually shoot anything, but he gave me a twenty-minute lesson on safety and how to operate the gun. As he leads me back to the front cash, a figure shifts in the shadows near one of the back shelves.

"Here you go," Jones says, distracting me from the movement.

I reach for my new gun hidden inside the brown bag and thank him. But before I turn away, the figure comes out of the darkness.

"All done, Jones."

That man.

My heart hammers in my chest as I stare at his chestnut curls and bright green eyes. He looks even taller, standing right next to me.

But what the hell is he doing here?

First, in the grocery store, and now, in the gun shop?

He's following you. You were right to think that something was off.

The man bows his head slightly, a handsome smile tugging at his perfectly shaped lips. "Ma'am," he says, his sparkly eyes glued to me.

I stare at his square cleft chin hiding under a bit of stubble. When I don't say anything, he clears his throat awkwardly and turns to Jones. "I'll grab a box of nines."

Jones laughs. "Someone sleeping on the job?"

The tall man rolls his eyes playfully. "Something to do with contractor delays. Wish we had more space, to be honest."

We?

What is he talking about?

Clutching the paper bag against my chest, I thank Jones with what sounds like more of a breath than an actual *thank you* and rush out of the gun shop.

I want to get back to the house and load this thing as soon as possible.

With shaky hands, I reach for my keys.

Behind me, the store's bell jingles, and footsteps follow.

But they aren't slow, the way one might walk on a Monday morning. They're hastened, determined.

And they're coming straight for me.

Breathless, I tuck a few of my metal keys between my knuckles. I've never had to fight anyone off this way, but I've always known about it, and I've dug keys into my skin more times than I can count while walking alone.

The footsteps draw in closer.

My eyes dart from left to right.

There's no other car in sight. This isn't a coincidence. That man is coming straight for me.

I'm almost at my car, but I won't make it in time. He's walking too fast. His strides are too long. A sloshing sound fills my ears, matching the rhythm of my chaotic pulse. It's so loud that I can't even hear his steps anymore.

I turn sideways, spotting his shadow growing nearer.

He's right behind me.

Without thinking, I drop my paper bag and swing back with my keys aimed at his throat. Concurrently, an involuntary cry slips out of my mouth.

His strong, warm hand catches my wrist in midair.

"Whoa," he says, his eyes bulging from their sockets.

My arm shakes in his grasp, the tips of my keys gleaming in the bright morning sun.

"Easy," he says. "I only wanted to talk to you."

His bright eyes widen at me, and he raises his free hand in submission as if to say, *I mean no harm.*

He slowly lets go of my wrist and takes two steps back, clearly sensing how terrified I am.

"I'm so sorry," he says. "I called out to you, but it didn't seem like you could hear me."

Is he lying? Or was all that pulsating in my ears masking his voice?

"I— I wanted to apologize to you," he says. "For bumping into you twice this morning. You must think I'm some creep who's following you."

I don't say anything because that's exactly what I'm thinking.

With his left palm still flat in the air, he presses his other hand on his chest. "Listen, this was all a coincidence. It's my day off, and I always do my groceries Monday morning before popping over to the gun shop to help Jones stock his shelves. Takes an hour of my time, and it helps him, since he has a terrible back."

I raise a brow. He's not making much sense. "I thought you said it was your day off."

He smiles, revealing a set of superbly white teeth. "It is. Sorry. Let me restart." He stiffens, draws in a breath, and blows it out through a partial crooked smile. "Wyatt."

He sticks out a hand, but I don't accept. My knuckles are aching around the sharp edges of my keys, but I can't seem to ease my tension.

"Officer Wyatt Daniels," he says. He wiggles a finger toward a green and white police cruiser parked on the side of the gun shop. It's barely noticeable next to a row of pine trees.

This time, my grip around my keys loosens. "You're a cop?"

He shrugs with one shoulder. "Yeah."

"So you don't work here?" My eyes shift from his handsome face to the gun shop.

He shakes his head and lets out a chuckle, the little curl over his brows springing slightly. "No, I volunteer. Well, not officially. I only help him out. I've known Jones for a long time, and he helps out our office a lot when we need ammunition in a bind." He raises a box of bullets—ones that read 9 mm. "He's a good guy."

"So you're a cop," I say. "And it's your day off, and this whole bumping into you has all been a coincidence because of timing?"

He beams, offering me his hand again. "Exactly. I'm Wyatt. Also known as Officer Daniels around here."

This time, I take it. "A— Emma. Emma Collins."

My new name sounds weird coming out of my mouth. Like it doesn't belong to me.

His grip is firm yet gentle. "Nice to meet you, Emma. And again, I'm so sorry about how things played out this morning."

He seems genuine. I gaze into his green eyes, noticing little blue flecks. He looks nothing like James, and even his demeanor is different.

He's confident, but not in an arrogant way. It's a maturity that tells me he's seen a lot in his lifetime.

"Nice to meet you too," I manage.

"Are you new around here?" he asks.

I hesitate. I hate who I've become. I feel like I have to hide my identity from everyone.

"Hey, I didn't mean to pry." He lets go of my hand and raises those two flat palms again. "You don't have to tell me anything."

It's simply a question of time before he discovers that I'm the new owner of Victor's old house. And if I'm secretive about my identity, he'll start to wonder why.

Besides, he's a cop.

Not that that makes any difference. The cops didn't help you when James wanted you dead.

I push this thought away.

That's not entirely true.

"No, it's okay," I say. "I just moved in. Sorry, I guess I'm hesitant to tell people where I live, because apparently, the place is cursed."

His eyes narrow playfully on me. "Let me guess. You bought the big house on Thorn Lake Drive."

I breathe out through a faint smile. "See, even you know about the stories. But no, I didn't buy it. It was inherited. Victor was my uncle."

"O-oh," he says, surprise slowly creeping in. "I-I'm sorry. For your loss, I mean."

I'm not sure how to accept his condolences, given that I haven't seen Victor in over twenty years. This whole time, I thought he was dead.

"Thanks," I say because there's nothing else to say.

"And, yeah, I mean, I would know about the notes," he says, changing the subject. "I was assigned to the investigation."

I stiffen. "Did you find anything? I mean, did Victor really do those awful things?"

Wyatt places his hands on his hips and bows his head. "Honestly, we still don't know. There was no proof of anything."

"Any idea who wrote the letters?" I ask.

What I really want to ask is, *Am I safe in that house, or does someone have a vendetta against it*?

Another shake of the head. "No, but the notes stopped after he died."

I raise a brow. "And that's not suspicious? What if—"

"I know what you're thinking," he says, "that whoever wrote those letters also killed Mr. Huxley. But I can assure you that Mr. Huxley died comfortably in palliative care at St. Maria Hospital.

St. Maria . . . I recognize that name.

I drove through the small city before arriving at Thorn Lake. It is quite a bit bigger than this town and also happens to be where the nearest hospital is located.

"And no visitors?" I ask.

He crosses his arms, an amused smile on his lips. "May I ask if you're a detective, Ms. Collins? Did you come here to solve the suspected murder of your uncle?"

I realize now how this must look—I'm interrogating a

cop. Heat rushes to my face. "No, sorry. I didn't even suspect murder until people started talking about all those weird notes. And it's not even about that. I have two boys. I want to know they're safe. If there's some lunatic out there—"

Wyatt places a gentle hand on my shoulder, and strangely, it comforts me.

"I wouldn't worry about that. I'm not technically supposed to talk about the case, but I can assure you that no one visited him in the hospital. No one poisoned him, if that's what you're thinking. I don't believe anyone killed him. Wanted him dead? Possibly. I mean, based on the horrific things written in those notes. But his death was completely natural. It was even confirmed by the autopsy. You're not in any danger, Emma."

He pulls his hand away and rests it back on his hip before eyeing the paper bag I dropped on the gravel lot. "Anyway, it looks like you know how to handle yourself."

I scoff. "I've never even shot a gun."

You shouldn't be telling him this. You have no idea who this man is.

I regret the words immediately after they come out of my mouth.

"No?" he says. "Well, I was about to go work on some renovations at home, but I'd be happy to take you to the shooting range. It's at the edge of town, by the water."

He isn't asking me to get into his car, which is a plus.

When I hesitate, he says, "Seriously, I don't mind. It's the Thorn Lake Shooting Range. If you're not comfortable shooting with a stranger, I can get back to my renovations and you can go alone. I completely understand. A lot of weirdos these days. But regardless, I'm happy to show you the way."

He flashes me a smile.

I could technically look it up on my GPS and go alone. But the whole idea of shooting a gun intimidates me. Even with Jones's short lesson, I don't exactly feel confident firing a gun for the first time by myself.

Besides, if there's one person who can teach me how to shoot properly, it's a cop.

CHAPTER 10

BEFORE

Things between James and me have gotten better since I called him out on his drinking. The next day, he apologized profusely. He even came home with takeout from an expensive restaurant and a bouquet of roses.

It made it difficult to stay angry with him.

He's been home early every evening to have supper with us and has even offered to cook twice in the last few weeks.

He's making an effort, and that means a lot to me.

Today, he comes home with a single rose and a smile on his stubbled face. He kisses my cheek and compliments my hair, even though I did nothing special with it.

"Look what I found," he says excitedly. "Fifty percent off."

He drops the rose on the sofa. He's so excited about his deal that he forgets to hand the flower to me.

Out from a paper bag come several white boxes with the words *high-definition camera* sprawled across their sides.

"What for?" I ask him.

"So I can still be with you guys, even when I'm not around. And so I know you're safe. There's this homeless guy who's been lingering at the corner of the block. I hate that I'm not home to keep you safe." He peels tape off the box and pulls out one of the circular-shaped cameras. At the base of it are little dots—assumedly a speaker.

"Two-way audio," he says, tapping his finger against the speaker.

"Two way?" I repeat.

"Yeah," he says. "So we can talk to each other."

"While you're at work?" I ask.

He must sense my lack of enthusiasm. He drops the cameras on the sofa like a child who's been told that their Christmas gifts need to be returned to the store.

"What's your problem, Alice? I thought you'd be happy about this."

"Happy about having cameras in our house?" I say.

Is he out of his mind? It's creepy. Why on earth would I want him watching me all day?"

"You think I'm gonna sit at work and watch you all day?" he says.

That's exactly what I was thinking.

He lets out a laugh. "Relax, honey. I'm not a creep. I'll text you before I even open the app."

"I don't think—" I try.

The smile on his face vanishes instantly. "Why are you so adamant about not having cameras in the house? Is there something you're hiding from me?"

"What?" I blurt. "No, not at—"

"If there's nothing to hide, then you shouldn't care that I can see you. What's the difference between me being home to see you or at work able to see you on a screen? The only difference is you can't see me. But I'll get to see my kids. I rarely see them as it is."

I suppose he has a point.

I'm being irrational about this.

He's my husband, after all. I shouldn't be this uneasy about it.

And he's right—I don't have anything to hide.

Surely, I'll get over myself.

This is for him. He wants to be more involved. Let him have this.

I sigh. "Fine."

"Fine?" he says. "Damn it, Alice. Why do you have to be such a downer? It's almost like you *want* to keep me away from the kids. Like you *want* me out of the picture."

"No," I say. "Not at all. I'm sorry, James." I close my eyes and force a laugh, hoping that if I act like it's nothing, it'll start to feel that way, too. "This is new to me. It's a great buy, really. I'll get over it."

"Get over what?" he says, his forehead creasing.

"Well, I find it creepy that—"

His eyes go huge. "Creepy? For fuck's sake. I'm your husband. And now you think I'm creepy . . ." He shakes his head and storms off.

"James, I didn't say that!" I call out after him. "I meant having cameras indoors on me at all times. Th-that's what I'm— James!"

He storms off into the bedroom and slams the door.

I really messed this up.

CHAPTER 11

I pull up to an old wooden sign that reads, Thorn Lake Shooting Range.

The place must be several decades old, with a small wooden cabin that I can only assume is the reception area. Behind this is a vast open field of sand.

I pull up next to Wyatt's green-and-white Ford police car, little rocks crunching under my tires.

I can't believe I'm doing this. Going to a random shooting range in the middle of nowhere with a cop. But there's no way he's lying about who he is. He's driving a real cop car.

Part of me wants to turn around, slam on the gas, and go home, but the other part of me wants real training. I want to know how to load a gun quickly and safely. And not based on some theoretical training provided by Jones, but through real-life experience.

If James finds us, I need to be ready. I can't miss.

I can't hesitate, either.

If that awful day ever comes, I need to fight back through muscle memory—not rely on my brain, which may not be functioning properly with a ton of adrenaline coursing through me.

"Save your rounds," Wyatt says, stepping out of his car. He slips a forest-green ball cap over his head. "Training is covered by the office. Rita has plenty of twenty-two rimfire inside."

He smirks, and I'm grateful for not having to spend any more money than I have to.

"Bring your new gun, though," he says.

I do as I'm told and follow him up a gravel path toward the wooden shack. Once inside, he greets a middle-aged woman behind the counter and signs something.

I assume that's Rita.

"Hey, Rita," he says cheerfully.

"Wyatt," she says, beaming at him. "How you doing, love?"

"Oh, the usual," he says.

She chuckles.

"Where's Dan?" he asks.

Rita rolls her eyes. "Got a man cold. I'm running the shop today."

Wyatt laughs and puts the pen down. "Rita, this is Emma. Emma, Rita. She and her husband own the range."

I nod briefly and try to smile.

"Wyatt here will take good care of ya," she says. She then winks at him, which makes me very uncomfortable.

Does she think we're on a date?

I just met the man.

Chewing a large piece of gum, Rita hands Wyatt two headsets and two pairs of clear glasses.

Protection, I assume.

Wyatt thanks her, then asks her for a case of twenty-twos. He tells her to put it on his account. He then grabs the equipment along with the box of ammunition and leads me through the back door.

It's quiet outside.

Almost too quiet.

In the distance are multiple green-and-white targets that spread backward into the sloping, sandy hill.

Wyatt helps me unpack my brand-new gun and, like Jones, shows me the mechanisms. He then pops out the magazine like he's done this a thousand times over and starts filling it with bullets.

Click.

When the magazine is back in place, he sets the gun down on a narrow wooden platform in front of us, its muzzle facing toward the target. He then hands me the protective gear.

I put on the ear coverings despite them seeming excessively large for my head. When he notices my struggle, he adjusts the top band until it fits comfortably, and all sound vanishes.

"Better?" he mouths.

I nod, then place the clear protective glasses over the bridge of my nose.

He points at the loaded gun on the table and smiles as if to say, *Give it a shot . . . literally.*

Although I'm a little nervous about shooting a real gun, it's comforting to know this place is designed for that. I can't hurt anyone so long as I keep my gun aimed straight ahead.

The metal is cold in my palm, and its weight is slightly heavier now that it's loaded.

I stand as Jones taught me, with my feet at shoulder's width and my eyes aimed straight ahead. I turn my face slightly, wanting Wyatt to approve of the stance before I fire my first round, when I realize I'm alone.

I whip around to find Wyatt standing near the cabin with his back turned to me and his shoulders rounded.

What is he doing?

Slowly, I place the gun down and remove my earmuffs to ask him whether he's all right. But right as I slide them down my neck, he turns around with a small cell phone pressed to his ear.

"Mm-hmm," he says when he catches me watching him. "All right, I'll be there soon."

And with that, he hangs up.

I feel rude watching him and immediately want to turn around, but it's too late now.

"Sorry," I say. "I was about to shoot, and—"

He forces a smile, though it looks strained. "Don't be. Listen, I'm so sorry, but I have to go."

"Oh no," I say. "I hope they didn't call you into work."

His eyes glaze over for a moment like he's lost in

thought. Then, they slowly regain focus, and he shakes his head. "Not quite."

Not quite?

I don't pry.

It's none of my business.

But he sounded very authoritative on the phone—not the way a husband or boyfriend might sound. And the last thing I want to do is be a home-wrecker.

I'm not that person.

Not that I'm even interested in Wyatt, but we are here alone, out in the middle of nowhere. If I *were* his girlfriend or wife, I wouldn't be happy about him being alone with another woman.

"Um, listen, you go ahead and practice all you want. Use up all the rounds. They're paid for."

"You don't have to—" I try.

"No, I mean it. You go ahead and shoot. I'm really sorry about this."

"It's okay," I say. "Life happens."

"Yeah," he says absentmindedly.

Whatever that phone call was about, it had him bothered. Is it about a case, and he isn't allowed to tell me?

"I'll be fine," I say, forcing a smile. "Jones gave me some basic training. I'll keep shooting until I hit something."

I'm not sure he even heard me. He glances at his phone before tucking it into his pocket and pulls his keys from his suede jacket.

"It was . . . It was really nice to meet you," he says, his eyes meeting mine.

"You too," I say.

I'm not sure whether, or when, I'll see this man again.

Although I enjoyed spending time with him, I'm not looking for any sort of romantic relationship right now.

It's better we don't exchange information.

"I'll see you around, Emma," he says.

With that, he jogs around the side of the cabin and disappears.

CHAPTER 12

I try not to overthink the whole thing with Wyatt as I fire round after round at the targets up ahead.

By my third magazine, I'm starting to hit a few things.

It feels good.

Okay, really good.

It's empowering to know that if James ever enters my life again with the intention of taking it, I stand a chance at coming out alive.

Halfway through the box of ammo, my arms start to get tired, so I call it a day. There's still so much to do at home—get the Internet installed, call the utility providers to change the name on file, find someone to plow the snow this winter, and most importantly, start making money.

And I can only do that if I get to work.

I unload my gun and insert the empty magazine back into place, then slide the gun back into its original packaging. It isn't ideal, but I'll place it in its new safe when I get home.

On my way out, I thank Rita, who smiles at me as if she's known me for years. "Take care, honey. Hope to see you again sometime."

She also tells me I'm welcome to return anytime to finish off my rounds. It's very sweet of her, and I appreciate her kindness.

I drive through the quiet town of Thorn Lake, still in awe over how quiet it is around here. A few people are walking their dogs, and one woman wearing a pair of tight yoga pants and a blue headband jogs at a steady pace.

She looks to be around my age.

Will I make friends here?

I haven't had friends for years. James made sure of that. It took time for him to push everyone out of my life, but looking back, there's no doubt in my mind that he orchestrated everything.

He was the puppeteer.

The missing texts. The deleted emails. All of it. Eventually, the few remaining friends I had in my life stopped trying with someone who made *zero effort back*.

Little did they know that I wasn't even aware of their attempts to reach me. And every time I reached out and tried to make plans, James found a way to keep me home.

He was too ill to take care of the kids, or he had to run into work at the last minute, forcing me to cancel my plans. And the few times my friends came over, James made sure he was present.

It was awkward and uncomfortable and made it impossible for us to have any girl talk.

How did I not see the signs?

I suddenly realize I'm driving with my hands wrapped so tightly around my steering wheel that my knuckles have lost all color.

I shake the tension out and take a left turn onto Thorn Lake Drive.

When I return to the house I struggle to think of as my home, I park the car in the back again and enter through the back door. The space is cool and so quiet that it makes me want to walk right back out and go somewhere else.

Anywhere but here.

You'll get used to this place. It takes time.

I'm not so sure I will. The house is massive. Far too big for a small family of three.

The soles of my sneakers smack against the floor, echoing throughout the house as I make my way to the kitchen. Although uncomfortable about leaving a gun in here, I want it near the front door.

It takes a little over fifteen minutes to set up my fingerprint settings, but once done, I place everything inside the safe and slide the shiny black box into the cupboard next to the fridge, on the highest shelf.

The kids don't need to know about it.

It's better if they don't.

I spend the rest of the day on the phone with local Internet and utility providers and then move on to setting up a home office space.

Not that there's much to do.

Victor already had a study on the main floor. It looks like something out of a movie—something a mafia boss might use to conduct business, with its oversized mahogany table and a leather chair that probably cost more than my laptop.

A few bookcases line the back wall next to the window. When I have time, I might scour the spines and see whether there's anything of interest.

Tired from the long day, I sit down, crack open my laptop, and connect to my hot spot.

I haven't touched my blog in days.

Okay, weeks.

Not since finding out about Victor's passing and about this place. I haven't had the mind to do it.

I blink at my stats on my account's dashboard.

Subscribers: 4,302.

The numbers impress me, even still. These numbers may not be much to big influencers out there—but to me, someone who started from nothing, well, they mean the world.

My subscriber list grew overnight last month when I wrote an article about domestic abuse and the early signs to watch out for in a relationship. Of course, I used a pen name and even wrote a whole fake bio about myself—how I live in California with my two cats, my new husband, and no children. I even go as far as to use a VPN that connects to California before logging into my blog and posting an article.

I never talk about James, either.

Not specifically.

If he were to ever come across my blog, I wouldn't want him piecing things together.

I open a new browser and visit Dazner—an affiliate program I signed up for once I started gaining traction with my blog—and navigate to my earnings page.

$142.73.

It isn't much.

But that's a week's worth of groceries.

Okay, with prices at an all-time high right now, more like a few days' worth.

If I can continue to engage my audience and grow my subscriber list, that number should continue to rise each month.

All I need is to tie us over until the inheritance check comes in. But even then, I don't want to rely on Victor's money. I want to make a name for myself. I *want* to work hard and have something to show for it. It's important to me that my boys learn the importance of reaping what you sow.

I return to my blog and click on New Post, then allow my fingers to hover over the keyboard for several minutes.

What am I supposed to write about?

There's so much on my mind that I can't bring myself to latch onto a single thought.

Sighing, I close my laptop, and at once, a knock echoes from the front door.

I flinch, despite the knock being gentle.

Who could possibly be at my door in the middle of the day?

I get up and slowly move toward the front door.

Another knock.

The figure on the other side shifts, trying to peer inside. I have half a mind to grab my new gun, but the thought seems outrageous.

How would it look if I opened the door to a welcoming

neighbor, only to be holding a gun at my side and out of view?

This neighborhood is safe.

Even Wyatt said that Thorn Lake is very safe.

With clammy hands, I unlock the deadbolt and open the door.

CHAPTER 13

BEFORE

"Hey, kiddo," comes James's voice through the speaker. "How you feeling? Any better?"

"Hey, Dad," Grayson says with as much enthusiasm as a snail. He's still in his pajamas, and his almost-black hair is completely tousled. He coughs, then crosses his pale arm over his chest and glares at the little red dot on the camera.

It's how I know James is on the other end.

We've agreed that he'll always text first before connecting. He finally came around and said he understood how it would be weird to feel like he was always watching me.

But he assured me that he values my privacy and would never do anything to invade that, even though I've seen the little red dot go off a few times without being consulted. When I asked James about it, he swore up and down that he didn't open the app—that it must have been a malfunction and that he would have to call the company to troubleshoot.

He has yet to do it.

But I get it—he's busy.

"This is weird. Why can't we do FaceTime like normal people?" Grayson asks.

It's a perfectly valid question.

I've asked James this several times now, and he always has the same answer: his work is confidential.

"Do you have any idea how much my ideas are worth?" he said the first day I asked him. "If anyone hacks into the feed, they could make millions if they're faster at production than me."

I suggested he step outside for the phone call, but his business office is situated on the twenty-fifth floor of a rental building.

"I'd have to go through security each time, and by the time I come back to the office, I'll have lost half an hour," he said.

It seems like an excuse.

It could be that he's lazy.

Either way, I'd much prefer to see his face when we're talking. And apparently, so would Grayson.

"I know, buddy," James says. "This isn't ideal. But I can't have cameras on at work."

"So go outside," Grayson says.

There's a long pause, followed by background chatter. It sounds like James has turned his head to talk to someone.

"Sorry. Something came up. Hey, I'll talk to you guys later, okay? Love you lots. Feel better soon, buddy."

And the little red dot disappears.

"That was stupid," Grayson says.

"I know it wasn't ideal, sweetheart," I say. "But it was better than nothing, wasn't it?"

It's Grayson's third day in a row talking to his father through the camera. He's been home from school with a cough, sniffles, and a fever that finally broke this morning.

"Not really," he says. "I don't like it."

How can I tell that to James? He checks in around the same time every day to say hi to me, and for the last three days, he's seemed awfully concerned about Grayson.

If anything, I'm glad he's trying to be more involved, even if this is all a little weird.

"Sometimes, we have to do things we don't want to do to keep other people happy," I tell him.

Instinctively, I look at the camera, relieved to see that the little red dot is still off. If James heard me say that, he'd get upset. He's always been sensitive, sometimes to a fault. But he also loves deeply and cares a lot about his children.

It's a fair trade-off.

Grayson sniffs, and it sounds like there's barely any oxygen making its way into his lungs. "No, you don't. You don't always have to do everything Dad tells you, you know."

My palms get clammy.

"What?" I say.

"You do everything Dad tells you," he says. "And when you don't, he gets mad."

Is he right?

Has my complacency with James become that obvious? I tried to shield my children from my husband's anger, but it's clear that hasn't worked.

"Dad has a lot on his plate," I say, trying to defend James. "You know he can get stressed."

Grayson rolls his eyes. "He's always stressed . . . and mean."

I'm stunned to hear this coming out of my eight-year-old's mouth. If anything, James has been sweeter these last few weeks.

So what is Grayson talking about?

Am I that deluded that I believe James's behavior is worth being excused simply because he's making an effort? Effort isn't enough if you're still hurting the ones you supposedly love.

"Has he done anything to you, Grayson?" I ask, my tone stern.

My eyes flicker toward the camera again, and although I probably shouldn't do this, I reach to the back and unplug it. "No one's listening, sweetheart. Only me."

He hesitates.

"He's mean," he says.

"Has he ever hit you?" I ask.

He shakes his head, and I believe him. "No, Dad wouldn't do that. I don't mean he hurts me. He's always mad at me. I didn't pick up my toys the other night, and he threw one of them at my closet door. It broke in half."

His bottom lip quivers.

"Oh, honey," I say. I open my arms, and he comes in for a hug.

My heart is thumping so hard that I'm afraid he'll feel it against his shoulder.

James lied to me.

I remember that sound—the loud *crack*.

When I questioned James about it, he said he tripped over one of Grayson's toys and landed against his closet. And although I know kids can sometimes bend the truth, Grayson wouldn't make something like this up.

I believe him.

But why would James lie about it?

There's a chance this was a complete misunderstanding.

He could have fallen and dropped a toy in the process, and it *looked* like he threw it.

Because how can I choose to believe one story over the other when they're coming from two of the people I love most in this world?

CHAPTER 14

The man startles when I swing the door open.

"Oh, hi there," he says. "I was beginning to think no one was home."

He's clad in a blue uniform with a name tag that reads: Charles.

Late-sixties. A thin frame, gray and brown hair, and a hesitant smile that suggests he suffers from mild social anxiety.

Behind him is a white van with a huge blue label on it that reads, Allister Wi-Fi.

I must be making a face; he scratches his forearm sheepishly and says, "I know our appointment is tomorrow, but I just repaired a line down the road, and I figured I could pop in now to set up your Internet."

"Oh," I say.

"I can come tomorrow if now's a bad time," he says. "I didn't mean to interrupt." He pauses, scratches his neck again, and adds, "I should have called. I'm sorry—"

"No, no," I say. "It's all right. Come on in."

I hate that I'm already sizing him up. He's nowhere near as tall as James, and if he were to try anything, I'd have a fighting chance.

Stop thinking like that. He's only here to install your Internet.

I feel ashamed for even having these thoughts. I've always been a bit fearful around men—after all, my mother made sure to warn me time and time again not to put myself in dangerous situations and how there are plenty of *psychos* out there.

But I never absorbed her fear.

Not until James.

Now, I know what men are capable of. I know what it's like to be held down, completely helpless, and at the mercy of someone else.

And it's something I never want to feel again.

Charles walks in, his boots heavy against the foyer's white tiles. He's about to remove them when I say, "That's all right, you can keep them on."

He hesitates, half bent, and scans the overly shiny floors. "You sure?"

"I'm sure," I say.

I want to wash these floors anyway. There's a residual smell in this house. It's not unpleasant—a lemony scent mixed with an herb I can't quite place—but it isn't *our* smell. It makes me feel like we're living in someone else's house temporarily.

"O-okay," Charles says. "Do you know if Wi-Fi was ever installed in this house before?"

I purse my lips. "I have no idea. But I doubt it."

"Phone line?"

I shrug.

Avoiding eye contact, he nods slowly and starts searching the walls, the high ceilings, and the floorboards.

"Where do you want your modem?" he asks.

"Anywhere in here is fine," I say.

The man pauses in thought before planting two hands on his hips.

"I didn't see any line running to your house out there, so I may need to run one. Mind if I check your basement to see what's been previously installed?"

"Sure, right this way," I say.

I lead him to the basement's oak door next to the staircase. He reaches for the handle and cracks it open. Before stepping in, a spider falls from the top of the door frame, and Charles swats at a large cobweb.

"Basement isn't used too much, is it?" he jokes.

A black, yellow-striped spider races away from his large boot and disappears under a floorboard.

"Haven't gone down there yet," I admit.

"Spiders don't bother me," he says. "I'll clear the path for you."

I smile but don't say anything.

"Do you need me down there?" I ask.

What I'm really thinking is, *I'm not following you into some creepy basement, where no one can hear me scream if you decide to attack me.*

The thought makes me feel crazy.

Charles seems like a very nice man. A husband, and likely a grandfather, who works part-time to supplement his retirement money.

So why do I feel like he's a threat? Like every man is a threat?

James did this to you.

"Oh, not at all," he says cheerfully. "Most basements are standard. I'll find my way. You go ahead and do whatever you need to do, and I'll let you know when I'm done or if I have any questions."

I appreciate his words, but I don't thank him. Instead, I nod politely and return to the kitchen, where I spend the next hour scrolling through my phone, trying to come up with article ideas for my blog.

I don't dare go upstairs or into my office and leave a strange man out of my sight.

When he finishes his work in the basement, he starts moving in and out of the house with equipment.

"All done, miss," he finally says. "Here's the password. Why don't you test it out?"

I pretend to look up from my phone, even though I've been keeping an eye on him since he returned upstairs.

"Thank you," I say. Then, the most dreaded part. "How does payment work?"

He waves a hand in the air dismissively. "Oh, don't worry about that now. It comes off on your first bill, which will be in thirty days. There's an installation fee of a hundred and fifty dollars, but I'll add a hundred-dollar credit to your file to reduce that."

I'm a bit taken aback by his kindness. He is, after all, standing in a multimillion-dollar home. Shouldn't he be trying to gouge me?

"Oh, that's very nice of you," I say.

He smiles like it's nothing. "Happy to have you as a new customer. Thank you for trusting us to deliver your Wi-Fi."

He remains quiet as I enter the new password to test out the connection.

"It works," I tell him.

Grayson will be happy.

I thank him and walk him out through the front door. When he's gone, I stand in the kitchen, but my eyes are immediately drawn to the basement door he left partially open.

Although irrational, I can't help but picture James's face appearing from the darkness of that crack. First, his dark eye, then, his symmetrical nose, and finally, a crooked, malevolent smile.

I blink the vision away.

The longer I stand around here avoiding the basement, the worse things will get for me.

You're a grown-ass woman, Alice. Plus, you have a gun now. Take it with you if you're scared.

It's ridiculous.

I shouldn't be this scared.

What is wrong with me?

Darkness never bothered me before.

Not until James.

Now, he lurks in the shadows everywhere I turn. I swallow hard, still staring at the darkness clinging to the edge of the door.

It may be preposterous to walk around my own house with a gun, but it would make me feel a lot safer.

I hurry to the cabinet next to the fridge and reach

inside for the small gun safe. It beeps when I press my thumb against the sensor, then clicks open.

I did as Jones instructed. I kept the magazine out of the gun for storage. But if someone is hiding down there—okay, there's most definitely no one waiting for me down there—I want to be able to defend myself.

I click the magazine into place and pull the slide back. It makes a satisfying clicking sound as the bullet enters the chamber. I may be acting irrationally, but I still have enough of my sanity to remember to keep my finger off the trigger of a loaded gun.

The sight of a spider might put a hole through my foundation.

"James isn't here," I say aloud.

The sound of my own voice makes me feel like I've lost my mind. Of course he isn't here. How could he possibly know about this place?

You took every precaution. You're safe now.

Heart battering in my chest and gun at my side, I reach for the door and slowly swing it open.

CHAPTER 15

The air is cool and damp and smells musty.

As I descend a set of old wooden stairs, the light bulb above me flickers.

Creak.

Crack.

Each step has been painted gray, though it doesn't do much to add to the aesthetics of this place.

Drywall surrounds me as I descend, but halfway down, the walls turn to what I assume used to be red brick. For the most part, they've all turned white, except for a few spots that showcase the remnants of a once beautiful storage space.

I didn't expect the basement to be this archaic. It looks as though it hasn't been touched since the late eighteen hundreds, and instead, left to rot in the humidity.

The space is also smaller than I expected. I spot the furnace and some old wooden crates that look empty. Plumbing travels along the ceiling, though it looks like it doesn't even belong in a space this old.

I reach for a light switch and flick it on.

A yellow glow fills the confined space, though it isn't very bright.

It looks like Charles took care of most of the cobwebs for me, which was very kind of him. Either that, or there weren't as many as he predicted. A few electrical wires run down from the ceiling into a large gray box that looks rather new. A few little lights flicker, some green, others red. I have no idea what they mean, but that's what electricians are for.

Hopefully, I won't need one anytime soon.

At the far back wall is a huge rectangular wine rack that stands pressed up against the wall. It looks new with its shiny rich brown wood.

I'm surprised to see so many wine bottles sitting here. Victor must have spent his time collecting wine rather than drinking it.

Keeping my gun at my side, I approach the dusty bottles.

There's some vintage stuff here. I don't know much about wine, but when I spot dates like 1942, I know they're worth a lot of money.

I wonder how much money I could make selling these old wine bottles. I pick one up and brush a strip of dust off the glass with my thumb, trying to estimate a price point. Right before I can read any text, something nearby squeaks. I flinch and drop the bottle.

Clash.

It shatters at the neck, and blood-colored liquid spills, creeping toward my shoes.

"Shit," I mutter.

A small grayish-brown mouse races across the bottles, slipping and sliding through the holes between each shelf.

Note to self: get mousetraps.

Mice weren't something I had to worry much about in the city, but here . . . I get the feeling it'll be an ongoing problem. I've used catch-and-release traps before. I don't have the heart to kill them.

And yet here you are, standing with a gun, prepared to kill a human.

I can't say for certain that I'd have it in me to actually fire the thing. Even if faced with a threat.

No, if James came at you or the boys, you wouldn't hesitate. You'd kill that bastard.

I take a deep breath when I realize I'm squeezing the handle of my gun a little too tightly.

I look around until I spot an old broom and a mop in the corner. I spend the next fifteen minutes cleaning up the mess I made while internally blaming the mouse for my problems.

Right as I toss the broken glass into a small plastic garbage can, a strange creaking sound pulls my attention to the ceiling.

What is *that*?

It's slow, deliberate . . . like someone is walking.

My mouth goes dry.

I reach for my phone in my back pocket, but it isn't there.

Damn it.

I must have left it on the kitchen island. I couldn't call the cops if I wanted to.

This doesn't make any sense.

After Charles left, I locked the door.

It could be another mouse traveling through the pipes.

You're being paranoid, Alice.

The sound grows louder, traveling right over the top of my head.

That's not a mouse.

Those are definitely footsteps.

My heart hammers inside my chest, and my legs start to tremble. Why is someone in my house?

See, you weren't crazy to bring a gun.

No, this doesn't make sense.

It must be Grayson and Lucas.

It can't be. It was 1:54 when you came downstairs, and their buses arrive at 3:15.

I've only been down here for fifteen minutes—twenty, tops.

Part of me wants to stay down here. It's the right thing to do, isn't it? To hide? Wait? If someone broke in, they're looking to rob me. They can take what they want, so long as they get out before my boys get home.

My phone is up there. My wallet. My new identity. If they take my wallet, along with my new cards, it'll be a nightmare trying to get all that back.

Besides, it's probably some teenager who got dared to break into Mr. Huxley's creepy old house.

I can handle a teenager. And if I do it right—if I scare the living hell out of him, or her—it might prevent other kids from ever setting foot inside this house again.

Or it's James.

The thought causes my throat to constrict.

Still shaking, I reach for my Glock on the floor and try to steady my quivering hands.

More creaking comes from overhead, and there isn't a doubt in my mind that someone is in my house.

CHAPTER 16

I walk slowly, one step at a time, with my gun held firmly in both hands. My entire body shakes so badly that even if I tried to fire a shot, I'd probably miss and shatter one of my windows.

A loud thump echoes upstairs, and I freeze, saucer eyed in the dim lighting of the basement staircase.

Right now, my earlier mouse problem seems so minute.

I'd take a whole mouse infestation over a stranger lurking around in my home.

I take another step, the bright kitchen light creeping through the crack of the basement door.

Almost there.

I'm about to take another step when Grayson's voice echoes on the other side. "Mom?"

The door suddenly blasts open, and I whip my gun around my back.

"Mom?" Grayson repeats.

He looks confused, likely wondering what I'm doing hiding in the creepy basement staircase.

"What're you doing?" he asks, crinkling his nose.

His eyes flicker toward my hand behind my back.

"Was just checking out the basement," I say, steadying my breath. My heart is still pounding so hard I can barely hear myself talk. "I— I'll be up in a minute."

"'Kay," he says and turns around.

I shove the gun under one of the steps and hurry upstairs.

"What're you doing home?" I ask, my tone clipped.

Lucas comes running from out of the living room with a grin on his face.

They're *both* home.

What's going on?

Grayson cocks a brow at me. I hate it when he looks at me like that. I know his teenage hormones are to blame for his incessant attitude, but it's a look that says, *Are you all right in the head?*

"What do you mean?" he asks. "School's over."

Lucas runs up to me and throws his arms around my waist. I should hug him back and smile at him, but I can't find it in me to do it.

I'm too confused.

"It's 2:20," I point out. "Why are you home so—"

"It's 3:20," Grayson says. "The oven clock is wrong, remember?"

It all comes back to me now.

I noticed it when we first entered our new home, and I told myself I'd change the clocks today. And then Charles showed up, which completely threw me off. And before I went into the basement, I glanced over at the oven clock, forgetting that the time was wrong.

"I didn't unlock the door," I say. "How—"

"You gave me the spare," Grayson says, dangling a navy-blue lanyard between us.

I rub my temples. "I'm sorry. I've had a long day."

When Grayson doesn't respond, I force a smile. "How was your first day at school?"

He looks annoyed.

I can't tell whether it's because he came home to an empty house and got spooked himself or whether he had a bad day.

"Was all right," he says.

That's not promising.

It's imperative that he like this new school. There aren't any other options in town. If things didn't work out, he'd have to go to St. Maria, which is half an hour away. And I don't think we're in the zone for transportation, which means I'd have to drive him every day.

I'd do it, but I don't want to.

"Just *all right*?" I ask.

"Yeah. That's what I said," he says.

"Don't," I say threateningly.

He can sense my anger. I can understand he's a hormonal teenager, and for the most part, I'm patient with him, and I let a lot slide.

Especially his eye rolls.

But I'm only willing to tolerate so much attitude from him. If he's going to outright treat me like garbage, I'm going to put him in his place.

He is *not* going to turn out like his father.

Not as long as I'm still breathing.

"Sorry," he mumbles. "It was fine, okay? I just miss my old school. I didn't mean to be rude."

"I understand that," I say. "And thank you for your apology." I wrap an arm around his shoulder, and he seems to appreciate the affection. "I know this is hard. It's hard for me, too. This place is weird. This house is huge. There's freaking mice in the basement."

His eyes go a little rounder. "Seriously?"

"Yeah," I say. "And the basement is creepy as hell. Looks like a place a vampire might have once lived in."

"Can I see?" he asks, more excited than I've seen him in days.

I rub his back. "Yeah. Clean out your lunch box first, and go put your bag in your room." I point at Lucas. "That goes for you, too, mister."

Lucas doesn't hear me. He plays on his tablet on the living room sofa, eyes shining brightly.

"Lucas," I say more sternly. "No screen time until your chores are done."

He looks up at me, then presses the power button and immediately drops his tablet.

For the most part, Lucas listens. Well, when he isn't so consumed by one of his games that he can't even hear me.

"Go on," I say.

They do as they're told, then hurry upstairs to drop their bags off in their rooms. I use this time to take the magazine out of the Glock, remove the bullet from the chamber, and store the gun back in its safe.

Right as I close the cupboard door, Grayson and Lucas come running down the large flight of stairs as if we're about to embark on some adventure to Disney Land.

Who knew an old basement could prove so entertaining?

"Ready," Grayson says.

"Are *you* ready?" I ask Lucas.

He looks scared, but in an excited way. He nods fast and latches onto his brother. Surprisingly, Grayson lets him, which is a role that suits him—protective big brother.

We venture down into the basement, which is a lot more enjoyable than my first time down here. Lucas and Grayson inspect the space with their jaws hanging agape.

"Old, isn't it?" I say.

"Why is it so small?" Grayson asks. "The upstairs is huge."

I shrug. "I don't know. I guess they didn't care much about basements back in the day."

I spot a few mouse droppings next to the wine rack. That can't be healthy. I'll have to get that cleaned up tomorrow.

"Come on," I say. "Let's go upstairs, and you guys can watch something."

"You got Wi-Fi?" Grayson asks, a hint of excitement flashing in his eyes.

"I did," I say.

That's all it takes to get him running up those stairs. Lucas follows, though he stays close to me.

They keep themselves entertained while I cook us some chicken and a side of rice and broccoli. It's nothing fancy, but it's healthy and filling. And with how much Grayson has been eating lately—that kid is growing like a weed—it needs to be filling.

An orange glow slips into the house as the sun begins to set. I make my way through the main floor, closing the blinds.

There's something about having open blinds at night that really gets to me. It makes me feel vulnerable because if someone out there is watching, they can see us perfectly.

I'm about to close the blinds next to the front door when I spot a figure standing at the very end of our driveway.

I squint, trying to get a better view of the man.

It's him.

The man from the other day.

He stands there, unmoving, with his long black trench coat and oversized yellow hat. Even in the dim light of the evening sun, his skin looks alabaster white.

I just joked about how a vampire might have once lived in our basement. What if *he's* that vampire?

And why is he standing on my property? He's literally at the end of my driveway.

Not in the road, not on the sidewalk, but on my driveway.

More importantly, why is he staring this way?

I'm tempted to run out there and yell at him to get lost, but something warns me against it. I get the feeling this man isn't playing with a full deck of cards.

There's something eerily frightening about him, and if I go out there on the attack, there's no telling what he might do.

A little tremble travels down my arm as I reach for the deadbolt and try to turn it. It's already locked, but I need to make sure it's *really* locked.

"What is it?" Grayson asks.

He's leaning over the couch, watching me.

"Nothing," I lie, and close the blinds.

CHAPTER 17

BEFORE

James has yet to have the manufacturer repair the camera. I've even considered asking him to swap it out with the one in the basement, or the kitchen, but he says he has them all programmed a certain way in his phone.

They're all labeled, or named, or something.

And if I go swapping them around, he'll have to reprogram them.

It sounds like he's making a big deal out of something small, but with how upset he gets when I bring up the red light glitch, I don't see the point in pursuing the matter.

I suppose it's not that big a deal.

If I really need privacy, say, to speak to my sister, Chloe, on the phone, I go outside and walk down the street. Both she and my parents have pointed out that it's a little odd—okay, very odd—that he wants cameras in the house like that.

I once made the mistake of throwing in my family's opinion in an argument, and he flipped out, saying that I valued their opinion more than my own husband's.

He also doesn't like to feel teamed up against.

I imagine James experiences a sense of isolation in this world. Especially given that he doesn't talk to his parents anymore. Several years ago, when they cut him off from financial support, he took it one step further and told them if they couldn't support his business ventures, then they were proving they no longer loved him as a son.

I thought it was extreme, but how can you argue about feelings?

He feels betrayed by them, and nothing I say will fix that.

Some days, I wish he had a brother or sister to talk to. Someone. I suspect he's jealous of my family.

It's like he thinks we're all out to get him. Or that they'll back up whatever suspicions I have, making him out to be the bad guy.

But that's not it at all.

I didn't even mention my concerns over the cameras. But of course, I had to let my sister know what was going on when she asked me how things were with James, and I told her to hold on while I made my way outside.

I shouldn't have done that.

My father has never been a fan of James. Even if they didn't live hundreds of miles away, I doubt they'd visit very often.

I always had the impression that they held a grudge against him for taking me away. But it was my decision to move this far across the country.

I stare at the camera as the red light turns on and off throughout the day. I really wish he'd have that damn thing fixed. It's stressful. It feels like I'm constantly being watched.

Only yesterday, I got so fed up that I turned the camera to face the wall. Since James is supposed to text before connecting to the camera, there shouldn't have been any harm.

But he called me minutes later to see whether I was okay.

"I was showing my colleague the app, and I noticed the camera wasn't working. I wanted to make sure you were all right," he said.

He'd sounded genuinely concerned.

When I explained my reasoning for moving it, he sighed heavily and reemphasized that there was no reason to do that. And that if I forgot to put the camera back, he wouldn't be able to check in in case of emergencies.

"What if someone breaks in? What if I don't hear from you?" he said. "What if you take a nap and the house sets on fire?"

"I thought you didn't check in randomly," I quipped.

"I do now and then, but only for a second," he said. "I told you that before I installed them. That I would text before checking in to talk but that I might sometimes open it to make sure everything was okay. What's gotten into you? You're acting paranoid."

He'd never said that.

Right?

Or had I forgotten?

And I wasn't being paranoid. The red light kept turning on, which made me feel like he was constantly checking in.

When the red light comes on again, I fight the urge to turn the camera around. If I do that, I might get another call. I grit my teeth and move into the kitchen to clean up dirty dishes, only to spot the kitchen camera's red light now lit up.

I want to yell at the camera's lens and tell James to back off.

I could be overthinking it.

He did get the cameras at a bargain store, which makes me wonder whether they were returned due to malfunctioning hardware.

My phone suddenly rings, then vibrates against the dining room table. I flinch and hurry to it.

It's James.

"Hi," I say coldly.

"Hey, honey," he says. "I have some good news."

"Oh?" I say.

Although I could use some good news, I don't exactly want to receive any from *him*.

"The cameras should be fixed," he says. "I just spoke to the company, and it's a known glitch. Apparently, hundreds of people have reported the same problem."

I start to feel very guilty for having made James out to

be some creep in my head. And for not having trusted him. He's my husband. Why did I make such a big deal out of this?

I glance at the camera in the living room. The red light is still on. Could it be that the company made a mistake?

"The red light has been coming on and off all day," I tell him.

Suddenly, another thought occurs to me. What if it isn't James? What if someone else has hacked into the feed? I've heard of horror stories like that. It's possible that this entire time, my paranoia has been focused on the wrong person.

"Oh," he says. "Okay, hold on. I have some notes." He goes quiet for a moment. "Okay, try resetting the cameras. All you have to do is hold down the power button on each one. I gotta go. If it keeps happening, shoot me a text. But it should fix it. I love you."

Before I can say it back, he hangs up.

I hurry to the cameras, resetting each one.

This better work.

I sit down and watch the black lens.

There's no light.

Nothing.

But it's on, that much I know—the little steady blue light is on at the base of the camera.

I'm so embarrassed and feel beyond guilty.

Especially after telling Chloe that I thought James was spying on me. Now my family probably thinks the worst of him, and they already weren't that fond to begin with.

I'd better call them to smooth all of this over.

CHAPTER 18

I tap my fingers against the island countertop, watching Grayson and Lucas. They're parked in front of the television, watching some pointless video on YouTube where people are shoving candy in their mouths and eating nonstop.

I don't understand entertainment these days.

It's mind-numbing and can't be good for their developing brains.

"You guys want to play a game?" I ask.

When they don't hear me, I get up and tell Grayson to pause the video. He does as told, and Lucas looks up at me like he's about to protest.

"Enough of that mindless stuff," I say. "How about we play a game?"

"What kind of game?" Grayson asks.

"Hide and seek," I say. "Imagine how hard that'll be in this big house."

Lucas bounces to his feet, but Grayson doesn't budge.

"I'm good," he says, prepared to press Play on the remote.

I lean forward and snatch it from him. "Either you play, or you go in your room and do nothing. You've been staring at that TV for over three hours now."

He sighs. "Fine."

"Can I start?" Lucas asks. "I wanna hide!"

How can I deny my seven-year-old a simple request like that?

"Of course," I say. "We'll close our eyes, and you hide.

You'll get thirty seconds."

"And ears!" Lucas says.

I smile and wink at him. "I'll turn the TV on really loud, and then you go hide. Got it?"

He nods fast.

I press Play, even though the last thing I want to hear is people chewing on candy. I turn up the volume, then sit down next to Grayson and wiggle a finger at him as if to say, *Go on, cover your eyes.*

He rolls them before closing them.

For effect, I use both hands to cover mine, and then I start shouting over the TV, "One, two . . ."

By thirty, I remove my hands and press Pause on the remote before I blow a gasket.

"We're coming!" I say.

Grayson doesn't get up.

"Would you at least make an effort?" I say. "Your little brother wants to play with you."

"He doesn't care who he plays with," Grayson argues. "As long as he plays."

"That's not true," I say. "He looks up to you."

Grayson gets up with an exaggerated sigh as if he's carrying a one-hundred-pound backpack.

"He probably went upstairs," Grayson says.

I aim my nose at the staircase to say, *Well, what are you waiting for? Go check.*

With heavy steps, Grayson makes his way upstairs while I search the main floor. I go out of my way to be dramatic by shouting things like, "Are you *here*? What about under here?"

That sort of thing usually gets Lucas giggling.

After several minutes of searching, Grayson comes downstairs. "He's not up there."

I hold back a sigh. Grayson has a habit of not looking with his eyeballs. "Did you look properly?"

"I looked everywhere," he says impatiently.

And so did I.

A surge of panic flows through me.

What if he went outside?

I glance at the front door. The deadbolt is unlocked.

Damn it.

Why didn't I tell him outside was off-limits?

"He might have gone outside," I say urgently.

"So what?" Grayson says.

So what? It's dark. It's cold. And a creepy old man sometimes stands at the end of our driveway. We also don't know this place. Not really. There could be plenty of threats out there.

"Help me find him," I say, fighting to keep my voice steady.

"That's what I'm doing," he says.

Ignoring the attitude, I rush to the front door, slip on my shoes, and run out into the darkness.

"Lucas! Time out! Come out, please. We need to pick a new hiding spot!"

Nothing.

"Lucas, the game is over. I need you to come out!"

Why isn't he listening?

Is he hiding in some corner, giggling to himself? Does he think I'm trying to trick him out of hiding?

Grayson smacks a few light switches, and the outdoor lights come on. Rather than thank him, I run to the back and search under my car with my phone's flashlight, around the hedges, and through the dark trees in the distance.

"Lucas! The game is over!"

"Mom!" Grayson calls out behind me.

Ignoring him, I keep searching.

Rapid footsteps approach me. "Mom," Grayson says.

"What?" I say impatiently.

Vapor plumes out of Grayson's mouth with every breath. "I think he might be in the basement."

I stop my search and stiffen. "What? Why would he be in the basement? And the deadbolt was unlocked. He has to be out here."

Grayson shrugs. "I don't know. But the basement door

is open."

With wobbly legs, I run back into the house and blast the basement door wide open.

"Lucas! I need you to come out!"

I race down the steps, my shoes smacking against the old wood.

Why would he have come down here by himself? It isn't like him. Last year, he said little monsters with prickly shaved heads like to live in everyone's basements.

"Lucas!" I shout.

My voice bounces off the brick walls and low-hanging ceiling.

"Um, Mom?" Grayson says.

I was so busy running down these stairs that I didn't even hear him follow me. I jolt at the sound of his voice. Before I can ask him what he wants, I see it—the huge wine rack.

The right side of it is pushed outward, and the left side, inward. A faint strip of yellow light slips out on both sides.

A secret swivel door.

I stick my fingers inside the crack on the right and pull back, revealing a long, cylindrical tunnel.

Cobwebs stick to nearly every surface in sight, and little footprints form a straight line all the way down the tunnel.

Lucas must have come down here.

At the end of the tunnel is a wavering light, almost as if the light fixture is convulsing.

What is that?

"Here," Grayson says, handing me a flashlight. "There's a bunch of them on the wall."

I turn sideways to spot a rack of old flashlights of various sizes. I grab one and flick the switch.

At once, a beam of light shoots down the tunnel.

I don't even think about running back upstairs to grab my gun. All I can think about is Lucas, and if I have to fight a ten-foot monster with nothing but my nails to protect him, I'll do exactly that.

I hurry through the tunnel, ducking to prevent my head from hitting the ceiling.

"Lucas?" I whisper.

My voice resonates down the tunnel, and at the same time, the distant light goes out.

My eyes bulge.

Why did it go out?

And what is that smell? It's faint, and not overpowering, but it smells like someone left a bucket of dead fish somewhere, and the scent has now seeped into the concrete walls.

"Lucas?" I shout in a whisper.

I don't like this place at all.

Why would someone have a secret tunnel in their house?

I round the corner but immediately stop when I come face to face with a room that looks to have been carved out of stone. The door's arch is narrow, low, and glaringly uneven. My flashlight shines right through it, hitting a concrete wall at the other end.

I don't want to step inside.

Something about this dark, ominous room has me wanting to run the other way.

But if Lucas is here, there's no question. I have to enter.

I point my flashlight to the left, hitting another wall. In the corner of the room is an old cot with a rusted metal frame. The mattress is missing, and next to this cot is a bucket.

The air around me is musty and earthy.

"Lucas?" I swing my flashlight to the right.

I jump when I spot Lucas facing away from me. He stands so still, his little round shoulders barely moving as he breathes. In his right hand is an unlit flashlight.

I stare at the back of his head—at his short brown curls and his adorable ears that stick out a little too much for his head.

"Lucas?" I repeat.

He doesn't respond.

What's going on?

"Lucas?" I try again.

When he still doesn't answer, I walk gingerly toward him.

"Hey, you okay?" I ask. I reach for his shoulder, my flashlight soaking him up entirely, along with the side wall he's facing.

Then, I see it, and I almost vomit.

CHAPTER 19

I wrap my hand over Lucas's face, covering his eyes, and pull him away from the horrid sight. Grayson tries to peek over my shoulder, but I shout at him, telling him to get out and to bring his brother upstairs.

"But—" Grayson tries.

I use my body to shield him from the view.

To protect him.

I've seen dead bodies before, at funerals. But this . . . this is something else. This is the remains of a body that's been left for nature to take its course for what I can only imagine is several months. The flesh, the muscles, the organs, they're all gone. They must have liquefied not too long ago because a dark stain spreads out under the skeleton. In some areas, bits of brown, almost black, flesh still cling to the bones. And that putrid smell. It isn't potent, but it's there, which means the body is still decomposing.

This death is fairly recent.

I turn away, the sight of the skeleton's loose-hanging jaw still engraved in my mind. It's all I can see as I navigate through the dark tunnel, back toward the house.

My legs shake so badly I'm afraid I might fall. I try to keep my flashlight steady for the boys, but it wavers from side to side, making me even dizzier.

When I reach the basement, I turn around and push the secret swivel wine rack door closed. It takes some effort because the wood is so heavy, but it clicks into place.

I breathe in, and out, trying to center myself.

I need to be strong for Grayson and Lucas.

"Mom?" Grayson asks, his voice almost squeaky.

"Take your brother upstairs," I tell him.

He's about to protest, so I add, "Now."

He goes quietly, asking Lucas to follow him.

When they're both gone, I reach for the bucket I used earlier to clean up the wine bottle shards. A loud retching sound echoes around me as I vomit my supper.

I wipe my mouth and hurry upstairs, slamming the basement door shut behind me. It's not like the body can follow us, but that sight was so disturbing that it feels like the entire house is now contaminated.

My mouth completely dry, I step away from my kids, snatch my phone and dial 911.

"911, what is your emergency?"

"I—I found a body," I say.

"Okay. Nonresponsive, not breathing?"

"Y-yes," I blurt. "A dead body. A corpse. A rotten skeleton. W-we just moved here, and we were playing hide-and-seek, and—"

"What's the address?"

"1472 Thorn Lake Drive," I say.

"That's in Thorn Lake?"

I nod, then realize she can't hear me. "Y-yes."

"Okay," she says, overly calmly. "We're dispatching an officer from Thorn Lake's local police department. It shouldn't be long. You're welcome to wait outside if the body is making you uncomfortable."

I nod again, then say, "Y-yeah, we'll do that. Thank you."

"It won't be long," she says again. "What's your name?"

"My name?" I ask.

For some odd reason, I feel like I'm going to become a suspect. Either that, or she'll figure out that I'm giving her a fake name.

It's not fake. You changed it legally.

"E-Emma," I say. "Emma Collins."

Her keys clack as she types this, along with my address and phone number.

"I've added the report to the system. If anything changes with your situation, give us a call back. Otherwise, your local police department will take care of it from here."

"T-thank you," I say, and hang up.

I urge Grayson and Lucas to go outside.

The air is cool and crisp and feels like it's cleaning my insides from the rotten air I breathed in that basement.

I blink hard, trying to rid my mind of the body's wide-open mouth, the hollow eye sockets, and its long, pointed fingers locked into each other.

I sit on the wooden bench on the front porch and exhale slowly, my breath unsteady.

"Are you okay?" Grayson finally asks me. "What was that down there?"

Lucas sits quietly, staring ahead.

He's not shaking, or crying, or asking questions.

"A body," I tell Grayson, matter-of-factly.

His eyes bulge. "A body? What the hell was a body—"

"I don't know," I cut him off. "The police will remove it and investigate."

"Well, I don't want to live here anymore," he says.

"Neither do I," I admit. "But this house is paid for. And Uncle Victor prepaid for all our services and property tax for a year, which means living here is completely free right now. We can't afford to live anywhere else."

He sighs through his nose and turns toward our driveway, staring at the tall streetlight at the very end. The house across from us is dark, aside from one window with a bright yellow light spilling through closed blinds.

Crickets chirp all around us, and something makes a yapping sound—possibly a coyote.

At least that creepy man isn't out here.

It's possible that's the reason he's been staring—he knows something.

Several minutes pass before a green-and-white police vehicle pulls into our driveway. A wave of relief washes over me.

Wyatt, possibly.

Hopefully.

I get up, holding onto myself as a cool breeze sweeps across the patio.

Once parked, Wyatt steps out of the driver's side wearing a police uniform—navy pants, a matching short-sleeve top, and a thick vest overtop. A shiny star clings to the front pocket of his vest, and on his sleeve is another badge of some sort. On both shoulders are three yellow chevrons that I assume represent his rank.

His official uniform makes me feel safe.

The passenger door opens, and out comes another man wearing a similar uniform, only with fewer chevrons on his sleeve. He walks with a puffed-out chest and a hand floating next to his duty belt.

From here, his hair looks jet black, and his face, clean shaven.

Wyatt leads the way, walking up the stone pathway and to the front porch. I hurry down the steps.

"Wyatt," I say.

"Emma," he says. "Are you okay? We received a call about a body."

I nod. "In the basement. There's some secret tunnel hiding behind the wine rack. I had no idea about it. Lucas went down there to hide while we were playing hide-and-seek, and—"

Wyatt stretches his jaw and rubs at his short stubble, his eyes bulging. "Shit, Emma . . . I-I'm so sorry he had to see that. I can't even imagine." He glances up at Lucas, who is still sitting quietly on the bench, unmoving. He wiggles a finger toward Lucas. "Mind if I—"

I shake my head. I'm grateful for Wyatt's willingness to try to talk to Lucas. Because he isn't talking to me.

The other police officer approaches but doesn't say anything. He doesn't smile, either. He's young—early twenties at most. I get the impression he's one of those cops looking to impress his superior and make a name for himself.

He inspects the house from the outside like he's looking for something. What? It's not like the killer would have left clues on my panels.

I shouldn't have such a sour attitude. He isn't doing anything wrong.

I'm just so overwhelmed that I can't think clearly, and I'm beyond upset that my seven-year-old son had to see that.

It seems as though someone neglected their responsibilities before giving us this house, and I want to identify that person and hold them accountable.

But you didn't buy this house. It's not like you hired an inspector. It was given to you.

"Hey, little man," Wyatt says.

He climbs the porch stairs and kneels in front of Lucas.

"How you doing?" he asks him.

Grayson watches with arms crossed, likely wondering the same thing as me—why isn't Lucas even looking at him? Responding? That isn't like him. I've put a lot of effort into raising my boys to be polite toward anyone they meet—even people who rub them the wrong way.

There's enough bad in this world as it is.

And although I want to correct Lucas—to tell him to respond to the kind police officer—I don't.

This has never happened before.

Lucas has never come across a dead body, so there's no telling what it's done to him. It's possible that, like me, he's feeling overwhelmed and unsure of how to respond.

"The cop's talking to you," Grayson says, looking irritated.

"Grayson," I say coldly, and shake my head. It's enough to get him to uncross his arms, sigh, and leave his little brother alone.

"Are you hurt?" Wyatt asks.

Lucas doesn't budge.

"Do you mind if I take a look at you?" Wyatt asks.

Still, no answer. Wyatt pulls out a penlight from his pocket. "I know things are scary right now, buddy. And it's okay to be scared. Heck, I get scared all the time, and I'm a cop." He pats his padded chest for emphasis. "So you take all the time you need, okay? My job is to make sure you, your mom, and your brother are safe. So I'm gonna go in there and check the place out, and we'll get rid of that body for you guys, okay?"

Lucas stares past him, at nothing.

It's a creepy look that sends chills up my arms.

"But before I do that," Wyatt continues. "I want to make sure you're not hurt, because I'm told you went into an old tunnel. Sometimes, these places carry germs, and we don't want you to get sick. So I'm going to make sure you don't have any cuts or anything that might get infected, okay? If you want me to stop, hold your hand up, and I'll stop."

Still, nothing.

Wyatt goes on to look at his feet, his ankles, and his hands. Finally, he says, "All good," and gets back up.

He approaches me, nudging his chin away from Lucas and Grayson as if to say, *Let's talk away from the kids.*

I follow Wyatt and his partner behind their cruiser.

"Emma, this is Officer Derek Garcia. He joined our office about six months ago."

Derek nods like a trained soldier.

Definitely young and eager.

The town might need that.

"He'll be taking notes and filing the report for today," Wyatt says. "Do you mind if we ask you some questions? Just so we know what we're dealing with? We'll document everything."

When I don't respond, he says, "You're not in any kind of trouble. Obviously, you didn't do this."

Derek walks to the car's passenger door, opens it, and reaches inside. When he slams the door, I flinch so hard I nearly let out an involuntary yelp. He comes back, carrying a clipboard with a pen and a few sheets of paper. He starts filling one out—likely with basic information such as the time, date, and location.

I go over everything that happened while Derek takes notes.

"I had no idea this house had a tunnel like that," Wyatt says.

How could he possibly have known?

Is this the first time he'll be entering Victor's house? Or has he been here before?

"And you said you saw a cot down there?" he asks.

I nod. "Y-yeah, a tiny one. Like a prison cot."

"Was there a lock anywhere?" he asks. "A gate?"

I shake my head. "I didn't see one."

Wyatt scratches at the scruff on his face, taking it all in.

"Derek and I are going to go in and investigate, and we'll have someone from the Forensic Center in St. Maria pick up the body."

I don't say anything.

I'm still too shocked.

He rests a warm hand on my shoulder, and I'm drawn back to reality.

"I doubt you want to stay here tonight. Forensics won't be here until tomorrow morning. I'll call Lambert Motel on the 18. I know the owner. He'll let you stay the night. No cost."

I part my lips, but nothing comes out.

"Do you want to get a change of clothes for tomorrow? Any belongings you want to pack? I'll come in with you."

Clutching onto myself, I nod.

The last thing I want to do is sleep here tonight.

There's a dead body in my house, and my uncle is probably the murderer.

Why would I want to stay in a house that once belonged to a monster?

CHAPTER 20

BEFORE

I haven't heard from Chloe in a few days despite sending her several messages.

"She always does this," James says. "Your whole family treats you like shit."

I don't think that's true . . . is it?

"You deserve better, Alice."

I'm not sure what he means by this. Sure, my family lives miles away, but we still talk on the phone every other week or so. And my sister and I keep in touch through text. I mean, she has three kids, a loving husband, and a house full of pets, including a parrot who she likes to call Demanding Deborah. The woman is busy. On top of this, she and Mark, my brother-in-law, are both very active—the type of couple that loads their kids up into their car and goes on a weekend hiking trip.

I wish I had that kind of energy.

Then again, even if I did, James wouldn't be up for it. He's always so busy chasing after his dreams . . . his business that he hopes one day will take off and become the new Apple.

"She's probably busy," I say.

"She read your messages," he says.

How does he know that? Has he been looking at my phone when I'm not around? Or has he been spying on me through those damn cameras again?

"Why are you looking at me like that?" he asks.

"Like what?" I say.

I must be scowling, even though I'm trying not to.

"Like you're accusing me of something," he says.

I press my lips together.

Because I am.

"Sweetheart, what's going on?" he asks. "It's not my fault your sister isn't talking to you. I feel like you're putting the blame on me."

I wave dismissively and put my phone down. "No, it's not that. You said she read my messages. How do you know that? Have you been looking at my phone?"

He scoffs. "Are you serious right now? You *just* said she read your messages. I'm only repeating what you said."

"I never said—"

His eyebrows slant, making me feel slightly crazy. "Alice, really? You literally *just* said it, right there—" He points at the couch I'm sitting on. "You said, 'I don't understand why she's reading my messages and not responding,' which is why I got so upset with her. You don't deserve that. It's like she's purposely ignoring you."

Did I say that?

I thought baby brain was only supposed to last during pregnancy. Lucas is going on a year soon.

"Are you okay, honey?" he asks. "I feel like you've been forgetting a lot lately. And I mean, a lot."

I rub my forehead, grime sticking to my fingertips. I can't remember the last time I showered. I've been so busy with Lucas and trying to keep the house nice for James, seeing as he's been rather vocal about how I have plenty of time on my hands and should be taking better care of the house.

I expect him to lean forward and reach for my hand. Offer to take me to the doctor or something. But instead, his jaw sets, and shadows form across his face.

It's terrifying how fast his moods can change.

"Let me see your phone," he says.

"Excuse me?"

"You were pretty quick to accuse me of spying on you," he says. "So if you have nothing to hide"—he sticks out an open palm—"prove it."

I'm so shocked that I have a hard time finding my words. Is he serious right now? I've never looked at his phone, even when I've had some suspicions.

"So you don't trust me," I say.

"I did," he says. "Up until right now. You got all weird, Alice. Is there someone else? I mean, you're home all day. And you've turned off the cameras several times now."

I frown. "So you *have* been spying on me! You've been watching me even when you said you wouldn't—"

Without warning, he slams his fist on the coffee table between us, and a coaster flops upward. I flinch, my shoulders tensing.

"Damn it, Alice! I'm not spying on you. I receive notifications on my phone when the camera goes offline! I don't have to be looking at the live feed to get a notification!"

Live feed.

Something about those words suddenly makes me feel sick to my stomach. If there's a live feed, that means there are recorded feeds, too. Is that his way around the little red dot? Has he figured out that he doesn't need to watch me live when he can simply go back and look at the previous videos?

"Let's swap phones, then," I tell him.

His nostrils flare. "Are you fucking kidding me? What do I have to do to get a bit of respect around here? You want to look at my phone? Here. Look at my fucking phone!"

Something dark zips past my face, and I instinctively raise my hands to protect myself. But the phone misses me and crashes into the wall, breaking apart into several pieces before landing hard on the floor.

The wall is now dented, with bits of drywall crumbled on top of the broken phone.

He gets up angrily, thrashing the coffee table over. I raise my legs and cower on the couch.

He's gotten angry before . . . but never *this* angry.

"I do everything in my power to keep you happy, Alice!"

He points a menacing finger inches from my nose. My heart pounds so hard that I'm afraid he'll hear it and it'll aggravate him even more. "And this is how you treat me? I work my ass off every day to take care of you and the boys . . . miss time with them, so I can build an amazing life for us. And this is the respect you give me?"

You asked me for my phone first.

I don't say this.

He's so angry that I can't be certain he won't hit me.

I want to believe that James would never lay his hands on me, but this is a side of him I've never seen before.

His eyes are dark and glossy, as if all the good inside of him has dissipated, leaving behind only rage and hate.

He breathes hard through wide nostrils, his finger still aimed at me.

"I've put up with your shit long enough," he says. "The messy house. How you do nothing around here. The suppers aren't even good. It's like you aren't even trying while I bust my ass all day. You have no job and a family that barely talks to you. So if you want to leave, go ahead. Leave. I'm a successful businessman who could have a new wife in a week, and I'd feel better taken care of if she gave me half of what you're giving me."

My throat constricts.

I'm too scared by his huge body towering over me to cry, even though that's all I want to do.

How could he say such awful things to me?

He's supposed to be my husband.

My loving partner in life.

I'm suddenly reminded of the fights we used to have when we first started dating. We were toxic together. Yet we loved each other fiercely, and the sex was beyond passionate.

I'd always thought that the timing hadn't been right.

That we were too young.

But as he stands here, eight years older than his twenty-year-old explosive self, I realize that he hasn't changed at all.

He's only gotten better at hiding who he really is.

CHAPTER 21

"Carla McKenzie speaking," says the woman at the other end of the line.

"Oh, hi," I say. "I'm sorry. I didn't expect anyone to pick up."

"That's quite all right," she says cheerfully. "I'm an early bird, so I come in early to get some work done before the students come in."

It's 6:04 a.m., and Lucas and Grayson are still sound asleep in the motel bed. I certainly didn't expect Lucas's teacher, Mrs. McKenzie, to pick up the phone at this hour.

"Are you calling about a student?" she asks.

"Yes," I say.

"Name?"

"Lucas R— Collins. Lucas Collins. I'd like to report an absence."

I blink hard, panicked by how close I came to blurting out his old last name.

"Oh, the new student," she says. I can hear the smile on her face through the phone. "Absences are usually handled by Administration, but I'll let them know you called today. They made a mistake in one of the emails they sent out and added the teacher list under absence contacts. I'm really sorry about that."

I thought calling his teacher to report an absence was simply a small-town thing. I'm about to apologize for the mistake when she continues. "Lucas is a sweetheart. I'm so glad to have him in my class. Little guy isn't feeling too well today?"

That's an understatement.

I'm not prepared to go into detail about the body that was found last night, so I simply agree. "No, he'll be staying home with me today."

"You must be Emma," she says.

I'm taken aback by this. But then again, it's a small town. Everyone knows everyone.

"I am," I say.

"I'm sorry we haven't yet formally met," she says with a chuckle. "I'm hoping I get to meet you soon. I so look forward to it."

I wish I could say the same, but I have so much on my mind right now.

And how can anyone be this chipper at six in the morning? She must not have kids. Either that, or she's younger than her voice sounds.

"Me too," I say, though I imagine my tone of voice says the opposite.

All I can think about is the body and whether or not the Forensics team will be coming by early. Wyatt mentioned they open at 8 a.m., and they're in St. Maria, so hopefully, they're at the house by nine.

I want that thing . . . that person . . . gone. And in all honesty, I want that entire tunnel collapsed or filled in.

"Ms. Collins?"

Am I still on the phone? I blink hard, realizing she called me Ms., and not Mrs., or Miss.

Small town. Big mouths.

She looks to be over thirty.

Why isn't she married?

Where's the father?

Somehow, I hate the sound of it.

Miz.

It's like an uncertain pronoun. I'm no longer a Miss or a Missus.

"Yes?" I ask.

"I think the phone cut out," she says. "I wanted to remind you that we're having pajama day on Friday."

"Oh," I say. "Thank you."

I say goodbye, hang up, and proceed to call Administration at Grayson's school to let them know he won't be attending class, either.

After what happened, I'd prefer they both stay home.

Lucas is still not talking, and I need Grayson to watch him while I return to the house and figure out what's going to happen next. I'm afraid I'll be asked to go to the police station for questioning. I don't want to drag my boys along with me for that.

I sneak out of the motel room and speedwalk to the reception desk. A friendly man with a short gray afro and a name tag that reads Arthur rolls toward me, the wheels of his chair clicking over tiles on the floor.

"Good morning!" he says with a smile. "How can I help you?"

"I'm Emma Collins," I say.

His smile vanishes. "Oh, yes—my colleague, Kyle, put some notes here about your stay." It looks like he wants to apologize for what I went through but doesn't know how. Instead, he taps his pen on the front desk while looking at his notes.

"H-how can I help you?" he repeats.

"Officer Daniels called last night, and he said that you guys graciously let us stay. I know checkout is typically at eleven, but—"

"Noon, here," he corrects me.

"Well," I continue, "I have to run out and take care of a few things. Speak with the police. Find out what's happening with my house."

My house.

It doesn't feel like *my* house. Not anymore.

He raises his hand like he already knows what I'm about to say. "Officer Daniels already cleared you for a week. He said investigations can take time, and you may need to stay a few extra nights."

Wyatt didn't tell me that last night.

He offered us one night, which made it sound like this

would all be over soon.

He probably didn't want to overwhelm you.

"That's very kind," I say, relief washing over me. "Thank you. Truly."

He smiles sweetly again and nods as if to say, *It's no problem at all.*

The moment I walk away, his face grows somber as if he's sad for me.

I send Grayson a text:

> *Heading out to do a few things. Please stay with your brother in the room. Don't leave. I'll be back in the afternoon. There are muffins and fruit by the microwave for breakfast. Text me if you need me. I love you.*

They'll be fine.

Lucas has his tablet, and Grayson, his phone. Those two are glued to their devices as if their lives depend on them. It's not ideal, but right now, I'll happily allow them unlimited screen time if it protects their minds from last night's events.

I step out into the parking lot, the morning sun barely piercing the sky.

I should be waiting for Wyatt's call, but I can't sit around. I tossed and turned all night, vividly picturing the body in my mind.

I want this over with.

And sitting around waiting for something to happen isn't me. So I drive down the 18 and toward a house that now feels tainted.

As I approach, I'm not surprised to see yellow tape across my front lawn. Several neighbors walk by, which is dismaying, given that I've barely seen anyone out here since we moved in.

It's like the news is already spreading, and everyone decided to walk their dog first thing in the morning to hear the latest gossip.

I drive slowly, watching people as they stop in front of

our house, point, and talk to each other.

Great.

Now the whole town will know.

To my surprise, Wyatt's car is parked in the driveway. Although, its position is different, which tells me he left last night and returned this morning.

Behind him is a black cruiser with shiny black rims. On the back bumper, large font reads, Regson Heights Regional Police Department.

I recognize that name.

It's a larger city about a hundred miles from here, past St. Maria.

Did Wyatt have to call in the big dogs?

Is there more to this than he's letting on?

I pull into the driveway, and a cop with huge, tattooed biceps, a long yet trimmed beard, and sunglasses even though it's still dawn, walks toward me aggressively, like he's about to tell me to get out of here.

Wyatt comes jogging toward him and says something.

The cop backs down.

Yeah, I live here, thank you very much.

I park my car and step out, trying to ignore the several sets of eyes that watch from the sidewalk.

"What's going on?" I ask Wyatt.

"We don't have any detectives here in Thorn Lake. And homicides, well, that's out of our jurisdiction."

"So it is a homicide," I say. "Victor killed—"

Wyatt raises a flat palm. "Hang on. I didn't say that." He gets distracted by my front door opening. "There isn't much left for the Forensics team to look at, but once we identify the body, we might have more answers."

A woman wearing a black business suit and a pensive scowl comes out of the house.

"Is she the detective?" I ask Wyatt.

He nods. "She's getting everything she needs. They're coming to pick up the body in twenty minutes. We'll have this tape cleared up for you after that."

"But you think it was a murder," I say.

I want him to confirm what he just said.

Wyatt crosses his arms and watches the detective speak with the macho, bearded cop who stands twice her size. "It's looking that way, unfortunately."

How am I supposed to go back inside that house?

How are we supposed to live here, knowing someone was killed in the basement?

CHAPTER 22

"I wanted to call you after we had more answers," Wyatt says.

He says that like he feels guilty about me showing up here—like he should have warned me that there was so much chaos on my property. But it isn't his fault.

"I couldn't sleep," I say.

We walk away from the house and toward the cedar shrubs on the side.

"I'm so sorry about all of this, Emma."

Me too.

"You said it was a homicide," I say, nausea creeping into my stomach. Could it have been Victor?"

He takes a sip of his coffee with a brown label that reads Beans & Stuff. I drove by it in Thorn Lake on Monday. It looks like a typical quaint local coffee shop. The kind that goes out of its way to keep its customers happy by always brewing coffee fresh and adding little personal touches, like Wyatt's name and a smiley face on the side of the cup.

"I don't think so," he says, "but we need more answers from Forensics first. It'll help us piece the timeline together."

That body was definitely older than a month, which means Victor *could* be responsible.

"Mr. Huxley was in palliative care for about a month after that anonymous call came in," Wyatt adds.

I stiffen. "Anonymous call?"

He takes another sip of his coffee. "Yeah. The

department received a call stating that Mr. Huxley had collapsed in his home."

"That's so suspicious," I say, "that a person would report that anonymously."

He hesitates.

It's definitely suspicious.

"There could be countless reasons someone might call in anonymously like that," he says.

"I wouldn't say *countless*," I say.

Someone waves at Wyatt, urging him over. "I have to go," he says. He takes a few steps, then stops and turns around. "Oh, I meant to ask—how's Lucas doing?"

"He hasn't said a word," I say.

Wyatt averts his gaze and drums his thumb against the side of his coffee cup. "I'm sure that was traumatic for him."

It was.

And I wish I could go back in time. If I hadn't brought them into the basement, this would never have happened. The thought is irrational, of course. It was inevitable that one of us would find that secret passageway.

Wyatt shifts his body to the side and pulls a shiny blue card out of his pants pocket. "Here. She's good. Really good."

I grab the card and read the text on the front:

Dr. Maya Jackson
Registered Psychologist
204 Limestone Street
Thorn Lake

I must raise a brow or something, because Wyatt is quick to talk after I'm done with reading the card.

"For your son," he says.

"You think he needs to see someone?" I ask.

"It wouldn't hurt," he says. "Kids don't see dead bodies every day, and especially not in that state."

Nausea sours my stomach as I think back to the blackened flesh.

He aims his chin at the business card in my hands. "Think about it."

I thank him and tuck it into my jacket's side pocket.

I suddenly feel guilty over having left Grayson and Lucas alone in that motel room. It wasn't right. They should have come with me. I was trying to protect them from all of this, but what if they don't need protection? What if they need *me*?

"I better go," I say.

"Of course," Wyatt says.

"Also, Arthur—the man at the motel—"

Wyatt smiles like he knows exactly who I'm talking about.

"He said you made arrangements to have us stay there all week, if we'd like," I say.

Wyatt nods. "Of course. I figured you probably wouldn't want to come back here right away."

"That was very kind," I say. "Thank you."

He bows his head slightly. "Happy to help. I imagine this is extremely difficult for you. For all of you."

It is.

When I remain silent, he clears his throat. "I'll give you a call as soon as we're all done here, and you can come back whenever you'd like."

I thank him again and hurry back to my car. I drive a bit faster than I should, but I figured the entire police staff of Thorn Lake—all of two people—are too busy investigating a crime scene to be handing out speeding tickets.

My tires squeal as I come to an abrupt stop in the motel's parking lot. I hurry out, fingers fumbling through my purse to locate my motel keycard.

I rush to room 12 and unlock the door, a soft beeping sound filling the air.

When I walk inside, Grayson is sitting at the edge of the bed with a muffin in hand, and Lucas is lying down, facing away from the door.

I walk in slowly and mouth, "Is he sleeping?"

Grayson shakes his head. "No. But he won't eat. He

won't talk to me." He grabs a pillow and throws it at Lucas's head.

It makes a soft *thump* before bouncing off and landing on the floor.

"Grayson!" I shout.

"What?" he says. "I'm trying to get him to get up. He's lying there with his eyes wide open. It's creepy."

I shut the door and hurry inside, placing my purse down on my unmade bed.

"Lucas? Sweetheart?"

I walk around the bed and kneel in front of him.

He's staring past me . . . at nothing.

It's a glazed look that makes me think he isn't even in his body anymore. I grab his little shoulder and shake him gently.

"Lucas? Come on, honey. You need to get up and eat something."

He doesn't move.

I squeeze my fingers around his shoulder a bit harder, trying to draw his attention to me.

"Lucas," I say sternly.

Slowly, his brown eyes roll at me.

It should come as a relief, but it doesn't—there's a hollowness to him that I don't recognize. As if the sight of the body stole a piece of his soul.

It makes me want to yell and cling to him simultaneously.

My sweet little Lucas.

Only yesterday, he was bouncing around the house with a grin on that adorable, dimple-cheeked face of his.

"Come on," I urge, pulling him up.

I expect him to stay exactly where he is, but he gets up and slides his legs over the edge of the bed.

"What kinds of muffins are there?" I ask Grayson.

"Blueberry and chocolate chip," he says. "Well, one chocolate chip left."

On any other day, I wouldn't give Lucas a chocolate chip muffin for breakfast. Not unless it was whole grain or healthy in one way or another. Otherwise, it's basically cake. But right now, I'd let him eat candy for breakfast if it meant pulling him out of his thoughts.

"You want chocolate chip?" I ask him.

He nods but doesn't smile.

I run a hand through his curly locks and grab him a chocolate chip muffin. I watch him as he sits there chewing on the fluffy bread with zero expression on his face. He may as well be eating dirt.

I reach into my jacket pocket and pull out Maya Jackson's business card.

I've never worked with a psychologist before. After James and I split, my mom urged me to go to therapy the few times we spoke. She said it would do me some good to talk to a professional.

But I never went.

That was probably my dad's doing. Every time my mom brought it up, he scoffed in the background and said I didn't need a therapist who was going to suck me dry. I needed time and distance from James.

But as I watch Lucas finish his muffin, chocolate chips bouncing off his knees and landing on the floor, I can't help but wonder whether this whole situation is something the professionals need to handle.

Because I have no idea what to do.

CHAPTER 23

BEFORE

I've thought of opening up to Chloe about James lately, but I'm afraid to put her in danger.

"I love your family like they're my own, Alice, but if you try to take my kids away from me . . . you'll regret it. And so will your family."

He said the words a few months ago, but they were out of anger, and he was drunk, so he likely didn't mean them.

Or the truth came out.

My husband wouldn't hurt my family, would he?

He often makes comments about how no one will love me the way he does, and that he'd even go as far as to kill any man who laid his hands on me. Including any guy I met if we were to divorce. But that's the territorial side of him, isn't it? I don't think it would extend to my family. And I don't think he'd actually hurt anyone.

It's probably all talk.

But you aren't sure, Alice. Do you really want to find out?

I want to talk to someone about it, but ever since I moved out here, I've been out of touch with my best friend, Reese. It was odd, really. We used to talk on the phone for hours after the move, and then out of nowhere, her calls stopped coming in. I sent her a long message, asking whether I'd upset her in any way, and her answer was: *Life has gotten really busy with work. I'm so sorry.*

Now, I don't hear from her anymore.

James is convinced that she's always been secretly in love with me and that our marriage, along with the long-distance move, is what pushed her away.

I mean, we were *really* close. And she's been single for as long as I've known her.

Is he right?

I miss her terribly.

And right now, I wish I could talk to her about everything that's happening. I need an outsider's opinion. Some days, I think I'm the one who isn't trying hard enough, and James has every right to get as upset as he does.

But then other days, I know I don't deserve this.

Which emotion is valid? Talking to someone about it might help me gain more insight.

I used to love James, and now, I'm uncertain. Occasionally, he's still the sweet man I fell in love with. He comes home with flowers and kisses me passionately. But more and more often, his eyes take on an almost black hue, giving the impression that he isn't even in his own body anymore.

And although I hate to admit it, I think I'm afraid of my own husband.

CHAPTER 24

"You must be Ms. Collins," says Mrs. McKenzie.

"Oh, yes," I say. "Um, Emma is fine."

Her heels click as she walks toward me with a sad look in her eyes and an outstretched hand. Big brown curls, an average-sized frame, and bright-blue eyes that look to be heavily lidded due to genetics rather than fatigue.

"You can call me Carla," she says.

She's sporting a pair of fitted blue jeans and a white blouse with marker stains on the right sleeve. She's a bit on the plump side, and with her hourglass figure, the extra weight suits her nicely.

I grab her hand and shake it gently.

The boys have been back at school for a week, and her bright eyes linger on me as if she's been eager to meet me for a while.

Why?

To see whether I'm a bad mom?

Her eyes flicker toward my shoes, my pants, and then my shirt.

She's definitely trying to read me. Possibly to see how much effort I'm putting into caring for Lucas. And although I hate that, I remind myself that it must mean she cares for Lucas and wants the best for him.

It wouldn't be the first time a teacher has had to deal with a horrible parent.

"Thank you for coming in on such short notice," she says. "It's a lot easier to speak with you while the kids are having lunch."

I'm not sure what made her presume I didn't work a customary nine-to-five job. She didn't even ask. When she called me this morning, she asked whether I could come by the school at lunchtime to discuss Lucas's progress.

I suppose my career has no bearing when it comes to my son. Even if I worked long hours, it'd be up to me to take the time off to be here when needed. That's what it is to be a mom.

"Right this way," she says.

Her large curls sway behind her back as she leads me down the empty corridor and along a long row of gray lockers. We approach an open door with a sign that reads, Mrs. McKenzie, 103.

I walk into a large room with about twenty desks and vivid colors all over the walls. Crafts and art projects are sprawled across a few tables at the very back, and at the other end of the class is Mrs. McKenzie's desk, stationed in front of a whiteboard that covers the entire wall.

"Please, have a seat," she says.

I'm afraid to sit down. Did Lucas do something?

I spoke with the principals at each school to ensure the educational staff was aware of what my boys had gone through in case their behavior were to change.

Grayson apparently hasn't shown any behavior change aside from irritation, but that's to be expected when other kids are constantly asking you to explain what happened. He said he's sick of having to tell everyone that he doesn't want to talk about it.

And he's entitled to his privacy.

For Lucas, however, I've been receiving daily phone calls from the school with the same update—he won't talk.

But now I've been asked to come to the school in person, which makes me think something bad has happened.

Mrs. Mckenzie clears her throat.

I look up, remembering where I am, and reluctantly sit

at the edge of a desk, waiting for the bad news to spill.

"How bad is it?" I ask.

She forces a smile. "Well, it's not good. But Lucas isn't acting out, if that's what you're thinking. He hasn't done anything wrong, per se."

Then what could this possibly be about? Why get me to come in person when it could have simply been explained over the phone?

Not that I mind, actually.

I've been wanting a reason to get out of that house. It's been nearly two weeks since the body was removed, and I can't bring myself to go into the basement.

Oddly, Lucas avoids even the door. He'll walk a half moon around it as if it's contaminated. I'm glad—the last thing I want is for him to relive that awful day.

Unless something goes wrong with our electrical system or plumbing, there's no reason to reopen that door. I've even considered buying a secondhand bookshelf and placing it in front of the basement door to hide it. I don't even want to look at it.

Mrs. McKenzie walks away from me, then returns with a stack of papers. She places the pile down, and the first image has a knot forming in my stomach.

It's a dead body drawn with pencil scribbles. Amid all these scribbles are two white circles to showcase a pair of eye sockets that appear too big for the head.

That might be how Lucas remembers it.

As I sit here, going through terrible, colorless images of dead corpses, I have to consciously remind myself to breathe.

"It's apparent he's struggling—" Carla says.

Is that her professional opinion?

I frown. This is more than apparent.

Lucas won't talk to me at home. I've tried sitting down with him and telling him we need to discuss what happened. I've also tried the scientific route and explained to him what death is, and what happens to bodies after they die.

That it's natural and nothing to be afraid of, despite the horrendous images that flash in my mind seconds before I fall asleep, jolting me awake.

It doesn't take a genius to know that Lucas needs professional help.

Thankfully, I called Dr. Maya Jackson the first morning at the motel, and I did his intake meeting a few days ago.

"He's meeting a psychologist this evening," I tell Mrs. McKenzie.

"Oh," she says, taken aback. "Maya?"

I suppose it would make sense that everyone knows the only psychologist in town.

"She's wonderful," she says. "Many years of experience. That was going to be my next suggestion."

I try to force a smile, but nothing happens.

How can I smile when I'm staring at my son's pain on multiple sheets of paper?

"Do you want to keep these?" she asks.

My frown deepens. Why the hell would I want more reminders of my son's trauma?

"For his therapist," she quickly adds, and I reel in my defensiveness.

"Oh," I say. "Y-yeah. That might be a good idea. Thank you."

She scoops the papers and sorts them neatly into one pile before retrieving a bright orange file folder from one of her desk drawers.

It's strange to see my son's eerie depictions of his trauma be slid into a file folder intended for second-grade homework or report cards.

It doesn't feel right.

There's something off about all of this.

Carla hands me the folder but pauses just as I grab it. "Do you mind if I ask you something?"

I don't like the way she's wording that. It sounds as though she's about to ask whether I'm doing everything in my power to help Lucas heal.

I've been talking to him every night. Holding him

every night. Reminding him of how much I love him and how safe he is. Booking him an appointment with a psychologist.

I'm doing everything I can.

She isn't James. Stop thinking everyone is judging you.

"Sure," I say.

"How did he end up in that tunnel, anyway?" she asks. "Doesn't seem like an easy place to access."

And there it is.

Judgment.

How is it that my seven-year-old was left unsupervised long enough to venture into the basement to access a secret passageway?

He's seven—not three.

He doesn't need constant supervision. And this really isn't any of her business.

I pull the file folder out of her hands. She probably means well, but I'm sleep-deprived and extremely on edge. I just want Lucas to get better and for all of this to be over.

"Thank you for your time," I tell her as politely as I can.

"Oh, I'm so sorry if I upset you," she says.

I bet you are.

"I suppose that sounded rude, now that I think of it," she says.

I don't respond, and instead, make my way to the classroom's closed door. And although it's none of her business, part of me feels like I have to defend myself and my parenting skills. Also, I don't want to make enemies with Lucas's teacher.

I turn slightly and say, "We were playing hide-and-seek, and I had no idea there was a secret passageway down there. If I had known, I would have taken every precaution."

"Of course," she says. "Of course. Anyone would have done the same thing. I'm sorry I asked. I was just curious. Because no one knew about a secret passageway in Mr. Huxley's house, so I was curious how a seven-year-old discovered it when no one else did."

I watch her for a moment, suddenly realizing something.

How does she even know about the secret passageway? It's not like there was a news article written about the body found in my house. The only thing people know is that a body was found and extracted.

Did Wyatt reveal confidential information to someone? Did the news travel all over town? Does everyone know my house has a secret passageway?

"Can I ask you something?" I ask.

Now that I've been honest with her about how this all happened, it's only fair that she be honest with me.

She forces a wide grin and says, "Oh, Emma, of course. Ask away."

"How did you know about the secret tunnel?" I ask.

She pulls her face back slightly—something I might have missed if I weren't staring right at her. I can't tell whether she's embarrassed for gossiping with people of the town or whether someone told her something in confidence, and she just realized she'd opened her mouth about it.

She flicks a wrist at me. "Small towns. Honestly, it's horrible. I shouldn't have even known that. But news travels fast around here."

News only travels fast if someone with the information opens their big mouth. Grayson has been telling everyone he doesn't want to talk about it. And Lucas sure as hell didn't talk.

So who did?

CHAPTER 25

"You must be Emma," says the cheerful young woman behind the counter. "I have a bit of paperwork for you to fill out here."

There's nothing fancy about this place, which I appreciate. I'd always pictured a psychologist's office as filled with expensive plants, spotless windows, shiny tiled flooring, and leather chairs.

But this place is nothing like that.

It's homelike.

Carpet covers the floor, and although it smells fresh in here, it doesn't look all that clean. The baseboards look decades old with dirt staining their edges and cracks splitting the wood in certain areas.

This tells me one of two things—Dr. Jackson doesn't make enough money to invest in the appearance of her office or she doesn't care about appearances and would rather put her focus on her clients.

I suppose there's also a chance that she doesn't own the place and has no intention of renovating a rental property, but if she truly cared about appearances, she'd have contacted the landlord and made some arrangements to spiff things up.

Regardless of the reason, it makes me feel less taken advantage of. Had I walked into a high-end office with extravagant decor, I might have found myself wanting to turn around.

Lucas clings onto my arm like he doesn't want to be here. I've told him several times that this is good, and Dr.

Jackson will help him overcome whatever war is going on inside his head.

The worst part is that he won't even talk to me. So I don't know what's actually going on. I've never felt so helpless—not even with James beating me.

This is my child.

And I can't help him.

I approach the counter where the young woman watches me with a smile on her face. She's young, likely fresh out of college, and looks eager to please Dr. Jackson by ensuring her clients are contented.

She tightens her ponytail, but this does nothing to tame the little curls sticking out on either side of her head.

Likely bangs growing out.

I take a few steps closer to inspect the forms attached to a clipboard.

"Just a few confidentiality forms," she says. "Giving us permission to work with Lucas and yourself."

"With me?" I ask.

I didn't come here for therapy. This is for Lucas.

She flicks a wrist. "You're his guardian, I assume?"

"His mother," I correct.

"Yes, of course. Dr. Jackson may want to do a few family sessions."

I part my lips, and she quickly adds, "For Lucas. It's standard with young children."

I nod, pick up the pen, and start filling out the paperwork. It isn't long before Dr. Jackson steps out of her office with a warm smile pulling at her lips.

Her hair is short at the top, while both sides are shaved close to her skin. It's a look that suits her elongated face and high cheekbones. She's slim, taller than me, and has a dark complexion that makes her light-beige top really pop.

Someone who might have been a model in her younger days.

"Emma, yes?" she says.

When I nod, her smile grows even wider, revealing perfectly straight white teeth. She glances down at Lucas and says, "Well, hello there. I'm so happy to finally meet you, young man."

As expected, Lucas remains quiet, and his grip is so tight around my waist that it pinches, and I find myself prying away his little fingers.

"Lucas," says Dr. Jackson. "I have some cookies and Cheetos in my office. Do you like Cheetos?"

His eyes go huge.

Lucas loves Cheetos—so much so that I stopped myself from buying some at Thorn Lake Grocer because I'm afraid he'll put orange fingerprints all over the walls of our new house.

No matter how often I tell him to wash his hands, he forgets unless I stand there until he does it. I've had to use toothpicks to scrape orange dust out from the cracks of his tablets and under his fingernails.

Dr. Jackson looks up at me. "Is it all right if he—"

He can eat Skittles all day if it'll get him talking again. Right now, nutrition is the least of my worries, given everything that's happened and how it's affected him.

"Of course," I say.

"Right this way," she tells Lucas. He follows her, then enters her office when she points at the back. "See that little table with crayons? Right there. There's a snack bin. Feel free to grab yourself a little bag of Cheetos."

She then turns to me.

"Are you okay to wait out here? The initial assessment should take no longer than an hour." She skims through a pile of papers in her hands. "I already have all the notes I need from your first intake form and from our conversation."

"Do you think you can get him talking again?" I ask.

She smiles politely, almost like she's holding back way too much information to be delivered all at once. "I need to perform an assessment first. From there, I'll let you know what I think needs to happen for Lucas to get better."

She glances down at the intake form I filled out last week, frowning. Then, without warning, says, "Alice . . . "

My name feels like a stab to my chest.

The room spins, and it feels like little bugs are crawling up my fingertips.

How the hell does she know my old name?

"Did you happen to reschedule my three o'clock appointment for tomorrow?" she asks.

Slowly, her dark eyes roll up at the young girl behind the reception desk.

"I did," says the receptionist.

"Great, thanks, Alice," Dr. Jackson says.

I release a low, quivering breath.

The last thing I want to do is leave Lucas in there with a stranger. But Dr. Jackson is a professional, and she seems to know what she's doing. After all, both Wyatt and Mrs. McKenzie had nothing but great things to say about her.

I have to trust her.

What other option do I have?

CHAPTER 26

"Why are you only telling me this now?" I ask Grayson.

He shrugs. "I only found out about it now."

I sigh heavily, completely thrown off by Grayson's sudden birthday party invitation. The only thing I've been thinking about is Lucas's condition.

After his assessment, I was informed that he would require weekly sessions with Dr. Jackson. She'd had a lot to say, but I was so overwhelmed with the fact that Lucas would need real, professional therapy to talk again that I didn't take it all in.

But I do remember one thing—selective mutism.

The name had irked me. It made it sound like Lucas is simply choosing not to talk. Like he's made a *selection* regarding his speaking abilities.

But when I questioned Dr. Jackson on this, she was quick to explain that the condition isn't selective—it's a response to trauma, and he's unable to speak at the moment.

So now, every week, Lucas will sit down with Dr. Jackson for some one-on-one cognitive behavioral therapy sessions.

I hope she's as good as people say she is.

I know nothing about her—her background, how long she's been doing this, or why she got into the profession to begin with.

"Well?" Grayson asks, pulling me back to reality.

"Well, what?" I ask.

"Can you take me?" he asks.

"Yeah," I say. "Where is it?"

"Lilac Bridge Park," he says.

I know the place. It's a huge patch of green land on Thorn Lake's map. I've also seen signs there several times—something about gatherings and events.

"Whose birthday is it?" I ask. "Do you need a gift?"

He shakes his head. "Nope."

No gift for a birthday? That's odd. Shouldn't he want to bring his friend a gift?

"Don't you want to bring a little some—"

"No," he says. "Really, it's fine. We don't need a gift."

I don't argue. It's not like I want to spend the extra money on a gift right now.

For a moment, I consider dropping him off and returning home to spend time with Lucas. But he still isn't talking, and it's frustrating to ask him questions only to get silence in return.

Besides, Dr. Jackson said it's good for him to get exposure to other situations outside of the home. And a visit to the park on a beautiful autumn day is the perfect outing.

I get myself ready by slipping into a pair of old jeans and a blue-and-pink hoodie that makes me want to stay home and cuddle up on the couch.

After a bit of coaxing, Lucas gets up, yawns, and follows me to the front door. I slip a plain white baseball cap over my head—something that I hope will keep me out of the public eye.

It's stupid, but I can't help it.

What if someone recognizes me?

That's all it takes.

One person.

No one will recognize you. Not in this little town. Not this far north in the country.

Grayson walks out of the door without headphones around his neck.

He hurries down the porch stairs with a hop. Someone's in a good mood.

"I'm glad you made some new friends," I tell him, locking the door.

A half-hearted smile tugs at his lips. "Yeah."

It's like he doesn't want to show how happy he is. Like he wants to hold onto his resentment over having moved here. That's fine. I won't press.

Lucas hops into the back with his tablet and disappears into his own world.

We drive toward Lilac Bridge Park with our windows down. A cool breeze fills the car with a crisp smell that I love more than anything—it's fresh and makes your lungs feel like they're being cleaned out.

When we pull into the parking lot of Lilac Bridge Park, I'm a bit taken aback by how many cars are here.

Easily over fifty.

How popular is this kid?

"Whose birthday is it again?" I ask.

"It's not a birthday," he says.

I spin sideways fast, my seatbelt digging into my shoulder. "Excuse me? You said you had a birthday party to go to."

"I said anniversary," he says.

Did he? I can't even remember what he said. But why would a fourteen-year-old refer to a birthday as an anniversary?

I was too busy thinking about Lucas's mutism.

I sigh through my nose. "Okay . . . what kind of anniversary?"

He shrugs.

"If you don't know what it's for, then why'd you want to come?"

"To see my friend," he says. "My friends."

The way he quickly changes his word *friend* to plural makes me think he's here for one person but doesn't want to admit it.

A girl?

I want to ask him, but with how defensive he's been lately, he'll only get attitudey with me. And the last thing

I want to do is push him away.

"I suppose it's good to get out and get fresh air anyway," I say.

Before I can say anything else, Grayson unclips his belt and swings the door open. "See ya!"

I'm about to yell at him to get back over here so we can arrange where and when to meet up again, but he's got his cell phone. If I want to find him, I will.

Besides, I haven't seen him this excited in forever. He deserves the freedom.

"You ready?" I ask Lucas.

When I turn around, he's still tapping his screen and twirling his thumbs to do God knows what in that game of his. Bright flashes illuminate the tip of his nose and the underside of his chin.

"Lucas," I say.

When he still doesn't look up, I say his name louder.

His big brown eyes roll up at me, and he stops twirling his thumbs.

"Time to go," I say. "Leave the tablet here."

He pouts, turns off his tablet, and places it on the seat next to him.

He then climbs out of the back seat with his head bowed. I can't tell whether he's upset or anxious or simply doesn't want to be here.

Poor Lucas.

I wish I could take his pain away.

"Come on," I say, reaching for his hand. To my surprise, he doesn't take it. He brushes past me, slides out of the car, and lands on the gravel of the parking lot.

"Stay close," I tell him.

The last thing I want to do is lose him in a crowd full of people. If he doesn't talk, how is he supposed to communicate anything?

I lower my ball cap a little, trying to mask my face, before locking my doors and making my way down a narrow path toward an oversized outdoor gazebo.

Then, I see it.

A huge sign that reads, 50th Anniversary.

What is this all about?

People fill the entire gazebo, chatting away as if they're all one big happy family. There are probably over a hundred people here.

Instinctively, I reach for the back of Lucas's shirt and pull him closer to me.

Even though he's seven, now would be a good time to have one of those kid leashes. Though it would probably attract unwanted attention.

What kind of mother puts a leash on her seven-year-old child?

The kind who has a kid that doesn't speak at the moment.

I already feel like I'm being judged, even though no one has looked our way yet.

Then, something bright and red catches my eye.

A playground.

It looks brand new. Either that, or it was recently repainted. Wood chips fill the square around it rather than sand, which is so much less messy.

"Look at that," I tell Lucas. "Why don't you go play for a bit?"

A few other kids are already swinging from the bars, laughing and swatting at each other like monkeys.

"Go on," I tell him, giving him a gentle push.

He goes slowly with his hands in his pockets.

This might be exactly what he needs.

To be around kids his own age.

I watch him as he draws in closer to the park, hoping he'll have somewhat of a good time, when I feel someone standing next to me.

"Didn't think I'd see you here," the man says.

I turn around to spot a familiar face. Dark eyes, a squared-off jaw, little to no facial hair—he must have *just* shaved before coming here—and shoulders drawn a little too far back.

It's a stance that tells me he either has a big ego, or . . . no, I know what it is. It's the cop in him. That's where I recognize him from.

"Officer Garcia," I say.

A short smile appears on his face. "I'm sorry we first met under such awful circumstances."

I fluff it away with a quick hand gesture like it's nothing, even though it keeps me up at night.

"Not on duty?" I ask, noting his blue jeans and button-up flannel top.

His eyes scan the crowd—likely a cop instinct of his. "No, not today. It's my day off."

"I take it Wy— Officer Daniels is working, then?"

He lets out a little laugh. "Yeah. Small staff. He doesn't much care for social outings and said he'd cover today."

"That must be tough," I say. "To rotate shifts between the two of you."

He shrugs, then raises a red plastic cup I didn't notice and takes a sip out of some dark bubbly liquid. "It's not bad. We only work days, but we're on call at night. It's not too often that there's a police emergency at night around here."

Until I came around, that is.

"What is this, anyway?" I point at the big anniversary sign. "Whose anniversary is it?"

Derek smiles, which looks unnatural for him. "Lilac Bridge. It's a bridge they built over the river near the forest—back there." He points beyond the large crowd. "It's one of Thorn Lake's historic structures."

I part my lips but don't say anything.

"Well," he says, cutting through the awkward silence. "Welcome to Thorn Lake. Officially, I mean. Nice to have a new face around here."

As I look around at all the smiling faces and the far-reaching laughter, I know I should be happy to be here. Thankful, even.

I'm finally safe, away from James.

But now, my son doesn't speak, and I'm haunted by the image of a dead body in my basement.

I can't shake this feeling . . . that something else is

going to happen.

You're being paranoid. It's normal, after everything that's happened. But you're safe here.

Am I, though?

I'm starting to think that coming to Thorn Lake was a mistake.

CHAPTER 27

BEFORE

"Why are you wearing that dress?" James asks.

I run my hand down my black silk dress, suddenly feeling insecure. He used to love this dress. What changed?

"It shows too much cleavage," he says. "This is our third wedding anniversary, Alice. Are you happy to be with me, or are you looking to find someone else?"

I wish I wasn't with you. I wish I would find someone else.

But I don't say this aloud. He'd probably freak out. He says I can leave whenever I want, but then goes on to say how I have no life to run back to and how he'd ruin my life if I tried. He also threatens to take Lucas and Grayson away from me.

"Who do you think the courts will believe?" he asked the last time I said I was done. "Me, a successful businessman?"

You're hardly successful. You've launched several startups since we've been together and had to use my savings and our house as collateral for your latest business loan since your parents stopped funding you.

"Or will they believe a heavily medicated lunatic like you? No way am I letting you take my sons away from me. Do you hear me?"

I frowned but kept my mouth shut.

He's the reason I'm on antidepressants and antianxiety medication in the first place. If it weren't for those pills, I'd have probably killed myself by now.

Then again, I'd never leave my boys behind.

But before the medication numbed me, I spent every day crying in bed, wishing for a different life.

Looking back, everything happened gradually. I kept hoping he'd get better, that he'd stop drinking, or that there would simply be more good days than bad ones.

But now, two years later, he's managed to gain control of absolutely everything in my life. I can't even have a phone call with my sister or parents without him asking why I step outside every time.

And when I ask him why he's watching me, he snaps, calls me paranoid, and says that I need to add antipsychotic pills to my list of daily medications.

Then, in the next breath, he pulls me into his arms, kisses the top of my head, and tells me how worried he is about me. How he only wants the best for me, and how I deserve the most amazing life possible.

But this isn't a life.

This feels like prison.

If I need to go do groceries, he says it's something we do as a family and that I'm not to leave the house during the day—it's too dangerous with all the medication I'm on.

"Well?" James asks, pulling me back to reality. "Go put something else on before the babysitter gets here. Like the blue dress I got you."

I insecurely play with my earrings—two silver teardrops Chloe got me several years ago for my birthday.

"And what are those?" he asks with a disgusted look on his face. "I thought you'd put a bit more effort into our anniversary, Alice. It's hurtful, to be honest."

I walk away, feeling like a pig wrapped in a silk sheet despite my small frame. He makes me feel so small . . . so ugly. And although I used to lash back at him, I've lost the energy. My lashing back simply isn't worth the fight afterward. Somehow, he gets angrier than I do, no matter how right I feel I am.

Besides, I don't even have any anger left.

All I have is a feeling of worthlessness.

I return to our bedroom, forcing a smile at Grayson as he peeks through his bedroom door. He must have heard the way James was talking to me. But he knows better than to talk back to his dad—he learned that the hard way. At first, it was an earful, then shouting, and now, shouting combined with a fist through drywall or a broken gaming system.

And Grayson loves his games, so he's learned to keep quiet when his father gets upset.

I change into the blue dress James was talking about—the one that feels too tight on me now since I've gained a few pounds thanks to my new medication. It makes me feel even uglier than I did before, but if I don't wear it, James will throw a fit.

And it is our anniversary, after all.

I'd rather keep the peace.

I pull out my earrings and replace them with a gold pair he bought for me for our last anniversary. Hopefully, he'll have nothing to say about that.

I lean forward in the mirror and gaze into my hazel eyes. The eyeliner around them has smudged slightly, so I wipe a finger under my eyelid to smooth everything over; otherwise, James will say I look like I'm wearing cheap dollar-store makeup.

It wouldn't be the first time he said that.

"What's taking so long?" comes his blaring voice.

I flinch at the sound, and my gut tightens.

I hurry out of the room to spot Grayson still watching me through the crack of his door. I'm about to tell him that everything is okay when I hear the front door open, followed by James's overly charming voice.

"Hey there, Yannah," he says. "Right on time. Wow, it looks windy out there. Come on in, come on in. Here, let me help you with that."

Why can't he be that nice to me?

He used to be.

Now, it's like I'm his worst enemy half the time.

Yannah lets out a shy laugh and says something I can't make out. She's babysat for us before, and although she's only eighteen years old, I know she finds James attractive.

Why wouldn't she?

He's tall and rugged with his defined jaw and jet-black hair that he coifs messily to the side every day. His smile is almost too beautiful. The kind full of perfectly straight white teeth that make you want to kiss him. Plus, he always smells so good. Some crisp, manly cologne. I don't know the name. The scent makes me sick now. I used to love it, but when I smell it now, a knot forms in my stomach.

Despite all these positive physical attributes, I find him ugly. I guess that's because I know the real him. And no matter how good looking he is on the outside, it isn't enough to make up for the monster on the inside.

When I return downstairs, Yannah is beaming at James, and he's smiling back just as wide. His eyes even flicker toward her cleavage, and her cheeks blush.

Not that I care.

I might have when we were first married, but now, I'd be more than happy if someone else came along and swept him away.

Although, I'd feel awful for the unlucky girl.

"There's my beautiful wife," he says, placing a hand on the small of my back.

I fight the urge to pull away.

When he leans in to kiss me, it's awkward and strained. But I let him do it. If I don't, I'll never hear the end of it in the truck. He'll go on about how I embarrassed him in front of our babysitter.

And if there's one thing James values above all else—arguably even his own children—it's his image.

"See you later, Yannah," he says. "Thanks again for this."

He says goodbye with a smile, and the second he closes the door, his smile vanishes.

CHAPTER 28

"Emma!"

Her chipper voice catches me off guard. I've been sitting on one of the park benches, watching Lucas play with the other kids. He isn't talking, but he isn't running away from them, either.

I'd say that's a good sign.

I turn sideways just in time to see Carla McKenzie rushing toward me while clutching onto her purse.

She beams, revealing slightly coffee-stained teeth.

"Mrs. McKenzie—" I start.

"Carla," she corrects me warmly.

She sits down hard next to me, causing the bench to shake slightly. I scootch over a bit, not wanting my thigh pressed up against hers.

"I didn't expect to see you here," she says.

Before I can ask her why she's made such a presumption, she adds, "You know, what with Lucas and all—"

I suppose the fact that my son doesn't talk due to trauma would be a valid reason to stay out of large social gatherings.

She thinks you're a bad mom for bringing him here, when he should be someplace quiet, healing his trauma.

That's ridiculous.

She's smiling and seems genuinely happy to see me.

"How's he been?" I ask. "In class, I mean."

She lets out a long sigh and sets her purse down between us. "Well, I wouldn't say bad. He's still drawing, you know—" She wiggles a finger like she's drawing some invisible doodle in the air.

Yeah, I know.

Dead bodies.

Apparently, it's too awful for her to simply say it aloud. Either that, or she doesn't want anyone overhearing us. Which is respectable. I appreciate her keeping my life and my son's trauma a private matter.

"But he's doing his schoolwork," she says. "He understands instructions just fine. Mind you, he hasn't been playing with the kids as much. A bit like—" Her finger drifts toward him now, where he's crouched under the play structure, shuffling wood chips around.

"Yeah," I say. "He hasn't been very social."

"It'll take time," she says. "These things always do."

She goes quiet for a bit, almost like she's disappeared into her head to think about something traumatic that's happened in her life.

I don't press her.

Her life isn't my business, and I'm afraid if we get too personal, she'll start asking questions about my past.

"I hope it's all right that I've been giving him little treats here and there," she says.

"Treats?" I ask.

She offers me a little smirk like it's nothing. "Oh, you know, a little cookie, a piece of fudge . . . I should have asked you first, but—"

"It's fine," I tell her. In any other circumstance, I'd be upset that a teacher is giving my kid sugar behind my back.

Until he's a teenager, whatever goes into his body is up to me. I've always worked hard to keep my kids as healthy as possible by limiting sugar and pastries. But now, none of that matters. If it's helping him, I don't care.

"Does it help?" I ask.

"He perks up every time," she says.

I try to smile, but I don't have the strength.

"How are things going with Maya?" she asks.

I didn't realize she was on a first-name basis with the town's psychologist.

"Hard to say," I admit.

He's only had two sessions. It's not like he'll be cured overnight.

"Well, hang in there," she says.

Her warm hand catches me off guard. She pats my knee, then squeezes it. Instinctively, I pull away.

"Oh, I'm sorry—" she says.

She retreats, but right before her arm is tucked back against her side, I catch a glimpse of something. Scars? Burn marks? Whatever they are, they've disfigured her wrist.

She must have caught me staring.

Quickly, she yanks on her long sleeve to cover up her marred skin.

"No, *I'm* sorry," I say. "I—"

She wipes the air as if to erase everything that's happened. "You have nothing to apologize for. I've always been very touchy-feely, and I sometimes forget not everyone likes to be touched. Besides, it's normal to be jumpy when you're on the run."

I suck in a breath, feeling like the park is spinning around me. What sounded like innocent laughter coming from the picnic tables now sounds ominous, as if coming through a tunnel.

"Excuse me?" I blurt.

Did I hear her wrong? Because no way could she possibly figure me out so soon. I barely know her.

"What?" she says, looking confused.

"What did you just say?" I ask her.

I need her to repeat it. To explain herself.

She raises a brow as if nothing happened. It makes me feel crazy. I must have misheard her. I'm barely sleeping as it is.

"I said it's normal to be jumpy with everything that's going on with your son," she says. "I hope I didn't cross a line, or anything."

I let out a slow, quivering breath and shake my head. "N-no, you didn't. Sorry. I didn't hear you. And y-yeah, it's not been easy."

My eyes flicker toward her wrist again.

I didn't mean to look.

But she tugs at her sleeve like it's a compulsion now—like she has to pull it down over her palm to erase the fact that I saw it.

Should I ask her about them?

No. It's not your business.

"Emma," she says, her smile vanishing.

I'm afraid to hear what comes out of her mouth next.

"I know I'm only Lucas's teacher, but if you ever want to talk"—she pauses, her heavily lidded eyes scanning the crowd around us—"I'm here. I . . . I know a thing or two about trauma."

Is she referring to the scars on her wrists?

Did someone do that to her?

"And I know how awful it can be. I imagine you aren't sleeping much."

I don't say anything.

I can't tell whether she's speaking from experience or whether she's deducing this from the dark bags under my eyes.

"This town also likes to talk," she says. "Which is why I'm very careful about who I open up to because, as you know, some people around here have big mouths. But I get the feeling you're not like that. You seem like a private person, and I admire that. So if you ever want to talk, I promise you, it's going to stay between us."

She swipes sideways across her mouth as if closing an invisible zipper.

I appreciate her attempt at friendship.

Right now, however, I'm not looking for a friend. All I want is to keep my head down, look after my boys, and get back on my feet.

"That's very kind of you," I say.

I should probably tell her she can talk to me, too, but

that will open a door I'm afraid I'll never be able to close. If she starts talking about her trauma, whatever it is, she'll expect me to open up about my past.

And I can't have that.

Not if I want to stay safe . . . to stay alive.

I force a smile. "Thank you, Carla. You've been so kind to me, and I really appreciate it."

She reaches to tap my knee again but stops herself and nods curtly instead. "Life is hard, and I believe the only way through it is with each other. I'll keep you posted on Lucas next week."

She grabs her purse, drops it on her knee, and grins at me. "I have to go check on my kids, but it was really nice to see you again, Emma. I'll catch you later."

With that, she leaves, her big brown curls bouncing behind her back.

And although her scars are none of my business, I can't help but wonder whether she's in the same boat I used to be in. Is someone abusing her? Was this her attempt at reaching out for help?

If I'd opened up, she might have done the same.

It's none of your business, Alice. Stay out of it, and focus on yourself and your family.

Isn't it everyone's business, though, when another human being is in danger? When they're hurting? Maybe if more people started looking out for each other, this world would be a better place.

CHAPTER 29

BEFORE

James lifts two heavy grocery bags—one with each arm—which causes his deltoids to double in size. And while years ago, I might have found that sexy, right now, it makes me feel weak and small.

I hate it.

"It's fine, Alice. Sit on your ass and do nothing," he says as if he's struggling.

He isn't.

I pull my head out of his truck, vexed. Do *nothing*? I was buckling Lucas into his car seat.

"Is there anything left?" I ask.

"Obviously not," he huffs. "I took care of it."

"Thank you," I mumble.

You shouldn't even be thanking him. He's being an asshole.

But if I don't, it'll only make matters worse.

Without warning, Grayson lets out a squeal. My eyes double in size as I try to figure out what just happened.

"I was in a boss battle!" Grayson cries.

James towers over him on the other side of the truck. "How many fucking times do I have to tell you? My truck isn't your charging station. Unless you want to start paying me gas."

He tosses Grayson's Nintendo Switch into the back of the truck, and Grayson lets out another squeal before lunging at his system to ensure the screen hasn't shattered.

James tears the charger out of the back seat cigarette

lighter and chucks it at him. "Do that one more time, and I'm smashing your Switch. Do you hear me?"

Grayson glowers at him.

He's so hurt he's on the verge of tears.

"James," I say as sweetly as I can, trying to calm him down.

I want to point out that charging a Switch is hardly a use of his gas, but he cuts me off.

"I don't want to fucking hear it, Alice. Don't you dare undermine me in front of our son. Get your ass in the car, now."

At the same time, I catch a glimpse of a couple standing behind him. They're both frozen, with grocery bags held firmly against their chests.

It's like they want to say something but don't want to get involved. The man is half of James's size. If I were him, I'd probably stay out of it, too.

Yet I wish they *would* say something.

I wish someone would put James in his place once and for all. No one ever seems to have the courage to say anything. And I certainly can't put James in his place, no matter how angry I get. The only thing I'm good for is trying to keep the peace.

It's the only way to keep my kids safe.

James gets into the driver's seat and slams the door. At the same time, the bystanders quickly look away.

No one is going to save me.

If anyone is going to get me out of this, it's me.

CHAPTER 30

Grayson walks into the house with a silly grin on his face.

What's that about?

I haven't seen him smile that big in years. It's such a goofy smile—and such a needed distraction from Lucas's current inability to talk—that I find myself smiling back at him.

His face goes sour when he catches me. "What?"

"You look happy," I say.

He shrugs. "I had a good time."

I'm happy to hear it. It's little moments like these that make being a mom so rewarding. When I see my kid genuinely happy.

"Good," I say.

I don't interrogate him or ask him whether he made any new friends. He's fourteen. As soon as I start questioning, he'll get weird and tell me he doesn't want to share every detail of his life with me.

Besides, his newfound happiness is probably over a girl.

He used to tell me about his girlfriends in school. They'd last a week or two, but it was still sweet of him to talk about it. Then James started getting involved, telling him to never let some *broad* get in the way of his career or his studies. And while I agree that studies should come above relationships in high school, James spoke about women like they were the scum of the earth. Then, his eyes would linger on me, almost like he wanted Grayson to know that he had firsthand experience in dealing with a greedy, soul-sucking woman.

The worst of it was when Grayson started repeating some of what James was saying, like *bros before hos*, or *men should always be in charge*.

So while James implanted horrible lessons into my child's head, I spent most nights trying to reverse this by educating him on women's rights and equality.

He didn't always want to hear about it, but I know it had an impact on him.

We have enough sexism and hatred toward women in this world. I certainly don't want my boys to be a part of the problem; I want them to be a part of the solution.

"I'll be in my room," he tells me.

He climbs the stairs two steps at a time, assumedly in a rush to go talk on his phone in private.

Lucas brushes past me and plops himself down on the couch.

"You hungry, sweetheart?" I ask him, even though he just ate a burger at the park.

He shrugs.

"You want to watch TV for a bit?"

Another shrug.

I fight the urge to sigh. This isn't his fault. He's struggling on the inside. All I can do is be supportive and attentive to his needs.

It's funny how we live in a mansion with everything we need, yet I feel unhappy most days. With James, I always struggled financially—the main reason being that he kept "borrowing" money from me for his business and never returning it. And without a job, I wasn't able to earn it back.

Back then, I wondered if his business took off the way he wanted it to . . . whether he might come back to me. Whether his anger was misdirected due to his feelings of inadequacy in the world of entrepreneurship.

But it wasn't about the money. It never was.

I see that now.

Money, things . . . a nice house. It hasn't changed

anything for me. I still feel like I'm being hunted. I still go to sleep with a rotten feeling in my gut that no matter how thick my front door is, James is going to come blasting through it.

More money could get you a security system.

I make a mental note to call up Mr. Yonuk soon. He may be able to pull a few strings and get me that inheritance money sooner.

The thought of a security system has me racing to the front door to ensure the deadbolt is locked. It isn't, which sends a hot panic through my veins. How did I miss it? It's usually an automatic action.

All those medications fried your brain.

I stopped my antidepressants and antianxiety medication over six months ago when I first escaped James. The side effects were awful, but I pulled through. However, I can't help but wonder whether they caused long-term effects.

My memory has been awful these days.

Shaking my panic away, I move back into the kitchen to prepare Lucas and myself a snack. He may not be hungry now, but if he has a plate of carrots and dip in front of him, he'll eat it.

And after all the candy I've been letting him eat, I need to balance it somehow with good nutrients.

I pull a shiny knife out of the knife block, then open the island drawer where I spotted a large wooden cutting board the other day.

I pull it out, but just as I close the drawer, something wavers.

What is that? A slip of paper? It's sticking out of the utensil drawer.

An old receipt?

I open the drawer, and the crumpled paper slips out.

It lands on the tiled floor without a sound.

Appliance instructions left behind by Victor?

But when I open it completely, my mouth goes dry, and the kitchen whirls around me.

It's a short message typed out in red font:

YOU'RE NOT SAFE HERE.

CHAPTER 31

I whip open the door the moment Wyatt steps onto the front porch. With trembling hands, I give him the note.

"This is the note you called about?" he asks.

Behind him, Derek comes strolling toward the house like there's nothing to be concerned about.

I'm not sure I like that cop.

There's something about him.

A crease forms between Wyatt's thick dark brows. "Could be a warning."

"A warning?" I blurt.

I wrap myself up in my oversized bummy cardigan and step outside, lowering my tone to a whisper. "I don't care what the note says. How the hell did it get inside my house?"

Wyatt scratches at his morning scruff. He looks like he was *almost* ready when the call came in, forcing him to rush out the door.

Derek walks up to him, his shoulders square and his heavy boots clacking against the porch's wooden boards. Wyatt hands him the note.

"Printed," Derek says.

Obviously. Whoever did this doesn't want their handwriting out there. Doesn't take a cop to figure that one out.

I breathe in slowly, reminding myself that they're here to help. But it's that nonchalant look on Derek's face that's upsetting me. It's as if he doesn't realize that this poses a threat to not only me but to my sons. How am I supposed to sleep at night knowing someone managed to sneak a note inside my house?

"Could it be one of your sons?" Derek asks.

I'm insulted.

Why the hell would Grayson or Lucas write something like that? It's not like them. Grayson is very upfront about his displeasure when he isn't having a good time. He's like his father in that way. He wouldn't go leaving notes around the house to toy with me.

And Lucas is too young.

"We have to think of every option," Wyatt says, his features softening.

"Any other notes?" Derek asks.

My eyes bore into him. I wish he'd show even a modicum of concern. "No. Not that I've seen."

"Could it have been there before you moved in?" he asks.

I frown hard and part my lips, but Wyatt interrupts us both with a gentle wave of his hand. He turns to Derek and says, "Can you go get my notepad in the cruiser?"

The moment Derek steps off the patio, Wyatt turns to me. "He's still learning the ropes. Doesn't exactly have good bedside manner."

I scowl at the back of Derek's head as he walks like a gym rat on steroids.

Young and macho.

"I'm sorry about that," Wyatt says. "He'll cool down once he's comfortable on the job. The kid thinks he has to impress me."

"I don't see who he's impressing," I say.

A hint of a smile pulls at Wyatt's lips before he says, "He's asking all the right questions, though. We need to rule everything out. I mean, a note isn't typically enough to open an investigative case, but given what happened here—"

Our eyes lock.

"Are you sure the note wasn't there before you moved in?" he asks. "May I ask where you found it?"

"In the cutlery drawer," I say. "And no, it wasn't there. I use that drawer all the time."

"You're *sure*? It couldn't have been hiding in the corner, somewhere?"

I'm about to tell him I'm sure when I start to doubt myself. What if the note *was* there all along? What if it was a warning to the dead person in the basement? It might have nothing to do with me.

"I'm not here to downplay anything," Wyatt says. "Trust me. I want to make sure that you, Lucas, and Grayson are safe."

I like how he says their names, rather than refer to them as *the kids* or *your kids*. Somehow, it makes me feel close to him. It makes me feel like he genuinely cares about us and didn't simply show up here to appease a frightened woman.

"You have a Hawk Security system," he says.

Why would he say this? I don't have any security system in place. When he catches me squinting at him in confusion, he wiggles a finger toward the front door. "I saw the keypad the other day, during our investigation. The door and window sensors are all still in place. The only thing missing is your connection to the service provider."

I know what he's talking about—the touchscreen pad sitting next to the front door. I figured it was an old security system that was no longer operative.

"We have a local branch here in Thorn Lake," he says. "I know the owner. If you'd like, I could ask him to get everything set—"

"I appreciate the offer," I say. "But I can't afford—"

He politely hushes me with a wave of his large hand. "We'll say it's a police matter for now. That you need surveillance. And with only two members on staff, we can't exactly provide around-the-clock monitoring services."

Derek returns with a notepad and a pen.

I'm so taken aback by Wyatt's kindness that I don't

know what to say. Before I can respond, Wyatt says, "Derek, call up Hawk Security on Beverly Avenue and have them connect Ms. Collins's security system with monitoring.

Derek's lips curl. "What? Why would we—"

Wyatt plants his hands on his hips and turns to his partner. "Unless you want to park out front on surveillance duties for the next two weeks, day and night. Up to you."

Begrudgingly, Derek agrees and pulls out his cell phone. He trots down the patio stairs to make the call, and in the distance, I hear the mention of my name, the police department, and my address.

"I— I can't thank you enough," I say to Wyatt.

He brushes me off with an amiable smile. "Just doing my job as a police officer."

Is he trying to make me feel safer in my own home, or does he genuinely believe that there's a threat lurking nearby?

"So do you think someone left the note?" I ask. "Should I be taking any precautions?"

Biting his plush lower lip, he shrugs with one shoulder. "It's impossible to say. I wish I had more answers for you. I really do. Right now, let's hold onto the idea that it may have been there to begin with and may be connected to the body in the basement. I should have more answers any day now. Forensics was supposed to get back to me last week, but they're apparently behind."

He pauses like he's weighing his next words carefully. "Either way, we're going to have that security system up and running by evening, so if anyone tries to set foot inside your house, Hawk personnel will be dispatched to your house to take a look for any signs of a break-in, and if anything suspicious is found, I'll be on my way."

"Hawk personnel?" I ask.

"A guard," he clarifies. "False alarms happen all the time. If Derek and I were called to every alarm, we'd never get our jobs done."

I suppose that makes sense, even though I'd much rather Wyatt show up with that gun of his. But the desire makes me feel selfish. Of course this method makes the most sense in terms of resource management.

Besides, I have a gun, now.

If the alarm goes off, I'll be prepared.

As if reading my mind, Wyatt says, "Hey, have you gone back to the shooting range?"

I shake my head.

A charming smile pulls at the corners of his lips. "Well, I go every Wednesday around noon. I'd be happy to shoot some targets with you."

I try to smile back, but I'm too distraught over everything right now. Despite this, I appreciate the invitation. I may take him up on it.

Derek returns, wiggling his cell phone next to his face. "It's connected." He hops up the stairs, two at a time, and shows me his screen.

EmCo

1234

"What's this?" I ask.

"Your login and password."

It takes me a moment to understand what EmCo stands for.

Emma Collins.

The name still sounds weird in my head. Sometimes, I'm afraid that even thinking of my own name will give me away.

Alice. Your name is Alice.

A bead of sweat drips down the arch of my brow.

"You all right?" Wyatt asks.

"Y-yes," I say. "This is great. Thank you."

"Do you need help setting it up?" he asks.

I'm about to accept the offer when I spot Derek standing as stiff as a statue, arms crossed over his chest. It's a stance that says, *We're police officers, not technicians. You're wasting our time.*

"I should be okay," I tell him. "Thank you. Both of you,

for all your help."

Derek nods like a trained soldier, and Wyatt reaches for my shoulder but pulls away.

It would be unprofessional.

Especially with Derek watching.

"Absolutely," Wyatt says. "If anything else happens, Ms. Collins, please don't hesitate to give the police department a call. That's what we're here for."

I believe him, though it's hard to hold onto that belief with the way Derek carries himself. Like I'm siphoning their resources and am an utter waste of time.

Wyatt raises the crumpled note. "We'll keep this in your file if that's all right. Until it's ruled out, we have to assume it's related to the VIC." He clears his throat. "The victim. The body."

"I understand," I say, eager to get back inside.

The sooner I'm inside, the sooner I can set up the security system and prevent something like this from happening again.

CHAPTER 32

I toss and turn most of the night, picturing someone sneaking in through a window or somehow breaking through the back door.

How did they get in?

How did they leave that note behind?

And more importantly, why?

I push these thoughts away—Wyatt might be right. What if the note was there all along? I can't be certain. It's not like I've done much cooking in this house and have thoroughly inspected my kitchen drawers. I could have missed it, and it was there, right under my nose.

Thump.

My eyes pop open.

What the hell was that?

It came from downstairs. It was loud, too, like someone dropping something heavy.

I reach for my phone and open my new Hawk Security app. All entry points are secure. There's no break-in activity. And before going to bed, I went around the entire house to ensure that each door and window had a sensor.

Maybe one of them is broken.

Or you're imagining things, and there was no loud noise.

No, there was definitely a bang.

My gaze involuntarily drifts toward my nightstand in the dark.

My gun.

Am I overreacting?

What if it was a shift in the house? This house is rather

old. Or a branch hitting a window?

Something in my gut tells me it's more than that. I'm trying to calm myself down because I'm afraid, but there's someone down there.

I know it.

I slip my legs out from underneath the blanket and quietly open my drawer. Within seconds, my Glock is loaded and in my palm.

Quietly, I tiptoe to my bedroom door and creak it open. The sound makes me wince.

Thump. Bang.

It wasn't my imagination—someone is downstairs.

I retreat into my room that seems to swirl around me, and I call 911.

After a single ring, the line picks up.

"911, what's your emergency?"

"H-hi," I whisper as close to the phone as I can. "I think there's an intruder in my house."

The woman's voice at the other end is calm—almost too calm in a crisis like this.

"What's your address, ma'am?"

"1472 Thorn Lake Drive," I whisper.

I want to tell her to hurry and send the police, but I'm leaning next to the crack of my door, trying to listen for any other sound.

"Are you safe?" the woman asks.

"Y-yes," I whisper.

"Stay hidden," she says. "Police will be right over."

But the sound that follows next makes me think I'm having a heart attack.

Grayson.

I'd recognize his voice anywhere.

He lets out a faint cry from downstairs.

Grayson!

Without thinking, I drop my cell phone to the floor—*clack*—and hurry down, feeling like my legs aren't even attached to my body.

I can't feel anything.

Not with this much adrenaline pumping through me. It's a miracle I even make it down the stairs without falling, but this is my son. Nothing will stop me from protecting him. Not even if I were to tumble and break my legs. I'd crawl to him if I had to.

"Grayson!" I shout, gun sticking straight out in front of me.

Although, it's not entirely straight.

It's swaying from side to side as I run in my pajamas, probably looking like a total lunatic with disheveled hair and dark bags beneath my eyes.

I come barreling into the kitchen with wide eyes to find Grayson looking back at me, his features mirroring mine.

I jerk my gun around, trying to point it at an invisible enemy.

"Where is . . . Where are they? Where are—" I shout.

He throws two hands in the air, his round eyes aimed at me. "Mom! What are you doing?"

My eyes catch a glimpse of bright red trickling down his left hand.

"I— I'm sorry," he says. "I got hungry. And I wanted to make myself a sandwich. And I—"

In his other hand is a serrated bread knife.

"Mom, please!"

Suddenly, I realize what's going on. I'm standing in the kitchen aiming a gun at my son, my supposed intruder.

I immediately lower the Glock, having a hard time placing it on the kitchen island because my hands are shaking so badly.

And Grayson's quivering chin tells me he's on the verge of crying.

"What the hell are you doing?" I shout.

I should be apologizing for scaring him so badly, but my entire body is vibrating, and I feel like I might throw up. I'm too worked up to talk to him calmly.

"I— I told you," he says. "I got hungry."

"So you started banging cupboards?" I snap.

I can hear myself yelling at him—and I'm not one to yell

at my kids—but I can't stop. "I could have killed you!"

He slowly lowers his hands. They tremble.

"I could have shot you, Grayson." Slowly, my breath returns to normal.

"I wasn't trying to be loud." He lowers the knife on the counter and reaches for some paper towel. "I reached for the peanut butter, and it slipped, and then I tried to catch it, and the cupboard door slammed shut. And then—"

"It doesn't matter," I say. I inhale deeply, trying to steady my breathing. "I heard you cry out . . . I thought—"

"It's just a small cut." He raises his finger to show me the droplets of blood before rinsing it under the tap.

As the water trickles down his hand and turns pink, Grayson looks at me and then at my gun.

"It's for protection," I tell him.

"From dad?" he asks.

Our eyes lock.

Mostly. But I can't tell him that. I can't tell him that if James ever sets foot in this house, I'll kill him. He's still his father. And despite all the horrible things James did, he still tried to build happy memories with Grayson. It must all be very conflicting for a fourteen-year-old boy.

Blue and red lights flash through the glass of the front door, and Grayson frowns. "You called the cops?"

I sigh. "Yeah. Like I said, I thought someone was down here hurting you."

He blows air out through ballooned cheeks as if trying to take it all in. I can't even imagine how terrifying this must have been for him—me running down the stairs, screaming at the top of my lungs, swaying a gun in his direction, when all he was trying to do was make a sandwich.

"I'll talk to them," I say. "You can go to bed."

He hesitates, then reaches for his peanut butter and jelly sandwich and hurries upstairs.

I spot Derek through the window before I open the door. He approaches with two hands planted on his duty belt, casual as usual.

Shouldn't he be holding his gun or something?

Isn't it his job to be on high alert?

I open the door and step outside.

"I'm so sorry, Officer Garcia—"

He shrugs casually. "Derek is fine."

"It was a false alarm," I say.

He doesn't look surprised. Still, he comes up the steps, his large frame towering over me. "Mind if I take a look inside?"

Where's Wyatt? I want to ask. But I don't. It's three o'clock in the morning. They can't both be up at night.

"What for?" I ask. "I told you, it was a false alarm. It was my son—"

He crosses his arms. "I understand, Ms. Collins—"

"Emma is fine," I tell him.

He offers a half nod before continuing, "It's protocol. I have to ensure that the home is secure."

CHAPTER 33

BEFORE

James opens the door with a smile on his face. I watch him from the living room sofa, wishing the police could see *through* the house . . . see my crooked ponytail and the large gash across my face. Or how badly I'm shuddering.

"We received an anonymous call about a fight at this residence," says the male officer.

"A fight?" James says, forcing a laugh. "The only fighting going on in here is me and my son watching UFC. Could that be the source of the sound?"

But the boys aren't home tonight. They're at the babysitter's—Stacey's.

So who called?

The neighbor? Mr. Amir? Whoever did knows well enough to remain anonymous.

I think back to our fight, though it's blurry. We were shouting—well, James was shouting—and the next thing I knew, he was on top of me. I tried to get away and kicked a lamp down in the process.

My gaze drifts to the broken lamp on the floor.

I always hated that thing. James paid over $300 for it, saying it was highly energy efficient and well worth the money. But it's ugly and almost too modern, with a glass shade that reflects light in every direction imaginable.

As I stare at the shattered pieces on the carpet, I realize that it may very well be the reason I'm still alive right now.

"Hell of a fight," James adds.

One of the male cops says, "Oh, you're watching Anzi

versus Hefferson?"

James leans on the door, charming as always. "Wouldn't miss it. It's on the TV now. You're welcome to come in and take a look. Admittedly, I do watch TV a bit too loud. Bit of a hearing problem." He points at the side of his head and lets out a playful laugh. "But I can turn it down. I'm so sorry for the trouble."

There's nothing on the TV. In fact, the TV is cracked and sitting at an angle from one of James's outbursts last week—the result of him grabbing me by the hair and throwing me into it.

Pain starts to throb in my ribs.

James is taking a huge gamble by lying right now.

I want to shout at the cops to accept James's offer and to come in, but if I do that, I won't be alive by morning.

Say something, Alice. Anything. They'll protect you.

Will they, though?

I've heard countless stories of men being taken into custody, only to be released the next day due to lack of evidence. It's my word against his. And if I get him arrested right now, he'll come back in a day. Or two, if I'm lucky.

It would give you time to run.

How?

I have no money. No credit cards. James has made sure of that. I'm a prisoner. The only way out of this is by gathering evidence of his abuse—and a lot of it—or leaving in a body bag.

CHAPTER 34

I'm midblog when my phone starts to ring next to my laptop.

Thorn Lake Police Department.

If I didn't have such a history with them, I'd panic at the sight of that text scrolling across my screen. I might allow my imagination to run wild and think that something happened to Grayson or Lucas.

Instead, I find myself rushing to hit Accept.

"Hello?"

"Emma," Wyatt says. "How're you doing?"

"Fine," I lie.

I managed to sleep an hour, maybe two.

"Listen, I was wondering if you'd have a minute to come down to the station?"

My eyes narrow at the back wall of my office. Am I under investigation or something?

"The results came in," he says.

Results?

"Forensics," he quickly adds.

"Oh, right." I rub grime off my forehead. "Sorry, I barely slept—"

"I know," he says.

He knows? How does he know that?

"Derek left the police report on my desk this morning. I wanted to check in on you. Make sure everything is . . . okay?"

It depends on how I look at it. While there no intruder, I may very well have traumatized my fourteen-year-old.

"There was mention of a loaded gun in the kitchen," Wyatt adds.

A sinking feeling hits me in the gut.

A loaded gun. Inside my house. With my kids.

He must think I'm a terrible mother.

"You must have been terrified," he says.

"I— I was," I say.

"I'm sorry that happened," he says. "It's completely normal to be on edge after witnessing something traumatic."

On edge?

I heard someone in my house, followed by the sound of Grayson crying out in pain. How else was I supposed to respond? Call out gently and ask whether everything was okay?

When I don't say anything, Wyatt says, "Anyway, that's not why I'm calling. Like I said, some information came in from Forensics, and I have a few questions for you."

"Questions?" I say.

"You're not a suspect if that's what you're thinking," he says.

I would hope not. It wasn't like I even lived here when the person was killed or died. I might finally get answers today.

But the way he assures me that I'm not a suspect makes me feel like he doubts my sanity. Like he has to walk on eggshells around me.

"I wasn't thinking that," I say.

"Good, good," he says.

The conversation feels strained and awkward.

"When can you come by?" he asks.

"Anytime before three," I say. "I like to be home when the boys get back from school."

"I'm in the office now," he says. "Is now a good time?"

How urgent is this?

Should I be worried?

What information did he find that warrants him calling

me first thing in the morning for questioning?

"Now is good," I say.

He thanks me and ends the call.

And although I should be relieved that he has more answers, I can't help but feel a twinge of anxiety creeping into my chest.

***

The police station doesn't feel like a police station. The redbrick building feels like an old pizza shop that got new tenants.

Behind the counter is a young woman wearing a police uniform. Her hair is tucked neatly into a tight bun at the base of her skull, her hairline perfectly straight across her forehead.

"Hi there," she says. "Do you have an appointment?"

She's sitting behind an old wooden desk. No Plexiglass. No fancy security equipment. Nothing.

I thought there were only two cops in Thorn Lake?

Wyatt and Derek.

I spot a shiny nameplate next to a stack of papers and yellow folders.

Officer Teresa Diaz.

She's even younger than Derek, which would make her somewhere in her early twenties—fresh out of her teenage years. She doesn't smile at me, but she doesn't scrutinize me the way Derek does, either.

"Oh, um, hi," I say. "Yes. I received a call from W— Officer Daniels."

"Ah, Wyatt," she says.

So they're on a first-name basis.

She rolls her chair back. "You must be Emma Collins. One second."

She gets up, and moments later, Wyatt appears from behind a poorly painted blue door.

"Emma, please, come in," he says.

I thank the young cop and follow Wyatt into what appears to be an office. He picks up a stack of papers off a peeling leather chair and offers me the seat.

"Thank you for coming in so quickly," he says.

I don't say anything.

He closes the door behind us and takes a seat at his desk. A soapy smell enters my nostrils, followed by the strong scent of coffee. I spot a brown Beans & Stuff cup next to his keyboard.

"I'm sorry," he says, watching me. "Would you like a coffee? I can get Teresa to brew up a fresh batch."

"No, that's fine," I say. "Is she new?"

He's searching through paper notes, distracted. But finally, he looks up and says, "Hm? Oh, Teresa? She's been here about a month. Fresh out of Police Academy. Derek was the one handling the phones for about a year, so when he moved up, we needed to bring someone else in."

"I'm sure the extra hands help," I say.

"They do," he says, lacking any hint of emotion on his face.

When he finds what he's looking for, he pulls out the sheet of paper and spreads it flat on his desk with one hand.

"Marta Sanchez," he says matter-of-factly.

He pauses a moment, his green eyes rolling up at me.

What is he waiting for? A reaction? I thought he said I wasn't a suspect.

"What?" I ask, growing increasingly uncomfortable under his gaze.

He must not have received the reaction he was looking for. As if nothing happened, he taps his finger on his report and says, "That's the name of the woman who was found in your basement. Twenty-two years old. Does the name ring any bells?"

I suck in a breath, hold it, then shake my head.

Twenty-two years old?

In my uncle's basement?

How is that possible? Who was she to him? And did he

do this?

"We're still waiting for the official results from the Medical Examiner," he says. "Unfortunately, these things take time. And I imagine their job isn't easy given the condition of the body."

"What do you mean?" I ask him.

He glances up at me again. "Well, the body. There wasn't much—"

I cut him off with a quick wave. It was a stupid question. I should have thought before I spoke. The last thing I want is to be reminded of that gruesome sight.

"She lived in Aspen Heights," he continues. "Small town about thirty minutes from here."

I know that name. I saw it on the map when researching Thorn Lake.

"Was she killed?" I ask.

"It's impossible to say just yet," he says. "But there was a lesion on the skull, which has Forensics suspecting blunt force trauma."

I blink hard, trying to take this all in.

"Are you saying my uncle hit her in the head and put her body in the basement?"

He shakes his head slowly. "We don't have all the answers. Right now, we're trying to find out more about her and why she was in Victor Huxley's house to begin with. I'm heading to Aspen Heights next week to talk to her boyfriend."

I gaze at the report under his tapping fingers.

She had a boyfriend? Did she have children? Who was this woman?

Her name is written upside down next to a whole paragraph of text.

None of this makes any sense.

Unless it does. It could be really simple; my uncle was a psychopath who kidnapped this woman and kept her confined to a small space in a secret room in his basement before he decided to kill her.

It's not the Victor I remember, but then again, I haven't

known him most of my life. And he was a recluse. People don't just live in isolation for no reason.

"Do you know if your uncle had a history of domestic violence?" he asks.

I raise a brow. How would I know that? I was only a kid when I last saw him. "I don't know. I'm sorry."

Wyatt shakes his head. "That's all right. Listen, I know this doesn't give you all the answers you wanted, but it's a step in the right direction."

When I don't answer, Wyatt tries to apologize for this dump of information.

Now that I know who the body belonged to, I can't help but try to reconstruct a face on that decomposing corpse.

I wish I could rid my mind of the image, but I can't.

And now, I can't help but wonder why Victor would do something like this. How sick was he?

I thank Wyatt for the information and leave, feeling worse than I did when there were no answers.

CHAPTER 35

"What do you mean, a fight?"

"A fight, Ms. Collins. An altercation."

I don't appreciate Sarah's tone. I'm not sure how she ended up replacing the original principal—Mrs. Matthews—but she somehow earned the title, and it seems to have gotten to her head.

I know what a fight is. But why the hell would Grayson get into a fight? It's not like him.

"As you're well aware, Ms. Collins—"

"You can call me Emma," I cut her off. I'm sick of the formalities.

She doesn't repeat my name but continues, "We have a zero-violence policy here at Thorn Lake Secondary School."

I try, "Grayson isn't usually—"

"We ask that you come pick him up as soon as possible. He's suspended until next Tuesday."

"That's four days," I say. "Isn't this his first offense?"

"He broke the kid's nose," she says coldly.

I almost choke on my own breath.

Is he like James, after all? Prone to violent outbursts?

"I— I'm so sorry," I say, feeling awful for whoever the kid is.

She ignores my apology. "When can you arrive?"

"I'll be there in ten minutes."

I hang up and hurry out the door.

***

I storm into the Administration office, suppressing the urge to grab Grayson by the ear and embarrass him in front of everyone.

But this is a first.

Grayson has never gotten into a fight before.

Give him the benefit of the doubt. He was probably defending himself.

And if there's one thing James always taught him, it was to defend himself.

"A kid punches you," he'd said, smashing a fist into his palm, "you punch back until they don't get up."

"James—" I'd said.

"Don't," he'd warned me. "This is a man thing. You wouldn't understand. If he lets one kid push him around, he'll become a target." He'd then jabbed a finger in Grayson's chest hard enough for Grayson to wince and reach for the tender spot. "You understand? You fight back. You show him that you aren't having any of that shit."

I catch Grayson sitting in one of the waiting chairs, slumped over with his red hood over his head. He barely makes eye contact.

He doesn't look injured.

I'm relieved about that.

But I'm not happy that he hurt another child.

"You must be Ms. Collins," comes Sarah's voice.

She sounds unimpressed—like I'm the last person she wants to see despite being the one who called me here in the first place.

"Y-yes," I say, turning away from Grayson.

"A word?" she says.

I follow her into her office, which is agonizingly clean. Too clean.

As if she spends every minute of every day scrubbing away the smallest speckles of dust. That's probably why she's so miserable.

"Have a seat." She aims a flat open palm at a leather chair that looks too expensive to belong in a secondary school.

I suddenly feel like I'm sitting in the office of one of those high-end psychologists I'd imagined. Someone very much the opposite of Maya Jackson—someone who profits off her clients and isn't afraid to show it through the acquisition of expensive furniture.

She sits at the other end, making me feel like one of her students.

I want to ask her what happened, but I have the feeling she's about to go into great detail about how horrible a boy Grayson is.

"We have the footage on camera," she says, "in case Grayson tries to bend the truth."

What makes her think Grayson is going to lie about it? I keep my mouth shut. This is the first time we've met, and I already feel as though she hates me and my kid. And with only one secondary school in town, it's not like I have any other options if she proceeds with expulsion.

Stay on her good side, even though she seems like a total witch.

"Anthony's parents have yet to decide whether they will be pressing charges," she says.

Anthony.

That must be the other kid involved.

I nod slowly.

Oh, no . . . I hope they don't. Grayson doesn't need that.

"I understand," I say.

When she doesn't respond, I ask, "Can I ask what happened?"

"Some argument," Sarah says. "The camera didn't catch that, and neither boy is willing to *rat* the other out." She rolls her eyes as if dealing with toddlers.

"Grayson shoved Anthony. Anthony shoved back before throwing a punch to the side of Grayson's head. Then Grayson punched him in the face."

Grayson? My Grayson? The news feels like a blow to the gut. But at least he didn't hit first. Then again, he shoved first. Either way, it's unacceptable. I'm beyond outraged that he would get into a physical altercation. He knows how I feel about violence.

"That's everything," she says in a snooty way, barely looking at me.

I clench my teeth but don't say anything.

Despite my embarrassment and anger, I do feel as though she's handling this rather unprofessionally. At the end of the day, Grayson is a child, and so is Anthony. I don't condone any of their behavior, but Sarah is treating me as if I'm the one who threw the punch.

Or like Carla—Lucas's teacher—she's judging my parenting skills.

Or you're overreacting. Grayson broke a kid's nose. This is bad press for her.

"Again, I'm so sorry about all of this," I tell her.

I creak my chair back and leave without another word.

***

Grayson sits quietly in the car on the way home.

"Want to tell me what that was about?" I ask.

"Nothing," he says.

I'm usually very patient with him and his habit of retreating into himself. But today, after I met with Wyatt at the police station and after finding out my son broke another kid's nose, I've had my fill.

I swerve onto the road's shoulder and slam on my brakes.

Grayson's dark eyes bulge as he smashes into his locked seatbelt.

"What the hell?" he says.

"What the *hell*?" I repeat his words back at him. "Don't even. How about you start talking? Why would you throw a fist at someone's face like that?"

"He punched me first," he says.

"I don't give a shit. You broke his nose. You know how I feel about violence."

I'm breathing hard through my nose, and he must sense my rage. I'm so angry that my entire body is vibrating. He shrinks in his seat a bit—it's barely noticeable, but I know Grayson, and I can tell when he's scared. Despite having outgrown me in physical size, he's afraid right now. Probably because I never get this angry.

"He was talking trash," he says.

I make my eyes go huge as if to say, *Trash? What's that supposed to mean?*

"About Amelia's mom," he says.

Who the hell is Amelia? And what does he care what some other kid says about someone else's mom? Unless . . . And then it all makes sense. Is that why he's been so chipper lately? I was right all along.

This is about a girl.

"Is she your girlfriend?" I ask.

His cheeks darken in blotches. "No."

"You want her to be?"

He shrugs with one shoulder.

"I understand wanting to defend a girl's honor, Grayson. I really do. But what did punching that kid solve?"

"He'll never talk about her mom again," Grayson says.

My knuckles whiten around the steering wheel, and I suck in so much air it hurts my lungs. "Do you want to be like your father?"

I don't mean to yell, but my voice fills the entire car.

My question seems to pierce him in the heart.

"No!" he snaps back. "Why would you even say that?"

He looks like he's on the verge of tears.

I take a pause, breathing slowly to gather myself.

He got into a fight at school. Kids fight all the time. That doesn't make him an abuser.

I shift the car back into Drive, and my tires squeal as I speed back onto the road.

"You'd better hope his parents don't press charges," I say.

He stays quiet.

I think I really hurt him with that comment about his dad. Grayson has seen James beat me to a pulp and was too young to do anything about it. Of course he doesn't want to be like his father. And I really need to stop putting that out there.

After several minutes of silence, I say, "Can I ask what the kid was saying? You know, about Amelia's mom?"

"That she's a deadbeat pill popper and deserves to be in an asylum."

I purse my lips, letting that one sink in.

That's a pretty harsh thing to say about someone's parent. I can understand the anger.

"I bet Amelia was upset about it," I say.

"She was crying," Grayson says.

Part of me begins to feel like Grayson wasn't exactly in the wrong. I mean, Anthony *did* punch first, and he said horrible things. But I immediately push this thought away. What kind of mother would I be if I fluffed this off like it was nothing? Like it was warranted?

The kid has a broken nose.

That's a big deal.

Grayson could have handled things much differently.

"Is it true?" I ask.

I probably shouldn't have asked, but I need to know who Grayson is spending his time with. Even more so given that he's taken a liking to this girl.

Grayson's jaw snaps open, and he looks over at me. "What he said? No, it's not true! Amelia says she used to suffer from depression, but it's all under control now."

"Where's her mother now?" I ask.

"What? How should I know?"

"Does she work? Is she a stay-at-home mom?"

I realize I'm interrogating him over something he may know nothing about. But that doesn't mean it isn't worth digging into.

"Amelia says her mom keeps busy with work every day, even during the evening."

"Doing what?" I ask.

His bushy brows meet above the bridge of his nose. "How should I know?"

I peel a hand off the steering wheel and raise it to keep the peace. "All right, I'll lay off. I'm just checking to see who you're spending your time with."

He sits back hard against his seat and crosses his arms. "Amelia is good. Doesn't smoke, vape, or any of that."

I'm happy to hear it.

"No more fights," I warn him.

He gives me a single nod.

"And you're grounded," I add.

CHAPTER 36

BEFORE

James pulls Grayson into his arms and twirls him in circles with a childish grin on his face. The two of them are having a blast.

I want to smile. I really do.

But after the fight James and I got into last night—after he called me a *selfish cunt* for wanting to visit my family in Florida—it's hard to enjoy a moment like this.

"Come on, Alice!" James says.

He looks so happy. As if last night never happened. He may have genuinely forgotten. He was rather drunk.

"I'm okay," I say.

He turns up the music and starts swaying his hips from side to side and clapping his large hands. It creates a rhythm that gets Grayson going. He stomps his feet and starts clapping with his dad.

Smile, damn it.

But I can't.

And James notices.

All the happiness on his face disappears in a flash. He stops dancing with Grayson and reaches for the Bluetooth speaker. With a single press of a button, the music stops.

Grayson stands midclap, confused by his father's sudden shift in energy.

"Goddamnit, Alice. Why do you sit there with a sour look on your face? I'm trying to lighten up the mood, and you have to go and ruin it."

Without warning, he kicks the chair underneath the

speaker, and the slick black cylinder crashes on the floor. I flinch and tell Grayson to go to his room. When he hesitates, James yells at him, his voice so deep and thunderous it shakes the house.

Grayson runs away faster than a mouse caught sneaking food.

James sweeps another big hand across the display shelf behind him, hurling picture frames and a wax candle my sister gave me.

Glass shatters against the wall, and I pull my legs closer to myself, though this provides no comfort at all.

James catches me cowering from the corner of his eye. "Yes, Alice, play the little victim."

When I don't respond, he says, "Is it that hard for you to put in a little effort? Our family needs stability, for fuck's sake. I'm doing the best I can, and you just sit there, pouting like a five-year-old. Grow the fuck up!"

Last year, this situation would have led to a full-blown fight. But James's anger has escalated daily, and I know if I open my mouth, things will get a whole lot worse for me.

So I stay quiet and hope the moment will pass.

"What?" he spits. "You're just going to sit there? Make me look like an asshole?" Without warning, veins bulge from his thick neck, and his face turns a deep red. "Say something!"

"James, please," I say. "You'll wake Lucas."

He glares at me, an all-too-familiar darkness filling his eyes. When he gets that look, it's as if James has vacated the house, leaving behind some nefarious entity.

The worst part is I have no idea what he's thinking.

Any second, he may return to me and plead for my forgiveness. Or he may lash out again. It's impossible to tell.

It takes a minute for him to stop looking at me like that before he storms off into the kitchen, rips the fridge door open, and reaches for something inside.

Bottles clink. He's grabbing a beer.

After a moment of silence, he lets out a satisfied breath, which tells me he chugged the whole thing. Then he cracks open another—*pshh*—and comes stomping back into the living room. "You see what you do? You see *this*?" He shakes the now half-empty bottle at me, and the liquid sloshes inside. "You're the reason I have to drink."

He takes another swig.

Three bottles later, he comes stumbling back out and plops himself down into his well-worn recliner. With a sigh, he leans back.

He closes his eyes, and I can't tell whether he's falling asleep. So I get up. There's no reason for me to be here, and I'm not about to stick around for him to flip out on me again.

But the moment the floor creaks underneath me, James's dark eyes blast open. "Where are you going?"

"To bed," I say. "I'm not fighting with you."

"Fighting?" he says. "We aren't fighting, Alice. I got a little upset because you didn't want to spend family time with me and my son."

His son.

I hate it when he says that.

Grayson is *ours*. And if we were to analyze *ownership* of Grayson based on who is more of a parent to him, I'd win, hands down.

James is never around despite him thinking he's made an improvement with that.

"You just yelled at me," I tell him.

He scoffs, his head still leaning back. "Oh, don't be dramatic. You always do that. I raise my voice a bit, and you think I'm yelling at you."

"You *were* yelling at me," I say, "and Grayson."

His recliner straightens instantly, and he slams the footrest closed—*clack*.

"Don't you bring my son into this," he says with a threatening finger aimed my way.

I can't do this.

He's drunk.

"I'm going to bed," I say again.

But before I can move, James lunges to his feet and grabs me by the arm.

"James, you're hurting me!"

"You think you can walk away from me when I'm talking to you?" he growls.

His breath reeks of alcohol, which leads me to think he drank more than a few beers. He keeps several bottles of whiskey in the cupboard over the fridge and seeks comfort in them anytime he's stressed, which has become a perpetual occurrence.

"Let me go!" I try to pull away, but his grip is too tight.

James has gotten in my face before, but he's never grabbed me like this. I try to yank away again, but he doesn't let go.

Instinctively, I shove back. "Let me go!"

Without warning, he swings an open palm across my face.

Smack.

The whole left side of my face burns and throbs. I reach for my cheek, stunned.

Did he just . . . hit me?

Our eyes lock.

I expect him to break down and apologize, but he's looking at me in a way that has me treading very carefully. Inside, I want to rage—push him, crack a beer bottle over his head, or pull a knife on him.

But there's a little voice inside my head that tells me otherwise. If I do anything right now, he'll hit me again. I can see it in his seemingly black, soulless eyes.

He suddenly grabs me by the face so hard that my cheeks dig into my molars. I let out a soft squeal, tears prickling my eyes.

"James . . . please—"

If he squeezes any harder, I'm afraid he'll unhinge my jaw.

"You listen to me, you little bitch." His hot, alcohol-laced breath slips into my nose and mouth. "I've had enough of your shit. Do you hear me? You're going to start respecting me around here."

Respect him?

I won't be here tomorrow. I'm taking the kids and running as far as I can.

"And if you even *think* of leaving me—"

I try to shut off my thoughts. It's like he can read my mind. And if he knows what I'm thinking, who knows what he'll do.

"I'll kill you. Do you hear me? I'll fucking kill you."

He squeezes my face a little harder, then shoves me back into the couch, and I topple over, sobbing harder than I've ever sobbed before.

He walks away and slams the bedroom door while I lower myself to the floor and cry, feeling utterly shattered.

CHAPTER 37

I feel like I'm losing them.

Lucas sits quietly, watching some show about superheroes turned into domestic animals. It's the strangest thing, he seems riveted.

Grayson sits next to him because he has nothing better to do. I considered forcing him to stay in his room given that he's grounded—no phone, no electronics—but it's good for him and Lucas to spend some time together, even if they don't talk.

I wish I could walk over there cheerfully and join them.

But there's nothing cheerful about our lives anymore.

Everything is falling apart.

I spend most evenings on my phone, connected to a VPN while I search for James Remington on Google.

I keep hoping he's posted something on Facebook—an engagement, a successful business launch—anything to keep his mind off my sons and me.

When I'm not busy worrying about him finding us, I'm thinking about the body in the basement and the note in the drawer.

Why is my life so dreadful? If I were single and childless, I'd find a way to cope. I'd move to a different country and start a whole new life. Or I'd drink myself into oblivion.

But I can't do that.

The idea of my children being miserable is eating away at me. They deserve happiness. Not a life filled with trauma. I'm supposed to protect them from all of this.

They don't even have their grandparents in their lives anymore, or their aunt.

God, I miss my family.

But it isn't safe. Not until I know James has given up on ever finding me. Either that, or he turns up dead.

I hope he does.

A knock on the door makes me flinch so hard that I drop the potato masher I was holding over a pot of now-burning potatoes.

Shit.

I turn the burner off and hurry to the door, wiping my potato-soiled hands onto my pants.

Grayson leans his head on the sofa to watch but doesn't get up. The only person who seems to show up here unannounced is Wyatt. For a moment, a sense of relief washes over me. Something about that man makes me feel at ease, even though I don't entirely trust him yet.

But when I open the door, I'm met with an unfamiliar face.

"Oh, hi there," the woman says.

Her eyes drift to the interior of my home, then back at me. I step sideways, blocking her view of my children, and step outside, forcing her to take a few steps back.

"Can I help you?" I ask.

She seems nice, and I'm probably coming across like a complete bitch.

"S-sorry," she says, no doubt realizing that I'm not in the mood to socialize with anyone. She raises a tray of muffins so fresh that steam has coated the inside of the plastic wrap that covers them. "I meant to come by sooner to introduce myself, but I haven't had the chance. My name's Stella. I live right across from you."

She beams, raising the muffins even higher until I grab them.

"Oh, that's very nice of you," I say.

The house across from me? I've never seen her before. And why did she wait weeks to come and introduce herself? No one is *that* busy. She certainly doesn't have any kids; otherwise, they'd be taking the bus in the morning.

Little gray hairs stick out like metal wires on either side of her head. Middle-aged, by the looks of her. If she does have children, they're likely all grown up by now.

She blinks at me expectantly.

"Oh, I'm Emma," I say.

"So nice to meet you," she says.

Her eyes roll toward the interior of my home again.

"What are you looking for?" I snap.

What's wrong with me?

"Oh, I'm so sorry. I'm being rude," she says. "It's the house, you know? Everyone talks about it. And then the police a few weeks ago, and the news about a body. I'm so sorry you went through that. How are your sons doing? Okay, I hope."

My sharp gaze turns into a scowl.

"How do you know about my children?" I ask.

She slaps a hand over her smiling mouth as if she's been caught gossiping. "You must think I'm a total nosy neighbor. It's not like that at all. I see them now and then, dear. Taking the bus." She pauses, then shakes her head as if she's embarrassed. "I'm sorry, love. I didn't mean to come across like that. I'm harmless. I promise."

I'm not convinced.

"Thank you for the muffins," I say coldly.

I can tell I've embarrassed her, but I have too much on my mind to be worrying about my neighbor's feelings.

"Oh . . . okay, dear. Well, welcome to the neighborhood. If you ever need anything—"

"Thank you," I say before stepping back inside and closing the door on her.

I place the muffins down on the island for a moment so I can rush to the bathroom to compose myself. Why am I quaking like this? I splash cold water on my face, then look fixedly at myself for a moment.

Get it together, Alice. She's probably harmless.

When I step back into the kitchen, I catch Grayson with

a muffin slowly moving toward his open mouth.

"Grayson!" I snap.

Even Lucas flinches before turning to look our way.

Grayson freezes with the muffin in midair, on the verge of entering his wide, salivating mouth. "What? It smells so good."

I stomp my way to him, tear the muffin out of his hand, and throw it in the trash. Then, I snatch the tray and do the same, smashing it through heaps of old garbage until I'm satisfied with how deep they've all gone.

Grayson throws his arms in the air. "What the hell, Mom?"

"Don't what the hell me!" I say. "We don't know that woman. I've never seen her before. And with how weird people are in this town, I wouldn't be surprised if she poisoned those muffins."

Grayson pulls his face back so far he barely looks like himself anymore.

I know that look.

He thinks I'm crazy.

But he doesn't know about the note. He also doesn't know to what lengths James would go to have you killed. You're not crazy. You're being cautious. You can't be too cautious.

Lucas looks disappointed, like he wanted a muffin, too.

But it's the look Grayson is giving me that has me bothered the most.

"What are you even doing out here?" I ask him. "You're grounded. Go to your room."

"What? But you said I could hang out with—"

"Go," I say. "I'll call you when supper's ready."

CHAPTER 38

All day, Grayson is quiet and keeps to himself. I suppose that's to be expected when he's restricted from using his phone or watching television. All he has is his music.

Lucas should be home from school any minute.

I step outside, and Grayson immediately shoves earbuds into his ears. Without looking at me, he sways on the porch swing and gazes into the distance like he's trying to ignore me.

That's fine.

We don't need to talk.

I walk to the end of the driveway and greet Lucas as he steps off his bus. When I return to the house, I click my fingers at Grayson to get his attention. When he still doesn't hear me, I shout his name.

He pulls one earbud out and arches a brow at me.

"I'm taking Lucas to the doctor. You okay here by yourself for a bit? You remember how to activate the system?"

He nods and shoves the earbud back into place.

I don't like leaving him home alone, but with the security system now active, no one is coming in without Hawk Security being alerted.

He should be fine.

I tell Lucas to throw his school bag in the car, and he listens like a little soldier. Despite his mutism, he's been listening rather well.

"Excited to see Dr. Jackson?" I ask him.

He nods animatedly.

That's a good sign.

When we enter Dr. Jackson's office, I'm a bit taken aback to spot a familiar face standing at the reception desk.

"Carla?" I ask.

She spins around, her usually perfectly coiffed curls looking like they haven't been washed in days.

"Emma," she blurts. "What are you—" Her eyes roll toward Lucas, and she parts her lips, then closes them like a fish.

"Every Thursday," I tell her.

But I've told her this before, so I'm not sure why she's confused to see us here. Every time I inquire about Lucas's progress in class, she starts asking about how his therapy is going.

How's that going?

Is Dr. Jackson making any progress?

I'm sure he'll get better.

She forces a laugh and tucks a strand of hair behind a red, swollen ear. As her hand comes back down, I spot those scars on her wrist again—pink, bubbly, and unsightly.

She immediately tugs on her sleeve to hide them and chuckles again.

Then, eyes glued to me, she says, "Alice—"

My real name feels like a punch to the gut.

I keep a straight face, but my heart feels like it's about to jump out of my throat and splatter on the floor, right next to Lucas's bright-blue sneakers.

She then pivots and leans on the reception desk. "Could you please book my daughter in for next week again?"

"Um, Mrs. McKenzie?"

There's a moment of silence.

It feels strained, as if Carla is trying to communicate with Alice telepathically. She leans forward again and taps her fingers rapidly between her and the young receptionist.

"Friday is fine," Carla says. "She can do Friday."

Alice clears her throat.

Carla reaches over and taps on the young girl's computer monitor, whispers something, then pulls away.

I feel like I shouldn't be standing so close.

Whatever this is, it's none of my business, and it's clear that Carla doesn't want me hearing any of it.

"We'll wait outside," I say.

She spins around so fast that a breeze sweeps through the small office space.

"Don't be silly," she says.

At the same time, Dr. Jackson steps out of her office, a warm smile splitting her face. "Hey, Lucas!"

I love how she greets him—like they're best friends.

Lucas beams and runs right into her office.

Even though he isn't yet talking, this makes me feel like we're so close.

Dr. Jackson's warm, narrowed eyes turn on me. "See you soon, Emma."

With that, she closes the door, and I'm left standing with an unkempt version of Carla that I don't recognize.

"I'm sorry about that," she whispers.

Why is she whispering?

"Walk me out?" she asks.

I nod and follow her out into the parking lot.

"It's been a rough few days," she says. "My daughter's been threatening suicide, and I'm just beside myself."

She squeezes the bridge of her nose, not bothering to pull her sleeves down this time.

Should I comfort her? Reach for a shoulder? I used to be touchy, once, like her. I'd squeeze someone's shoulder or brush an arm to comfort them. But James took that away from me. He told me it was weird that I touched other people—that if I wanted to be single, all I had to do was tell him.

Not that there was even the slightest bit of romance or sexuality behind my touches. It was for human connection.

"I— I'm so sorry to hear that," I say.

She wipes a tear from the corner of her eye and lets out a big sigh. "Please don't tell anyone I was here. My daughter said if the kids at school find out she's seeing a psychologist, she'll never hear the end of it, and she'll never forgive me."

I can understand that.

Kids can be cruel.

"I won't say anything," I say.

Her lips quiver as she tries to steady her breath.

"Can I ask you something?" I say.

I probably shouldn't be asking. Carla's personal life is none of my business. But seeing her like this makes me feel awful for her. For the first time, I feel like I'm seeing the real her.

She nods, her red, bloodshot eyes fixed on me.

"Is there a father in the picture that can help?" I ask.

A scoff slips out of her mouth, though the way she immediately composes herself tells me she didn't mean to react so impulsively.

"I'm sorry," she says. "There is. But there isn't, you know? He's not much help. He's . . . Never mind."

The scars. The troubled kid. I can't keep my mouth shut any longer.

"Does he hurt you?" I ask.

She seems taken aback by this. Almost as if in shock that I would have the audacity to speak of such things so openly.

Her surprised eyes quickly narrow. "Why would you say such a thing?"

"I'm sorry," I say. "It's just—" I point at her wrists. The more I look at them, the more they look like cigarette burns. Not cuts. If she'd done it to herself, they would likely be cuts. But cigarette burns . . . they're something an abusive piece of shit might do as a form of punishment.

At first, I think she's going to lash out at me. But then, her lip starts to quiver again. "I— I can't talk about that."

Her eyes dart from side to side.

I know that look; she's scared.

Despite years of being told not to touch anyone, I reach out and rest a warm hand on her shoulder. "It's possible to get out, you know."

She's staring so intently at me now that it's like she's trying to siphon information out of my brain. Like she wants all the answers contained within . . . all my life experience as an abuse survivor.

Because she knows now.

I don't have to say anything else for her to know that we're both living the same thing. The only difference is, I managed to escape.

Finally, she looks away. "It's too complicated."

"It is," I say. "But that doesn't make it impossible."

Teeth now chattering, she reaches for something in her pocket, then fishes out a phone. "I— I have to go."

He's probably waiting for her at home.

A ball of anxiety builds inside of my gut.

I want to help . . . I want to do something. But what can I do? Follow her home? Call the police? Although I had bad luck with getting the police to protect me from James, things seem different here in Thorn Lake.

Wyatt may know what to do.

"I'm okay," she says, her fake smile suddenly returning. She wipes away the last bit of moisture off her plump cheeks, then shakes her hands as if to rid her body of all the negative energy.

"You're a true friend, Emma," she says. She thanks me with a pat on the shoulder. "I'll be okay. Really."

As she gets into her small silver hatchback, I can't help but feel like she won't be okay. Something is telling me that she's in a lot of trouble. That if something isn't done soon, things could get really bad.

CHAPTER 39

The house is exceptionally quiet tonight.

Grayson is still upstairs, likely reading or staring at the ceiling. It makes me feel awful to put him through this, but if I don't set boundaries, how will he ever learn in life? There needs to be consequences for his actions. And breaking a kid's nose warrants a consequence.

I ask Lucas whether he wants to play a card game, but he points at the television instead.

He pointed.

He's communicating.

I smile at him, then wrap my arms around him. I rake a hand through his hair. "I love you, Lucas. You know that, right?"

He nods.

"You take all the time you need to talk again," I tell him. "But I'm here, whenever you're ready. Okay?"

Another nod.

"No homework today?" I ask.

He shakes his head.

Smiling, I mess his hair up playfully, then shoo him off to the couch. He hurries to grab the remote while I leisurely stroll toward the kitchen, trying to think of what to make for supper. I sigh, and I'm placing my phone on the island countertop when a notification lights up my phone.

Views: 141.2K.

What is this?

I swipe my screen open.

My last blog post. I barely remember writing it—it was three o'clock in the morning, and I was running on fumes. Unlike my other posts about surviving abuse, this one was focused on the traits of an abuser—"5 Signs to Watch Out for in a Narcissistic Asshole."

Admittedly, I was angry when I wrote it.

As I scroll through the comments, my pulse throbs in my neck. How did it blow up like this? Is a hundred and forty-one thousand views considered going *viral*?

How many likes are there?

Forty-six thousand.

Holy crap.

The most my posts ever get is several hundred views and dozens of likes, hence my very limited income as a blogger.

Comments are coming in from all over the world.

"*I'm starting to think my husband is an abuser waiting to snap.*"

"*I never realized how toxic my relationships were until I started reading all your other blog posts. Thx, EmStar. For being so brave!*"

I stare at my blogger name—EmStar.

It was a spur-of-the-moment thing, combining my new name with the word *Star*, as if this would somehow make me feel anything other than a worthless human being. I thought that if I kept telling myself I was a star, I might forget the way James made me feel for so many years.

But now, as I look at those numbers and how they literally keep refreshing every few seconds, I *do* feel like a star.

People are actually reading my stuff. And it's having an impact. A sense of pride washes over me, though it's immediately squandered.

Don't get so excited. This is one lucky post. You'll never get anywhere in life as a blogger, Alice. Wake the fuck up.

No, this is James's voice.

Not my own.

I've been at this for months, and it's finally paying off. I'm not about to give up now. If anything, I need to start posting more often.

I finish supper distractedly, all the while pondering what I want to write about next.

Finding peace?

Escaping?

Learning to love yourself again?

Though I'm not quite there yet.

I probably shouldn't write about what I haven't yet achieved.

"Supper's ready," I call out.

Spaghetti with vegetarian sauce.

The boys grab their plates as I've been teaching them to do these last few weeks—I refuse to serve them the way James expected me to serve him, almost on my hands and knees.

They're old enough to grab their own plates and wash them when they're done.

We sit at the oversized dining room table, the chandelier light above us making our faces look yellow.

"Where's the meatballs?" Grayson comments, forking through the noodles, making a scraping sound on his plate.

"You don't need meat with every meal," I say.

He parts his lips like he's about to argue, but then his mouth snaps shut; he knows better. I know how much he loves his meatball spaghetti, but the beef was rather expensive, and I'm scraping pennies now.

Not for long.

Not once you get your affiliate payment.

I smile at the thought.

"What is it?" Grayson asks.

I consider sharing this exciting news with him, but I refrain from doing so. Grayson doesn't know that I run a blog. And if he did, he might start reading some of my old posts—all of which are about his father.

I don't want that.

"Nothing important," I lie.

He doesn't believe me but doesn't press, either.

I'm so excited about my new success that I hurry to eat, wash my plate, and declare to the household that I will be busy in my office for the next hour and that they can keep themselves busy.

I sit in my office chair, scrolling through my phone images for inspiration. I haven't taken many since I moved here, but I did snap a few at the Lilac Bridge Anniversary BBQ a few weeks ago. The leaves were turning orange and yellow—some a deep red. And they were everywhere.

The sight was astonishing.

Even now, as I look at the pictures, they are even more vibrant than the memory in my mind.

At one point, after Carla left, I moved to the edge of the park near a ravine and snapped a picture of a rabbit in the leaves. It immediately took off after my phone made that photo-snapping sound, but it was well worth it.

I smile at the image.

There's something here . . . an idea . . . a creative story.

I open my laptop and start typing away about rabbits and their prey instincts. I talk about how abusers want us to become like little rabbits—they want us to fear them so they can control us. Cage us. Some rabbits never escape and remain captive forever.

I stare at my post, wondering whether publishing it is the best idea. But it's not my real name on there. I was extremely prudent in setting up my blog. Everything is under a fake name—not even Emma Collins. I used a business name, instead.

James won't trace this back to me. Especially not since I'm connected to my VPN again.

Besides, there are countless women out there—millions—who are probably in the same boat as me.

I send myself the image of the rabbit sitting amid an array of vividly colored leaves.

It's so beautiful I can't stop looking at it.

And they do say that images help boost posts. So maybe it's time I start including pictures. I already changed the settings in my phone to exclude GPS data from my images. No one who looks at its properties will be able to decipher where it's been taken.

I only learned that a year ago, and I'm still in utter shock that most people don't know about it. It's extremely dangerous, and this data should be excluded by default.

Once the picture is added to my post, I hover over the Publish button. Then, my eyes wander to my stats at the top of the page.

163.8K views.

They're still climbing.

Smiling with pride, I click *Publish.*

***

When I return downstairs, Lucas is still parked in front of the television, and Grayson is sitting next to him.

They must not have heard me coming out of my office because Grayson is talking to his little brother.

"Why don't you just say something? You know you're upsetting Mom, right?"

Lucas remains quiet.

"Just talk, damn it," Grayson says.

He gives his brother a shove, and Lucas smacks him with the controller. At the same time, Grayson raises a fist.

"Hey!" I storm up to both of them, but in reality, my anger is directed at Grayson. "Don't you ever raise a fist at your little brother like that again, do you hear me? He's half your fucking size."

I didn't mean to swear.

But the sight of that triggered something in me. If Grayson is willing to hit a child half his size, what's to stop him from beating on his future girlfriend or wife? Or me, for that matter, once he's big enough?

His forehead bunches. "It was a reflex. I wasn't really gonna hit him."

"You're sixteen in two years," I say, pointing a threatening finger at him. "I swear to God, if you ever lay a finger on him, or on me, you're out of here on your birthday. Do you understand me?"

He swallows hard but doesn't say anything.

I should have left the *or on me* part out of it. I basically insinuated that I'm afraid of him—that I believe he's capable of hitting me.

Grayson hates James. If I keep talking to him like this, he'll end up hating himself. He hasn't done anything to deserve being treated like an abuser. He's a teenage boy with hormones flooding through him. There's going to be anger, and there will most definitely be fights.

That doesn't make him his father.

The problem is that he's the spitting image of him, and when he does act out in anger or violence, all I see is James.

I sigh. "I've had a long day. I know you'd never really hurt your little brother. Or me. I'm sorry I said that, honey."

Lip trembling, he throws one of the couch pillows on the ground and storms past me. His footsteps are heavy all the way up to his room. When he slams his bedroom door, the whole house shakes.

Despite the anger he's showing, I know how he's really feeling—he's hurt. Deeply. And I'd be willing to bet he's now sobbing into his pillow for the way I made him feel.

Not only did I make him out to be a monster capable of hurting me and his seven-year-old brother, but I also threatened to kick him out onto the streets on his sixteenth birthday, which must make him feel like I can't wait to get rid of him.

Only minutes ago, I was riding a high from my online success. Now, I feel like absolute shit.

I should never have said those things to him.

Worst Mother of the Year Award goes to me.

If he'll let me.

I tidy up the kitchen and move over to the security control hub to ensure everything is activated for the night.

All doors and windows have a green checkmark next to them.

"Time for bed—" I start to say, but then I catch a glimpse of something through the front door's glass window.

At the end of my driveway is that man again. The one who watches my house. I haven't seen him in a week or so. I thought he'd given up watching us.

What the hell does he want?

He stands under a light post, wearing that long brown trench coat and that ugly yellow hat that conceals the upper half of his face.

But there's no denying it.

He's watching my house.

He's watching me.

I'm tempted to run out there and tell him to get lost, but a burst of anxiety causes pins and needles to tickle the tips of my fingers.

I can't do that because I'm too afraid to face another man.

Because what if he's like James?

Or worse, what if he's working for James?

CHAPTER 40

I spend most of the night tossing and turning, and by midnight, I'm pacing in my room with my loaded Glock. I peer through the curtains, watching.

He's gone.

I'm not sure when he left, but he was still standing there when I last peeked out of my bedroom curtains twenty minutes ago. That means he watched our house for at least an hour. What kind of a person does that? What does he want from me?

It's not like he walked up your driveway.

He's likely just some creep, and you're overreacting.

No, this isn't normal.

People don't just stand outside for an hour staring at someone's house.

I should call Wyatt.

Then again, the police department is probably sick of hearing from me. The body was one thing, but then the note? And now, a man standing outside my house? The more I think about it, the more I wonder whether I'm the one imagining things.

And then if something serious does happen, the police may not be in a rush to come to my rescue, because they'll think, *Oh, that woman again . . . the one who thinks everyone is out to get her.*

No, this is serious, Alice. Someone is stalking your house.

By the time morning comes, I've easily logged over ten thousand steps pacing back and forth, and I've only managed to get an hour of sleep.

Still lying in bed, I reach for my phone and write out a message.

Can we talk? Off record.

I add Wyatt as the recipient and allow my thumb to hover over the Send button.

But then, I delete the message.

That man isn't some hitman James hired. You're overreacting.

The morning sun has pierced the sky, causing an elongated strip of orange to stretch across my bedroom and up the end of my bed.

I sigh, force myself out of bed, and do what I do best—function as a mother despite feeling as though I have less than two percent battery function in my cells.

***

The smile on Lucas's face was worth the drive down to Thorn Lake's dollar store. It was also worth the twenty bucks I spent on cheap plastic Nerf guns.

While Grayson looks about as excited as a kid being offered coal for Christmas, I appreciate him making an effort to play with his little brother on the front lawn. It's not like he has anything better to do since he's grounded.

And although he runs lamely in circles for the first few minutes of playtime, I can tell he's starting to have fun. After a while, he starts darting behind cedar shrubs and shouting playful insults at his little brother like poopstick, dirteater, and leafmuncher.

It's cute and reminds me of eight-year-old Grayson.

Lucas giggles as he runs after his big brother, his Nerf gun swaying wildly from side to side.

It's the most heartwarming thing I've seen since we moved here.

Good, wholesome fun between brothers. I especially love it when Grayson sets aside the fact that he's now a teenager and acts silly for his little brother.

Eventually, both start to slow down, breathing big clouds of white into the cold autumn air. Lucas's cheeks are so red it looks like he's wearing blush.

I tell them to come back in to take a break. Besides, my cheeks are cold, and the tips of my fingers feel like they've been sitting in a bucket of ice water.

Lucas hurries to the dining room table to play with a small Lego set Dr. Jackson gave him. It's a wizard with a green dragon—a very generous gift, considering how expensive Lego can be.

"I'll be in my room," Grayson mumbles.

I feel bad watching him climb those stairs, his shoulders slumped. I told him he could have his phone back once his suspension is over; otherwise, what's the point in suspending a kid? For them to stay at home and have a grand time?

"I'll be back," I tell Lucas, making my way toward the washroom.

I pass in front of the basement door—the one I still haven't passed through since that woman's body was found. If it weren't for the electric box being in the basement, I'd have half a mind to board that door up permanently. Maybe even have someone come by, tear it out, and add drywall to the opening. For now, I've settled for the bookshelf from my office. I managed to slide it out with Grayson's help, and although it isn't a permanent solution, it helps.

I've also noticed that Lucas is bothered by the door. Every time he walks by the bookshelf, his little legs start scissoring twice as fast.

Maybe I should hang a tapestry there instead. Something to make it look like the door doesn't exist at all. At least that way, I wouldn't see the brown edges of that calamitous door, followed by flashes of that woman's skeletal frame.

Once money is no longer an issue, I'll order something nice online. I'm about to turn away and resume my path to the bathroom when I spot a crumpled piece of paper sitting on the bottom shelf of the unit.

Or is that a tissue?

Lucas has a habit of blowing his nose and leaving the tissues lying around in crumpled balls. The front door must have sent a breeze through the house and carried the tissue to the basement door.

I don't want to go anywhere near the bookshelf, but I can't very well leave garbage lying around.

Clenching my teeth, I move toward the little white ball. Only, it doesn't look like a tissue at all. It's thick and has countless noticeable creases in it.

It's paper.

I bend down, my throat constricting as my fingers touch the crumpled paper.

Another note?

No. That's ridiculous. The note I found in the kitchen was a fluke. Something left behind by either Victor or the woman from the basement. Maybe she was his prisoner before he locked her up down there, and she wanted to warn someone else.

A crackling sound fills the air as I pry open the paper.

No . . . it can't be.

An involuntary gasp slips past my lips.

I stare at the note in my hands, on the verge of throwing up.

Why is this happening?

Who is doing this?

My hands tremble so badly that I accidentally drop the paper onto the floor and take a step back.

The message isn't a warning this time.

It's a threat.

CHAPTER 41

Derek Garcia looks a bit more concerned this time. Does he finally realize that I'm not making any of this up? That it's extremely concerning that I'm finding notes in my house despite having a security system in place?

"Could have been in there all along." He twiddles his thumbs.

If I had superpowers, I'd shoot laser beams at him with my gaze.

All along?

No way.

This note is fresh.

"Maybe it was under the couch, and a breeze swept it up—" he continues. But I can tell he isn't sure. He's hoping there's a reasonable explanation for this.

Wyatt sighs. "What about your son?" he asks. "Do you think—"

"Grayson?" I blurt. "Why would he do something like this?"

Wyatt repositions his weight onto his opposite leg, and the porch creaks under him. "I'm not saying it was him. But didn't you mention that he was unhappy here?"

"He's been better," I say, leaving out the part about him breaking a kid's nose.

Derek watches me with scrutiny. "Has he?"

What's that supposed to mean? Does he know about the fight? And how would he know about it? I thought the police weren't involved.

"Small town." A sheepish smile creases his face. "I heard

he broke some kid's nose at school."

Wyatt looks at me in surprise, and I feel a hot tinge of embarrassment creeping up my neck and cheeks.

"It was one fight," I say. "He didn't mean it."

"Breaking a nose is pretty bad," Derek says.

"Point is," I say, "I don't think Grayson would do this. Why would he?"

"To get you out of the house," Derek says. "Maybe he's hoping you'll go back home, wherever that is."

I don't like how he ends that sentence—*wherever that is*. He's pointing out that my past is mysterious. I'm entitled to keep my history a private matter.

I dismiss him with a wave through the cold autumn air. "No, he wouldn't want that. Aside from the fight, he's seemed better. He met a girl, and he has a crush. I don't think—"

"Why don't you let us talk to him?" Derek cuts me off.

I clench my jaw, then turn to Wyatt, hoping he'll tell Derek to back off. But he doesn't, and it's humiliating. Do they really want to interrogate my son over this?

They're just doing their jobs. They have to consider all possibilities.

Still, I don't like it.

Grayson has already been distant with me. How much worse will that get if he's interrogated by the police because of me?

"Ms. Collins?" Derek asks.

Wyatt steps in front of him. "Look, Emma . . . I think it's worth a shot. Why don't you let us talk to him? There's a good chance he has nothing to do with this. Best case, we'll know it isn't him, and he'll be on higher alert. If someone is messing with you, wouldn't it be good to have everyone in the family on the same page? To let them know to keep their eyes open?"

I suppose he's right.

"Not Lucas," I tell him. "Not yet."

Wyatt nods. He understands. Lucas doesn't need this right now. At least, not until he can talk so I can have a proper conversation with him. Otherwise, how am I supposed to approach this?

Someone is trying to scare us, honey. I don't know who it is. It might be your dad, but I can't say for sure.

"Do you want to bring him out here, or would you prefer we go see him?" Wyatt asks.

When I don't respond, Derek clears his throat. "How about I go see him? Where is he?"

"In his room," I say.

He nods and brushes past me, opens the door, and steps in. The sound of his heavy boots fades as he climbs the century-old stairs.

"Despite his bedside manner, he's pretty good with kids," Wyatt says.

This brings me a bit of relief.

I pull my coat around myself a bit tighter to keep the cool air out.

"I think someone's watching me," I tell Wyatt.

His brows knit, and he takes a step toward me. "What makes you say that?"

"There's this man," I say. "I've seen him at the end of my driveway at night. It looks like he's watching me . . . or the house. Or something."

"Have your children seen him, too?" Wyatt asks.

"What?"

He's watching me with scrutiny.

And then it hits me. Is he wondering whether I'm delusional? Whether I'm experiencing hallucinations?

"They saw him the first time," I say coldly. "I'm not imagining it."

"I didn't say you were, Emma. I don't think that." He pauses, his gaze fixed on the end of my driveway. "Can I ask you something?"

I stare at those beautiful green eyes sitting beneath thick dark brows.

The way he asks me makes me uneasy—like he knows something. But it's not like I can say, *No, you can't ask me anything.*

"Sure," I say.

His eyes slowly shift to the wooden panels under his boots. He looks lost in thought, trying to formulate his words in the best way possible.

"Are you in some sort of danger that I should know about?" he finally asks.

He knows about James. He knows you're not really Emma. He knows everything.

No, he doesn't.

"Isn't that *your* job to tell me?" I say.

I realize how rude I sound the moment the words come out of my mouth.

"I'm sorry," I blurt. "I didn't mean it like that. I mean . . . I feel like I'm in danger, yes. I told you. I think someone is stalking me. And then the notes—"

He brushes my words by raking a large hand through his hair. "No, Emma. Not that. I'm talking about your past. Are you running away from something? Could someone have followed you here?"

I frown at him. "W-what? What makes you say that?"

"I'm a cop," he says. "It's my job to piece things together. I mean, you're alone with your boys, and you never talk about your past. Is there a father in the picture?"

Is he asking as a cop or as Wyatt?

Something tells me both.

"Father's dead," I lie.

What the hell am I doing? Wyatt's a cop. He's on my side. Isn't he? Why am I so afraid to tell him about James?

Because James could be anywhere . . . he could have gotten to anyone, including Wyatt. It wouldn't be the first time James turned police officers against me and made me out to be some psychopath who stole his children from him.

And if James finally got his business up and running, it would mean he has money, and money can get just about anyone to do just about anything.

I can't trust Wyatt even though I want to.

No one can know about my past.

"He's dead?" Wyatt repeats.

He watches me attentively. His gaze is so intense that I have to look away; otherwise, I'm afraid he might see right through me.

"Passed away several years ago," I say. "I don't like to talk about it. So yeah, I'm private. I want to move on. I want my boys to move on."

His eyes soften.

I'm in the clear.

"I'm so sorry, Emma. I had no idea." He pauses, looking perturbed by this new information. "I didn't mean to press."

"It's okay," I say. "You're only doing your job. And I get it. Single mom. No dad in the picture. You must have thought my ex was after us or something."

His eyes meet mine again, and my mouth goes dry.

"Yeah, that's exactly what I thought."

I force a smile. "My ex isn't rising from the dead to kill me."

He isn't smiling back. Instead, it looks like he's disappeared into his head again.

"Wyatt?" I ask.

"Hm? Oh, sorry. No, I— I'm happy to hear that. I'm just trying to figure out who would be bothering you in a town like this. Thorn Lake has an extremely low crime rate. It's the kind of place you want your kids growing up, you know? And now, these notes, and the man outside your house."

For the first time, I feel like he's really listening to me. Like he isn't trying to shove the blame away from the actual threat.

"So you believe me?" I ask.

"I do," he says. "One could be passed off as a coincidence." He wiggles the paper note between us. "But a second one? That's not a coincidence anymore. That's a pattern."

"Do you think we're in danger?" I ask.

He mulls this over. "I'm not sure. Right now, I think

whoever is behind this is trying to scare you."

"Well, it's working," I admit.

"No kidding," he says. "I'll reach out to Hawk Security again and have them come install cameras."

"Wyatt, you don't have to—" I say.

He raises a flat palm. "It's not a suggestion, Emma. I need eyes on your house, and I can't be around at all times for that. This is for our investigation."

So there's an open investigation? I'm extremely grateful for Wyatt and his willingness to take this seriously. Somehow, I get the feeling that if I were in any other town, the police wouldn't go this far to get answers.

"Once you're back on your feet financially, you can pick up the monthly payments," he says. "This is the best way to monitor what's happening around your house."

Then, a thought hits me; maybe this is exactly what Wyatt wants. If he's working with James, what better way to keep tabs on me than to have cameras watching my every move?

Don't be ridiculous. Wyatt isn't working with James. He's only doing his job. He cares about you.

Does he, though? You barely know the guy. And he's the most handsome man you've seen in this town so far. He's got a good career. Smart. Excellent listening skills. A real catch . . . So why is he still single? What's wrong with him?

I push these thoughts away, afraid that if I keep ruminating on this, he'll somehow read my mind.

"The cameras are for outside, right?" I ask.

An indent forms between his brows. "Of course. Where else would they go? Inside your house? That's a complete invasion of privacy."

"I was only wondering," I say. "Will I have access to see the camera's footage?"

He must think I'm crazy for asking questions like this. But James had access to several cameras in our house and never allowed me access to any of the apps.

"Of course," he says. "We both will."

Derek suddenly comes out of the house with his chest

puffed out, and the screen door swings once before snapping shut.

"It's not the kid," he says.

I cross my arms over my chest. "His name is Grayson."

His dark eyes linger on me, but he doesn't say anything.

Wyatt clears his throat. "You should hear from Hawk Security later this afternoon. And I'll add this note to the file."

He raises it again, and I gape at the bold red font stretched across the creases in the paper.

LEAVE BEFORE IT'S TOO LATE.

"I thought they already came," Derek says.

"Cameras," Wyatt says.

Derek scoffs. "Do you really think Chief Madden is going to approve that expense? No one's been hurt. They're just threats. From an ex, or—"

"She'll approve it," Wyatt says, his tone clipped. "And this isn't an ex problem."

Derek parts his lips to add something, but Wyatt jerks his head sideways and says, "Let's go. I'll be in touch again soon, Emma."

CHAPTER 42

BEFORE

I'm sick of overhearing the nurses ask why I don't just leave.

This is my third time in the hospital in the last few months. If it weren't for James trying to hide my injuries from the world, I'd have been here at least a dozen times by now. But some things can't be fixed at home. And despite my best efforts to deny James's abuse through grandiose stories about tripping or falling, everyone here knows what's really going on.

"Why doesn't she just leave him?" someone whispers.

"He's obviously a piece of shit."

"Shh, Mal, keep your voice down."

"No," says the upset nurse. "She should have told the cops the truth."

"How can she? She's probably scared he'll kill her if she presses charges."

"He might kill her soon anyway!"

"That's enough," comes a different voice.

She sounds authoritative—likely the head nurse or one of the doctors.

I lie quietly in the hospital bed, my forehead throbbing. The worst part is that I barely remember what happened. One second, we were fighting, and the next, he was on top of me.

He fractured your skull.

"I'm looking for Mrs. Remington," asks a woman with a self-assured tone of voice.

I recognize that voice.

It belongs to the cop who interrogated me about fifteen minutes ago. Only then, there were three police in total, and each one of them eyeballed me in disbelief when I told them I slipped on oil and smashed my skull against the kitchen counter. When they asked me to explain the bruises around my throat, I told them I must have hit my neck, too, but that I couldn't remember it.

Yeah, not the best story.

I don't want to defend James—I don't want to protect him. But I have to protect my children. He's become so unpredictable that there's no telling what he'll do. And he's already threatened to hurt Grayson and Lucas by burning down the house while we sleep.

"Alice?" says the cop. She sounds a lot more friendly this time and doesn't have her chest puffed out anymore. It's almost as if she left her police badge behind and has decided to approach me as a friend, even though I don't know her.

She pushes my curtain aside and comes in.

I watch her through my one good eye, unable to see her through the swelling of my other.

She's a large woman—the kind that could easily bring a man to his knees with the right kind of swing. Also the kind of woman you'd expect to see playing professional basketball.

Her blond hair is pulled back into a tight bun and looks to be a permanent fixture on her head.

She points at a chair. "May I?"

I nod.

She sits down heavily, her gaze on nothing in particular, then says, "I know what's going on, Alice. You don't need to say anything. You'll deny it. Most women do. Because if you press charges, you know he'll come at you again, and maybe this time, you won't survive."

Our eyes lock.

For the first time, I feel like someone truly understands what I'm going through.

She reaches for my arm, and I don't pull away. "There's

a way out, you know. For you and your children."

I want to believe her, but I just don't see how it's possible. I've already called several shelters, and they're all full. I thought maybe I could take the kids there with me until I figure out how to escape him for good. But how can I do that if I can't even leave?

And going to my parents, or my sister's, is out of the question. If James finds out I sought refuge with my family, there's no telling what he'd do to them.

If he's threatening to hurt his own children, that means he's more than capable of hurting anyone else I love.

And I can't allow that to happen.

"There's a shelter in Colorado you can go to," she says.

"Colorado?" It hurts to talk. I swallow hard before adding, "That's miles from here."

"It's a different state," she says. "That's a *good* thing. I also have a friend there who is a lawyer. She can help. What you need to do is go to court and file for an emergency protective order."

"What's that?" I ask.

I feel like I should know all of this. But the truth is, I haven't dared to look anything up online. If James were to look at my browser history, which I know he'd find a way to do even if I cleared it, he'd probably kill me. And it always feels like he's one step ahead of me. Like he can read my mind, which means I need to keep all thoughts of running away out of my head when I'm around him.

"Think of it as a temporary restraining order," she says. "Only you can obtain one much faster than going through the whole legal process of a restraining order. That way, you can flee with the kids, and he can't go anywhere near you."

"Maybe not legally," I say. "Doesn't mean it would stop him."

"You're right," she says, a deep sadness in her eyes. She's been through this before—no doubt more than once. I'm certainly not the first woman she's helped out of a domestic abuse situation. "But it will give you some protection. He won't know where you are. He might look for you, but that's why I'm suggesting you leave the state entirely. Court can be messy, and it can take a long time. You'll want to get full custody and a divorce."

It's all too overwhelming, and it's making my head throb painfully.

"Listen." She squeezes my arm gently. "One step at a time. Right now, you need that emergency protective order, and you need to go to a shelter. You need to get away from him."

I draw in a deep breath, trying to steady my heart's erratic rhythm.

"Alice," she says, "look at me."

I hesitate, then look into her soft blue eyes. "You can't keep living like this."

She's right. You need to leave. But how? James will hunt you. He won't stop until he kills you. He already tried. If it weren't for Grayson throwing himself onto his father's back while he was strangling me, I'd be dead.

"I know this is scary," she says. "But if you don't get out now, he *will* kill you. It's only a matter of time."

Her words weigh heavily on me.

She slowly pulls her hand away. "I've already reached out to the shelter, and they've reserved space for you and your sons."

I feel a bit violated. Why would she do this without my permission? What if James finds out she did that?

She's only trying to help.

"Are your sons in school now?" she asks.

I nod.

"If you'd like, I can pick them up for you."

I don't know how to respond.

Why is she doing this?

"You don't have any other option, Alice."

She's right—I don't. I've been trying to plan my escape for months, but it never happens.

It's now or never.

I part my cracked lips but can't find the words to say.

"I imagine he controls your finances," she says.

I nod.

"I'll drive you down myself," she says.

I blink hard. Did I hear her right? She's willing to drive over ten hours to bring me to a women's shelter?

"Why are you doing this?" I ask her.

A modest smile tugs at her lips, and she lets out a long breath as if prepared to share her entire life's story. But instead, she says, "What's the point of life if not to help each other? I've been where you are. Actually, I died. Paramedics resuscitated me on the scene. I was eighteen at the time."

"Is that why you became a cop?"

She lets out a gentle laugh. "No, my dad was a cop. I'd always wanted to be one. But this is why I now help women like you. So let me help you, Alice. A battle like this is almost impossible alone. Women need to stick together."

I want to thank her, but all I can do is cry.

She holds my hands for a few minutes, her touch warm and comforting. I feel like I've known this woman all my life, even though we just met.

"W-what's your name?" I ask.

She taps her badge and says, "Officer Wilson, but you can call me Emma."

CHAPTER 43

Lucas returns to school on Monday while Grayson spends his last day of suspension up in his room. I spend most of my day in my office watching footage from the night before.

Leaves blowing across my lawn.

A raccoon racing across my driveway.

And right before sunrise, a streetlight flickering and dying.

Nothing eventful.

I keep hoping to find something that can be used to track down whoever is leaving these notes. What I don't understand is how someone could get into the house with the security system on.

Unless the notes really have been in here all along.

Is it unrealistic to think that?

I sigh, frustrated by all of this.

As if it isn't enough that I have to worry about James finding us and killing us in our sleep. Security system or not, he'd be in and out before the cops showed up.

I toss my coffee spoon in the sink, the clanking sound somewhat satisfying, and pinch the bridge of my nose.

Maybe Wyatt will have more information for me at the shooting range on Wednesday. He's apparently driving up to meet Marta's boyfriend today. I'm hoping this gives him more answers about the woman in the basement. I wonder what her boyfriend is doing today and how he will react when he learns that his missing girlfriend has been found.

The thought makes me sick to my stomach.

Rather than stand around thinking about how those events might play out, I decide to be proactive by cleaning the house from top to bottom.

If there's another note, I'll find it.

***

By Wednesday, no other note has been found. I'm eager to hear from Wyatt, so after my morning routine, and after writing a new blog post for my now-somewhat-famous blog, I store my gun in its carrying case and head over to the shooting range.

Rita is the first to greet me.

"Emma, right?" she says cheerfully. She tucks a thick lock of gray-and-red hair behind her ear. It's too short to stay in her low ponytail but too long to be considered a bang.

She's wearing overalls overtop a plaid flannel shirt today. A real country woman. Despite her sweetness, I imagine she knows how to load a shotgun in under five seconds and blast someone's head off if they so much as threaten her or her husband.

"Yes, it's Emma," I tell her, smiling back.

"Wyatt said you'd be coming by today," she says, winking. Then, her forehead wrinkles. "Dan!"

I flinch at the sudden change in tone and volume.

A muffled grunt escapes the back room.

She rolls her eyes. "Don't mind Dan," she says more softly. "He's a man of few words."

She looks over her shoulder again. "Emma is here! You know, the new girl I told you about."

Another grunt.

Why was she talking about me?

Probably about my uncle's house and the body.

It's your house now. Not Victor's.

I wish I felt that way. But ever since I came to Thorn

Lake, it's been one nightmare after another. I'm seriously contemplating putting the house up for sale after I receive that inheritance money.

I have no idea where I'll go next, but it's becoming glaringly apparent that I'm not welcome here.

Even the note said it: "Leave before it's too late."

Maybe that's exactly what I need to do.

Leave. Forget this place and never look back.

"Emma?" Rita asks.

When I look at her again, she smiles sweetly and jolts her chin toward the back door. "Wyatt's waiting for you."

The way she waggles her brows makes me uncomfortable. It's like she wants Wyatt and me to become an item. But I just spent several years being emotionally, physically, and psychologically abused by a man.

I'm not ready for a relationship.

What I am ready for are answers.

"Hey, Rita?" I ask, stepping toward the counter.

She rests her arms on the platform between us and grins. "Yes, dear?"

"Can I ask you something?"

"Shoot," she says, making a gun with her hand and firing off fake shots.

"Wyatt," I say, attempting to come across as nonchalant. "He's single, right?"

She winks way harder than necessary, her mouth agape. "Sure is."

"I find that surprising," I say. "I mean, he's a catch."

She leans forward, her smile disappearing. "He really is, honey. And I can tell he likes you. I haven't seen him show interest in a woman since I've known the man. Truth be told, I thought he was gay for the longest time because of it."

"So, no girlfriend?" I ask. "No ex-wife?"

She purses her lips and shrugs. "There's an ex somewhere, but he doesn't talk about her. He moved here about five years ago. He was single then, and he's single now."

"I don't get it," I say. "I see women eyeing him all the time in Thorn Lake."

Another shrug. "Truth be told, I think some bitch tore his heart out, and he never recovered. But then you show up. And he's a different man."

The story sounds sweet, but I'm not buying it. He could have any woman he wants, and he somehow wants me—scraps that James tossed aside.

Okay, technically, he didn't toss me aside like garbage. I fought through the haze of fear and programming, fought back through the legal system, and despite the terror suffocating me from the inside, I ran.

The back door suddenly creaks open, and I jump back as if caught doing something wrong.

But it isn't Wyatt. It's a man I've never seen before. He thanks Rita and walks out. I do the same—thank her for the information she gave me—and join Wyatt out back.

When I step out, he seems genuinely happy to see me.

Is Rita right about him? Or is this some act?

"Hey," he says. "Glad you could make it."

I clear my throat. "Hey. So, did you talk to the boyfriend?"

His smile vanishes as if he's disappointed that I'm jumping right to business. Either that, or the memory of the event is enough to dampen the mood.

"I did," he says. "It wasn't easy."

I can't even imagine.

"But I did learn something," he says.

He pulls his earmuffs away from his neck and walks toward me. "You can't share this with anyone, Emma."

"Why would I?" I ask.

"Technically, I shouldn't even be sharing this with you. It's an active investigation. But you're a part of it, and I think it's only fair that you know everything."

I appreciate his words.

"It took a lot of prying, but I finally got the boyfriend to spill the truth about Marta."

What *truth*?

I set my gun case on the table next to his earmuffs, afraid that I might drop it if my hands start trembling.

"They were trying to save up to have a baby together. But they both had minimum-wage jobs. Marta was a personal shopper through an app called ZoomShop. You place your order through any local store, and someone does all the shopping for you and delivers it to your house."

"Yeah, I've heard of that," I say.

"Turns out, she delivered to Victor many times. The boyfriend—Manuel—said she came home with one-hundred-dollar tips sometimes. He thought Victor was hitting on her, but she promised him it wasn't like that. The guy was just filthy rich and wanted to thank her properly. She said she never even met Victor. It was all through the app, and he'd never show his face."

I don't understand where this is going. How does Marta go from delivering groceries to being held captive in his basement?

"Anyway," he continues. "After a few months of that, Victor asked if she'd want to start cleaning his house for him every two weeks. He said he'd pay her in cash—no trace, no taxes—hence why Manuel didn't want to talk to me about it."

"Did she take the job?" I ask.

He nods. "She did. She kept bringing him his groceries, too, but every two weeks, Victor paid her upward of five hundred dollars to clean his house. That's a grand a month."

My mouth falls open.

Five hundred per cleaning? I understand the house is big, but it sounds like Victor was overly generous with his money.

Was this how he lured her?

"So, what?" I say. "He asked her to come in, and he captured her?"

"That's the weird part," Wyatt says. "She worked for

him for almost six months before she disappeared. Every now and then, Manuel would check in—ask questions about this *Victor dude*, as he worded it, and whether or not he was hitting on her during the cleanings. But she swore to him that he never showed his face. He unlocked the door, and she didn't hear a peep from him. Apparently, Marta even commented on how strange it was, given that she cleaned the house from top to bottom and never saw him. It was like he was a ghost."

An image flashes in my mind—the basement, the wine rack, and the secret underground tunnel leading into a small concrete room.

I home in on this mental image.

There's a bed in the back corner.

Was Victor hiding down there? Sleeping in that creepy room?

"What is it?" Wyatt asks.

"N-nothing," I say. "Was just thinking that—"

"He was hiding out in the basement?" Wyatt says. "Yeah, me too."

"Why would he do that?" I ask.

His lips pull up on one corner like he's excited about this whole thing. I suppose finally getting some answers *is* something to be excited about.

"Well, that's what I was wondering. So I did some research into Victor Huxley. Military veteran. Dark past. Saw some brutal wars and served in several missions overseas to combat terrorism."

I arch a brow. This isn't exactly a secret. I already knew that my uncle served in the military. The only thing I didn't know was that he survived. He went missing at some point after returning from a mission, and my family assumed he died by suicide.

"I already knew he served," I tell Wyatt.

"That's not it," he says. "He was captured by a Korean militia. Tortured for six months before being rescued."

I swallow hard, not even wanting to imagine what this militia might have done to my uncle.

He pauses, then asks, "Your family never looked for him? Went to the police?"

I shake my head. "My biological dad didn't have the best relationship with his brother. There was a huge age gap, and they had a different father. I don't think he wanted to look for him, to be honest."

Wyatt nods slowly. "That's understandable."

"So, what do you think happened to Marta?" I ask.

He rubs at the scruff on his face. "I still don't know. But what I do know is that Victor was probably struggling with his mental health. There's no doubt in my mind that he suffered from severe PTSD, and who knows what else."

"Post-traumatic—" I start.

"Stress disorder," Wyatt finishes. "A lot of soldiers get it. But to be held captive by the enemy? Tortured? That messes a person up. Big time."

If Victor really was that messed up, maybe the rumors are true. Maybe he truly was a sick man who did horrendous things like skin rabbits.

"Anyway," Wyatt says. "If he did suffer from PTSD, which I'm sure he did, maybe he developed some other psychiatric disorder, like agoraphobia, or anthropophobia."

When I don't respond, he quickly says, "Severe fear of leaving your house, and fear of people."

It would explain the creepy basement. I never thought of it that way. I always imagined the basement as a prison cell for some unsuspecting victim—not as an isolation room for himself.

But something else doesn't add up. "Why didn't the boyfriend, Manuel, share this with police when she first went missing?" I ask.

Wyatt crosses his arms over his chest and bows his head. "I think he was scared. Turns out he spent two years in prison for fraud and was on parole. He thought if the cops knew about the cash job, he'd get sent back. I told him I'm not the IRS and all I care about is getting to the bottom of this case . . . which I guess I did. Aspen Heights

Police Department is already closing the case. Deeming it a murder."

But what if my uncle isn't responsible?

I feel stupid even thinking this. Why is my brain trying to defend my uncle? Because he's family? That man hasn't been part of the family for decades.

And he was obviously very deranged.

There's no denying the truth: this poor woman's body was found in his basement. He killed her.

CHAPTER 44

"Hi, you've reached Carla. I can't take your call right now, but if you leave a message, I promise to get back to you as soon as I can."

I hang up.

I haven't heard from Carla in two weeks. She usually sends me an update on Lucas, and she hasn't been answering my calls.

So, what's going on?

Although I shouldn't be sticking my nose where it doesn't belong, I find myself dialing the school's phone number in my cell.

She really should be keeping me apprised of my son's progress. I don't think calling the school to get a hold of her is stepping out of line.

When the woman at reception answers, I explain the situation and ask to leave an urgent message for Carla.

"Oh," she says, sounding surprised. "Carla has been away for several days now. She's off sick."

"Sick?" I ask.

She was supposed to reach out over a week ago. What kind of bug has you out of commission for over a week?

Several bugs, including the flu or a really bad stomach virus. Besides, she's around children all day long. It's respectable that she would take precautions and not want to spread her germs to every family in Thorn Lake.

"Yeah," the woman says. "We're playing it day by day, but I don't think she'll be back for the rest of the week."

"Oh," I manage to blurt out.

But then, I remember the scars on Carla's wrists, and my imagination starts firing off all over the place.

She isn't sick. She's probably missing. Maybe her husband killed her.

"Ms. Collins? Did you still want to leave a message?"

I hesitate.

No, I don't want to leave a message.

For all I know, things are really bad at home. Maybe she's hiding to keep bruises out of everyone's sight. It's not like I haven't done it before.

"Actually," I say. "Could I ask a huge favor?"

The woman doesn't respond right away, so I start talking again before she has the chance to say she's too busy with other priorities.

"I had Carla's address not long ago, but I seem to have lost it. Would you mind sharing it with me again?"

The line is silent.

"Oh, um, I'm sorry, Ms. Collins. That's personal information, and we really can't be giving that out—"

"No, no," I blurt. "I completely understand. I don't want to get you into any trouble. It's just that she's been so kind to me since I first moved here, and I'd like to give back by bringing her some homemade soup. Might make her feel better."

"Oh," the woman says, sounding a bit more chipper. "That's very sweet of you. I'm sure Carla would very much appreciate that."

"I won't tell a soul," I tell her. "Like I said—she gave me her address a while back. I was supposed to go over for coffee, so it isn't like you're giving me any new information."

That's not true. Carla never invited me for coffee, and I certainly never had her address. But if my gut is right, and something is wrong, then I can't stand around and do nothing.

I need to make sure she's okay.

I need to do what no one ever did for me until I met Officer Wilson.

"I suppose that would be all right," she says on the other end of the line. "I mean, if you already had it."

"I did, and I think I tossed it with some of my junk mail. You know how it is . . . Mom brain."

Does she even know how it is? I don't know this woman. And she sounds rather young.

To my surprise, she laughs and says, "Oh, yeah. Hold on one second. I'll grab it for you."

Minutes later, I have Carla's home address stored in my phone. I thank the woman profusely, hang up, and grab my car keys.

Don't worry, Carla. I'm coming.

***

I drive slowly down the street, wondering whether I'm out of line. I shouldn't be here. If Carla finds out I asked for her home address, she might be furious with me.

Then again, maybe she'll thank me. I might be the reason she gets to live another day.

Because what if my gut is right? What if she's in trouble? I don't plan to knock just yet. I want to drive by to scope out the place. Look for a car in her driveway. Something.

House number 9, number 11 . . . I keep driving until I reach number 15.

There it is.

It's not hard to miss with how it looks in contrast to the houses around it. Almost like it was pulled out of a different neighborhood and dropped here by a crane.

While her neighbors have your garden variety white picket fences, hers is only partially erect, and it's far from being white. It's a combination of brown and gray, half of it the result of missing paint, and the other half, mold and dirt.

No maintenance.

Her garden is full of weeds, and vines crawl up the

algae-stained white panels on the front of her house.

I can't stop here.

Not empty-handed. What I need to do is stick to my plan and bring her a pot of warm soup. I keep driving extra slowly, taking in every detail of her home. Maybe if I drive slowly enough, I'll catch a glimpse of her through her window.

Because right now, I'm starting to worry she's dead. I don't buy the whole sickness thing. Not after seeing those marks on her wrists.

As I pass her house, my eyes shift to the police cruiser parked in front of her house.

It looks exactly like Wyatt's car.

I squint as I drive by.

It *is* Wyatt's car. He has a small Goomba figure from the Super Mario Bros. on his dashboard—something I asked him about when we first met. He said he has a soft spot for video games, though he doesn't play as much as he'd like.

Does he live here?

Or is he responding to a call?

I keep driving, even though all I want to do is pull over until I have answers. But I can't do that. What if he sees me? How will I explain that I'm driving down Carla's road midafternoon?

I never drive out this way—it's at the opposite end of town.

When I reach a stop sign at the end of the road, I glance in my rearview mirror just in time to spot Derek stepping out of Carla's house. He says something, waves, and hurries down her steps before walking toward Wyatt's car.

Shit.

Wyatt could be out any minute.

I step on the gas and round the corner as fast as possible, the police cruiser disappearing from my mirror.

As much as I didn't want Wyatt to see me, there's a more pressing concern now.

A call was made to the police.

There's no telling whether Carla is the one to have called them or whether someone reported a disturbance.

Either way, this isn't good.

CHAPTER 45

This is a mistake.

My thumb hovers over the Call button. Hours ago, I sped away from Carla's house, not wanting Wyatt to see me driving in that neighborhood.

But I've been replaying the whole thing in my head.

Isn't honesty the best policy?

In my case—partial honesty.

I'll tell Wyatt about wanting to bring Carla soup. Hell, I'll even tell him I had soup in the car with me. And that's when I saw the cruiser. Isn't it normal for me to want to check up on a friend?

If Carla was your friend, you'd call her and get the information from the horse's mouth.

That's the problem.

I've tried calling Carla five times over the last week, and she isn't answering. That's the whole reason I contacted the school and tried to leave a message, and then why I intended to go see her in person.

Practicing the conversation over again in my head, I hit the green Call button and place the phone up against my ear.

"Emma?" Wyatt answers.

I expected him to pick up by saying, "Officer Daniels," but he must have stored my name under his contacts.

I'm not sure whether that's a good thing or a bad thing.

"Oh, hey, Wyatt," I say, attempting to sound nonchalant even though I've replayed this at least a dozen times in my mind.

"Everything okay?" he asks.

He sounds groggy, like I just woke him up from a much-needed nap.

"Y-yeah," I say. "I'm so sorry to bother you—"

"You're not bothering me," he says. Then, he groans, and I picture him sitting up in bed. "How can I help?"

I appreciate his kindness, especially after all the chaos I've brought into his life.

"I know this isn't any of my business, but I just wanted to check in to see if Carla is okay. I drove to her house to bring her soup today, because she's been sick, and I saw your cruiser. I wouldn't normally butt in, but I get the feeling she's in a bad situation, and especially after seeing those scars on her wrists—"

"Whoa, slow down," he says. "Who are we talking about? Who's Carla?"

He sounds genuinely confused.

How does he not know who I'm talking about? He was at her house only hours ago.

"Carla McKenzie," I say. "Lucas's teacher."

There's a long pause between us.

I might have crossed a line.

If a police report was filed, it's none of my business.

What was I thinking calling him like this? Taking advantage of his kindness? At the end of the day, he's still a police officer. It's not like we're friends. Yes, he's very sweet with me, and he's gone out of his way to help me, but that doesn't mean I can ask him anything I want. We've never even talked about anything other than all the chaos in my life—the body, the notes. And let's not forget my 911 call after thinking someone broke into my home, forcing both Derek and Wyatt out of their beds in the middle of the night.

We are not friends.

Although, I keep hoping we will be. One day.

I like Wyatt.

If I weren't dealing with so much right now, I'd consider exploring things with him. I admit he's attractive.

And I do find myself thinking about him that way sometimes . . . wondering how he kisses. How those plush lips might feel against mine. But then, my brain stops me. It's like a complete block.

I can't even go there.

Not after James.

The thought of a man touching me, even lovingly, is too much for my brain to process.

"Emma?" he says into the phone. "Did I cut out?"

"Sorry?" I say.

"I've heard the name," he says. "Small town. But I don't know her. And I wasn't at her house today. I'm actually home, sick."

"Sick?" I say.

"Yeah," he says. "Caught some stomach virus, and it hit me last night."

Is he lying, or did I hallucinate the whole thing today? I *saw* his cruiser, along with the little Goomba. It was *his* car.

"Oh," I say. "I'm so sorry to hear that. Stomach bugs are the worst."

"They are," he says.

Now that I think about it, he does sound very rough.

Maybe he's telling the truth.

"Sorry to have bothered you," I say. "I saw your car, and I was afraid something might have happened to Carla. But it's none of my business."

"Derek's cruiser has been in the shop all week," Wyatt says. "So if you saw my car, it was him."

Derek *was* the one who walked out of Carla's house. I assumed Wyatt was right behind him, but I guess he wasn't.

"I wish I could do more, but I can't share any information on reports that don't involve you. Have you tried calling Carla?"

"I have," I say. "Several times. I've sent messages, too. But she isn't responding. The school said she's been sick all week, but when I saw your car, I thought something terrible had happened."

"I'm sorry," he says. "I hope your friend is okay. I really do."

I get it.

He can't give me anything. He'd be risking his job. What did I think would happen? That he'd admit to receiving a domestic call? He's been very nice to me, but that would be crossing a line.

"I'm sorry to have bothered you," I tell him.

"Emma, you didn't—"

"I'm sure she's okay," I cut him off. "I didn't mean to be so paranoid. It's just . . . " I pause, wanting to tell him everything. But I can't. No one can know about my past; otherwise, they might start digging. "A friend of mine was in a really abusive relationship years ago, and it almost cost her her life."

I'm talking about me, but he doesn't need to know that.

"Wow, Emma—"

"I'm sorry," I blurt.

"Don't apologize," he says. "That's terrible. I can't say I've experienced many domestic cases here in Thorn Lake, but I know how it is . . . " There's an uncomfortable pause that almost has my mind spiraling for a second. "I've worked in a few bigger cities, so I know how these things play out. I admit the system isn't great at protecting women who need protection the most."

Whatever sick version of him I fabricated in my head only seconds ago is gone.

I want to reach through the phone and wrap my arms around him. To hear a police officer admit to there being a gap in the system brings me a certain comfort I didn't know I was missing.

"Thank you," I finally tell him.

"For what? I didn't do anything," he says.

"You did," I say. "You may not realize it, but you did."

His mouth makes a dry sticky sound that is no doubt the result of dehydration. "If it makes you feel any better, I wasn't asked to come in to assist with any crisis. And trust me, when there's a crisis, I still get a call—sick or not. So I hope that means that whatever happened at your friend's house isn't too serious. If that helps at all."

I suppose it does a bit.

But it still doesn't solve the fact that Carla's husband might be hurting her. This isn't something that happens once and stops once the police are involved. It happens over, and over again, and often escalates *because* the police got involved.

I appreciate everything Wyatt has done for me. And as much as I don't like Derek, he seems to be good at what he does. Which means Thorn Lake has two competent police officers.

Despite this, it isn't enough to protect Carla.

I can't rely on law enforcement to keep her safe.

Which means I need to go over there and make sure she's okay.

Is it a stupid thing to do?

Maybe.

But Derek was leaving as I was driving away from her house. If there's any time to go over to her place, it's right now.

I thank Wyatt for everything and hang up.

Then, I go upstairs and grab my gun safe.

Hopefully, I won't need it.

But if things go south, I need to protect myself.

CHAPTER 46

BEFORE

Dear Chloe,

I'm so sorry in advance for this letter.

I should have told you sooner, but I couldn't.

You were right to not like James. Everything you suspected was true . . . but even worse. Things have gotten so bad that I'm afraid for my life. I don't want to go into detail in this letter, but I want to let you know that you won't be hearing from me for a while.

I found a way out . . . a way to get away from James and to keep Lucas, Grayson, and me safe.

He's dangerous, Chloe. Stay away from him, and don't let him into your lives. He might try because he'll want answers, and he'll think we're talking, but don't let him, okay?

I can't tell you where I am, and I won't be calling because, at this point, I don't know how far James is willing to go to find us. He has friends in the tech world, and if they find a way to hack into your phone . . . or if he places hidden cameras at your place, or at Mom and Dad's . . . Anyway. I probably sound crazy right now. Maybe I am at this point.

But James is good at spotting a liar, so if

he DOES come to you, be honest and say you received a letter from me telling you I'm disappearing but that you haven't heard from me since.

That's why I'm doing this.

I don't want you to have to lie because that'll only upset him more.

Please tell Mom and Dad that I'm safe and that I'll reach out again one day soon once everything is official and I have full custody and am no longer married . . . I think then, maybe he'll back off.

Until then, don't come looking for me.

I hope you, Mark, and the kids are all doing great.

I miss you so much, and I love you.

—*Your sis, Alice*

CHAPTER 47

I pull up on the side of the road across from Carla's house and shift my car into Park.

I stare at my black metal safe lying on the floor of my car. Would it be dangerous to bring it with me? It might be best if I leave it here.

It's not like her husband will attack you in broad daylight.

Still.

I'd feel safer with it on me. I open the safe and slip the Glock into my black leather purse. It's not the smartest move, and it's probably a very reckless thing to do, but what if things get bad?

What if Carla's husband grabs me by the hair and pulls me into the house?

The fact that I'm having these thoughts is probably proof that I shouldn't even be here. But I can't do *nothing*. I can't be one of the countless people who stand by idly while someone else is suffering at the hands of their husband.

I can't.

Besides, I put a lot of thought into this plan.

It should go smoothly. The whole point is to check in on Carla and make sure she's alive and well.

I reach far behind the passenger seat and grab my lidded ceramic dish with both hands, the sides warming my palms.

Fresh soup.

Okay, not really. It isn't actually homemade. I

stopped at the grocery store, grabbed one of those made-in-house containers, and threw it into a pot to heat it.

No one will know.

Especially not Carla. Well, unless she recently bought the exact same soup. Let's hope not.

Awkwardly, I open my car door and step out into the street carrying my ceramic dish of warm soup in one arm and my purse on the other.

A dog barks down the road as I cross the quiet street.

I walk across Carla's interlock driveway, which looks like it hasn't been treated for weeds in years. It's too bad. Aside from the lack of maintenance, her house is beautiful.

It's small, but there's something charming about it. Or at least, there would be if there weren't smudges on the windows, bits of tar falling off the roof, and a huge crack in the foundation.

I pull the warm dish into the crook of my arm and raise my fist.

Knock, knock.

There's a muffled *thud* inside, followed by the deadbolt unlocking. The door cracks open a few inches, and a man with a dark, wiry beard and tousled hair appears. He stands wearing what I've always heard called a *wife beater*, which looks stained with macaroni and cheese sauce.

He looks at me with his almost black eyes, then glances down the street from side to side.

The door conceals the rest of his body.

"Yeah?" he says.

"Oh, hi there," I say. I force a smile, even though I already don't like this guy. "I heard Carla was sick." I raise the dish to offer my gift.

"Carla's sleeping," he says, his voice gruff. With that, he slams the door.

I stand there for a moment, nostrils flared.

Did he seriously just slam the door on me?

I should walk away. I am, after all, risking my safety by confronting someone who I think is physically dangerous.

But I can't walk away. Not after the way Carla spoke to me. There was something in those big blue eyes of hers that told me she understood what it felt like to be abused.

And I think this man is abusing her.

Fuming inside, I rap at the plexiglass of the screen door. The whole thing rattles with every hit, and the door cracks open again.

"What the hell, lady?"

"Where's Carla?" I ask.

"I just told you, she's sleeping."

"I don't believe you," I say.

He watches me with elongated bags under his eyes that make him look like he hasn't slept in over a week.

"What's it to you?" he asks.

"I want to know she's okay," I say.

"Of course, she's not okay!" he says. "But you must already know that if you're here. Anyway, who the hell are you, and what do you want?"

I want to threaten him—tell him that if he hurts her, I'll hunt him down. But I can't do that. If he really is hurting her, then I'm risking her life by calling him out. Because the second he's back inside, he'll take his anger out on her.

I need to be careful about this.

"My name's Emma," I say, evening out my tone. "Carla has been taking care of my son at school," I say. "And—"

"*Taking care*?" He snorts. "She's a teacher. Not a nurse."

"It's complicated," I say. "My son, Lucas—"

His lips part, and he nods slowly. "Ah. The boy who stopped talking. She told me."

For a moment, he seems sympathetic. Sad, even.

"Yeah," I say. "I'm his mom."

"I'm sorry that happened," he says. "But I don't understand why you're here."

"I heard Carla was sick," I say. "I just wanted to bring

some homemade soup."

He scoffs. "Soup? What for?"

What is wrong with this man? Does he not understand English? Or has he never eaten soup when sick? Maybe his parents never took good care of him.

"Doesn't she have the flu?" I ask.

He arches a brow, then looks down the street again as if trying to catch an eavesdropper red-handed.

"She doesn't have the flu." He lowers his voice to a whisper. "Who told you that?"

"Oh. U-um," I stammer. "The school did. I'm sorry. I think I misunderstood. Is it a stomach bug?"

Glowering at me, he pushes open his screen door and comes outside with heavy strides, forcing me to step back onto the interlock pathway. The screen door swings a few times before slamming shut behind him.

Now that I can see his entire body, it's apparent he doesn't exercise or do anything remotely physical. A gut hangs over his jogging pants which look as dirty as his top. His arms are flabby and pressed against his sides, causing dark scraggly hairs to stick out from under his pits.

"Carla's *sick*," he says, tapping his temple hard. "Not sick with a bug."

The smell of sweat combined with day-old deodorant sweeps up my nose. I get the feeling he hasn't showered in days and is trying to cover it up.

And what is that supposed to mean, anyway? Is he implying that she has mental problems? He sounds like James.

When I don't respond, he sighs. "Anyway, she's sleeping right now. I can give her the soup anyway, I guess. Since she won't eat anything I make."

I stare at the yellow stains on his shirt.

Well, if you made something other than macaroni and cheese, she'd eat.

"Did something happen?" I ask.

He scoffs. "Did something happen? Um, yeah. She

stopped taking her meds."

Right.

Blame the victim.

My fingers clench my ceramic dish.

Stay calm. Anger won't solve anything.

"Is there anything I can do?" I ask.

He scratches the back of his neck, and that potent smell assaults my nose again.

He sighs. "No, not really. I'll tell her you stopped by."

As he says that, I spot bruises across his knuckles, and I feel like I might throw up.

Stay calm, Alice. Stay calm.

But I can't. I'm shaking so badly that if I don't do or say something soon, I might implode.

Without thinking, I shove the dish of soup into his arms and some of the yellow broth spills out from underneath the lid. His eyes bulge, surprised by my sudden change in demeanor. I want to point at him, but I'm afraid he'll see my hand quivering.

"If I find out you're hurting her in any way, I will kill you. Do you hear me? You have no idea who I am or what I've been through. I'll kill you in your sleep."

I can't believe the words coming out of my mouth.

They don't even sound like my own.

They sound . . . psychotic.

But there's so much rage inside of me right now.

"Damn it, lady. What the hell is wrong with you? I've never laid a hand on Carla. Ever."

"Bullshit," I snap, and my voice cracks.

I'm so angry I could start crying. I hate it when that happens. But it's clear as day to me now. This man has pummeled his fists into Carla. Who knows the damage he's done. Maybe he did it after the police showed up. Found a way to avoid a report, then took his anger out on his wife.

I start walking away, feeling like my legs might give out. Although I want to blast inside the house to check on Carla, this man is three times my size.

It would be suicide.

And I have my boys to think about.

"Threaten me like that," he mutters to himself. He smashes a fist into the plexiglass of his door, and huge cracks spiderweb across the whole thing. "You stay the fuck off my property! You hear me?"

His voice carries throughout the neighborhood.

And then, I do the unthinkable.

I make a gun with my hands, point it at him, and pretend to shoot. Twice.

Bang. Bang.

He retreats into his house and slams the door. By the time I get into my car, I'm shaking so violently my car is vibrating. My teeth clatter, and breathing feels almost impossible.

Did that really just happen?

What the hell was I thinking?

That's just it . . . I wasn't thinking.

It's like someone else took over my body. Someone I always hoped would step in when James was bashing his fists into my ribs.

But now that the adrenaline is slowly wearing off, I realize the mistake I've made.

I already have an abuser after me.

Now, I might have two.

CHAPTER 48

BEFORE

"He keeps calling," Chloe says. "I've blocked his number countless times, and he somehow keeps calling from a new number."

"Is he threatening you?" I ask.

"A bit, but I can handle it. And Mark put him in his place."

I'm thankful for Mark, Chloe's husband. He's the size of a bear and used to be in a biker gang. So I know he has connections with dangerous people. If James were to try anything, he'd likely end up floating in a river.

Sometimes, I hope that Mark says something to his old buddies, and someone goes after James. But he doesn't want to be in that life anymore. He wants to be a good father and husband. Going after James jeopardizes that.

I'm happy for Chloe—truly.

She found herself an amazing guy.

But the fact that James keeps calling months after our court hearing tells me he hasn't given up on trying to hunt me down.

I've since left the shelter and managed to get myself a small house with cheap rent. I work full-time just to make ends meet. I thought after we got divorced and after the judge granted me full custody, along with a restraining order, James would realize he was in the wrong and he'd back off.

But that look he gave me in court—that deathly, soulless leer—sent chills throughout my entire body. He didn't have to say anything; I knew exactly what he was thinking.

I'm going to fucking kill you.

I felt it. And I believed it. I knew at that moment that if he ever found me again, I wouldn't live to see the sunrise.

I stayed away from my family for months and only recently started talking to them again from a burner phone.

Chloe doesn't ask where I am—she knows I won't tell her. All she needs to know right now is that I'm safe.

"You should change your number," I say.

"Yeah," she says quickly. "I was already thinking that. I'll give my phone service a call later."

"What about Mom and Dad?" I ask.

"They've gotten a few calls, but nothing like me," she says.

After a pause, she adds, "Alice, I'm a bit worried."

"Why?" I ask.

"What if he finds you? I mean, he's obviously still looking. It's only a matter of time."

I hate those words: only a matter of time.

But I know she's right.

I may be in a different state, but James is hell-bent on locating his sons and me. He won't stop. And the restraining order won't protect me, either.

"Can't you change your name or something?" she asks.

I've already thought about it. But I'm so tight on money right now that even *that* expense would be too much. The worst part is that, although I deleted all my social media accounts, I created a fake one to keep tabs on James. And a few weeks ago, he posted, "Colorado seems like a nice place."

I almost threw up.

He knows.

He may not have my exact address, but he somehow found out that I'm in Colorado. Which means it's only a matter of time before he finds me.

"Yeah, I might do a name change," I say.

Even though what I really want to do is run away again.

But I don't have the money.

I swear, Chloe can read my mind. "Is it a money thing? Because I already told you—I'll send you some."

I appreciate her willingness to help. I may just take her up on the offer.

"That's sweet—" I start.

"I'm sending you two grand right now," she says.

"What? Shit, Chloe, that's way too much—"

"Not really," she says. "I have Google open now. Apparently, it can cost anywhere from one hundred to five hundred dollars for a name change. And you should probably be changing the kids' names, too."

I'm both embarrassed and incredibly thankful. I part my lips to tell her that I'll pick up overtime to pay her back when another call rings on my phone.

Something *Associates*.

A lawyer's office?

"Um, Chloe, I'll call you back. Some lawyer's office is trying to get a hold of me."

What could a lawyer possibly want?

Oh, God . . . Is James going to try to come at me again legally? Try to reopen the custody battle?

I hang up with my sister and pick up the phone call.

"Hello?"

"Hi, this is William Yonuk. I'm looking to speak with Mrs. Alice Remington."

I hesitate, not wanting to confirm who I am. I also hold off on correcting him and telling him that I now go by my maiden name—Winslow.

"What's this about?" I ask.

He clears his throat, likely sensing my apprehension.

"I'm calling about an inheritance property left behind by Victor Huxley."

I stop breathing.

Victor?

Huxley?

I haven't heard that name in ages.

Besides, I thought he died years ago. He got deployed

and was never seen again after he returned.

"Um," I say. "Y-yeah. That's my uncle."

"Are you Alice?" he asks.

This must be a hoax.

Maybe James is trying to get a hold of me.

But there's no way. James knew nothing about Victor. I never spoke about him. My whole family acted like he never existed after his disappearance. My biological father grieved for a while and then turned to drugs. But after my mom left him, she never spoke Victor's name again and even changed our last names from Huxley to her maiden name, Winslow, because she wanted nothing to do with that family name.

"I— I am," I say despite the uneasy feeling in my gut.

"Well, Alice Remington, your uncle named you his beneficiary in his will."

"He *what*?" I blurt.

"He left you his estate. All of it."

Why would he do that? Sure, we got along great when I was a kid. He was my favorite uncle. But why wouldn't he leave everything to my father—his own brother?

Did he know about his addiction problem?

"I— I don't understand," I say.

"Are you free tomorrow at 1 p.m.?"

Free? In what sense? Does he expect me to drive all the way to his office? The number he's calling from shows New York.

He must sense my apprehension. "You're in Colorado, I believe, yes?" The riffling of papers echoes near his phone.

Shouldn't he know where I live if he called *me*?

"I'll have one of my associates book a virtual appointment with you for tomorrow at 1 p.m. I'll also send you some paperwork to fill out. Do you have a printer?"

"I do," I say.

"Great," he continues. "With technology these days, we can do everything virtually. You'll simply have to sign some forms and email them back to me. But I'd like to explain everything face to face, if you're all right with that."

What choice do I have? It's not like I'm driving to New York.

"You should receive an invite shortly," he says. "I look forward to meeting you in person.

Well, on camera, and answering any questions you might have for me."

When I hang up, I look up William Yonuk on Google. I find William Yonuk and Associates. The number matches the one he called from.

This seems legitimate.

I scroll down.

He has over a hundred five-star ratings, some dating back several years, which means he's been in business for quite some time.

Is this really happening?

Did my uncle Victor really leave me an inheritance?

In that instant, I receive an electronic transfer text from Chloe for the two thousand dollars she promised to send.

But I get the feeling I won't be needing that.

If this is real, which it seems to be, then our lives are about to change forever.

CHAPTER 49

I find myself walking down Thorn Lake Drive. How did I get here? I gaze up at the night sky, and little white snowflakes collect on my eyelashes.

I blink them away.

It looks cold out, but I don't feel cold.

Where's my house?

I continue walking down the elongated road, snow crunching under my feet.

Where's my car? Was I in an accident? And when did it start snowing?

"Found you," comes a gravelly voice.

I spin around to spot a figure standing in the distance. I can't make out any features, but I can tell it's a man by his large size and broad shoulders.

He walks toward me one long stride at a time.

But before I can even process what's happening, his long strides turn into a jog, and within seconds, a full-blown run.

My stomach clenches so hard it feels like I got kicked in the gut. I try to run, but my legs are as heavy as concrete blocks.

Why am I not moving?

He's getting closer, and closer.

But I can't escape.

My gun.

It's on me.

I reach into my purse for my Glock and rip it out. He's about to grab me when I pull back and fire a shot.

Bang.

The blackness of his figure explodes into a thousand little pieces that burst into the air like bats.

***

My eyes pop open.

Where am I?

I blink hard, my eyes adjusting to the darkness around me.

Home. In bed. I'm warm . . . safe. There's no man after me.

Everything is okay.

It was just a nightmare.

Thump.

What the hell was that?

It came from the main floor. Was that what woke me up? It sounds like someone tripped over the kitchen island's stools.

I grab my phone and open my Hawk Security app.

No alerts. No motion detected.

It's probably Grayson again. No need to fly off the handle like last time.

My brain is probably right. Still, I can't lie here and hope that Grayson is the cause of the noise downstairs.

I consider grabbing my Glock, but after what happened last time, it probably isn't a good idea. Instead, I'll check Grayson's room. If he's out of bed, then I can relax, knowing that no one broke into our home.

Peeling my blanket off of me, I swing my legs out of bed and slowly stand up. I reach for my door handle, careful not to make a sound, then inch it open just enough for me to slip through.

I pause at the top of the stairs, listening.

Footsteps.

It's Grayson. Relax. Stop panicking.

Then why does it sound like he's wearing shoes?

Grayson is usually barefoot. However, he does have a pair of hard-soled slippers that James bought for him last year.

Before allowing my brain to spiral, I hurry to Grayson's room and turn the handle. Thankfully, the door doesn't creak as I open it and peek inside.

It takes a few seconds to understand what I'm looking at.

Is that a blanket? Pillows?

No, it's Grayson.

He's sleeping on his side, a soft snoring sound slipping out of his parted lips with every breath.

Could it be Lucas downstairs?

I'm trying not to freak out, even though my heart is now pounding so hard I can hear it in my ears. I want to run to my room for the gun and call the police, but I don't want a repeat of last time.

And besides—there were no alerts in the security app. There's no way someone managed to break into my house without tripping the alarm. They'd need the security PIN, and no one knows it but Grayson and me.

What if Grayson told someone at school?

No, he wouldn't do that.

I tiptoe my way to Lucas's room and quietly open the door. When I see him lying curled on his bed, my head starts to spin.

Someone is downstairs.

I can't possibly be imagining it, can I?

One slow step at a time, I move closer to the top of the staircase to listen. If someone broke in, wouldn't they be making a bunch of noise? Breaking things as they try to collect valuables?

This doesn't make any sense.

I must have imagined it. I peel my hand away from the upstairs railing, my palm leaving a sweaty handprint against the wood.

This doesn't *feel* like my imagination.

But I did once read that people can experience

auditory and visual hallucinations when first waking up—when the body isn't yet alert but you aren't sleeping anymore, either.

That has to be it.

I breathe in deeply, trying to reassure myself that no one is downstairs.

Thud.

My eyes widen at the sound.

Okay—that wasn't my imagination.

A sharp pain radiates through my chest as I hurry back into my bedroom and grab my phone.

My whole body is quivering now, yet I somehow manage to dial 911.

We go through the same thing as last time, and I give the woman my location. This time, however, I make it a point to tell her that it isn't either one of my sons. She tells me to stay in my room until the police arrive.

What kind of advice is that?

If that person starts climbing my stairs, I'm going out there and shooting. There's no fucking way I'm letting anyone near my kids, no matter how terrified I am.

So I wait at the edge of my room, my shoulder pressed up against the door frame, the gun's metal slowly warming in my clammy palms.

With how badly I'm trembling, if I'm forced to shoot the intruder, I might miss entirely. I'd probably fire multiple holes through the wall, which might be enough to scare them off.

But if it's James ...

Or maybe it's Carla's husband, and he's furious over the way I spoke to him, and he's come here to teach me a lesson.

I don't hear anything anymore.

Why is there no sound?

I expected something ... a door closing. More footsteps. But it's so quiet I can hear the furnace running and the soft rattling of a loose screw in one of the heating vents.

Minutes pass, and there's still no sound.

Did they leave?

Or did you imagine the whole thing?

No way.

I heard it.

Maybe an animal broke in somehow.

My phone suddenly starts ringing, and I almost drop my gun.

It's Wyatt.

I slip back into my room and hurry to answer.

"Wyatt," I whisper.

"Emma, are you okay?" he asks. "I'm outside."

I peer through the window to spot rotating sweeps of blue and red lights.

"I heard someone," I whisper. "Downstairs. And it wasn't Lucas or Grayson."

"We've checked the doors and windows," Wyatt says. "There's no sign of a break-in. Do you still hear anything?"

"No," I admit.

"We have two options," he says, a little too matter-of-factly for my liking. "I can either break your lock—"

"What?" I blurt. "No, no, don't do that."

"You feel comfortable coming to the door yourself?" he asks.

I nod, then realize he can't see me.

"Y-yes," I say.

It's not true. I don't want to go down there. But I also don't want some dramatic entrance over nothing, only to be without a lockable door for several hours when James is after me.

"I'll stay on the phone with you," he says.

"Okay," I say, my mouth dry. I place my gun down on my bedside table and step back out into the upstairs hallway.

"I'm right here," he says. "If there's anything, you say the word, and we're blasting the door down."

We.

Derek is with him.

Despite how much I don't like his *machoness*, I'm thankful that they're both here.

I move down the staircase, the wood cooling the pads of my feet.

I hate this.

Any second now, James might jump out and grab me around the throat.

No, no one is here. You imagined it. Your senses were playing tricks on you.

No matter how hard I try to convince myself that no one is in my house, it doesn't lessen my anxiety or how hard my heart is beating right now.

I know I heard something.

The moment I reach the main floor, I dart across the dining room, past the kitchen, and unlock the deadbolt as fast as I can.

Wyatt opens the door, and it takes everything in me not to run behind him like a coward. Instead, I stand there, fingers digging into the doorframe.

"Are you all right?" he asks.

I don't know how to answer that. He must sense how terrified I am.

"Why don't you wait out here for a minute?" he asks.

I appreciate that he isn't staring at my pajamas. It's an old Christmas set with little reindeer and cartoon pine trees.

Not the kind of pajamas any grown woman wants to be seen wearing.

There's no wind outside, but the air is cold—easily in the low forties. I wrap my arms around my body to try to keep warm and step out onto the porch barefoot.

Derek looks at me, then at my pajamas.

I expect him to make a comment, but he doesn't. He looks exhausted, and it's obvious he doesn't want to be here.

"What kind of noise did you hear?" he asks grumpily.

"Footsteps," I say. "And some banging. Like someone tripped over the island stools."

He doesn't acknowledge my answer.

Instead, he follows Wyatt inside the house, his hand hovering over the gun attached to his belt. They aren't storming in with their guns raised, which tells me they don't think there's actually a threat.

And if there's no threat . . . I wasted their time.

Again.

At this point, I'm hoping they find something.

Not that I want an intruder in my house, but it would explain a lot, even the notes. The only question is: how the hell is someone breaking into my home undetected by the cameras and without setting off the alarm?

It makes no sense.

After a beat, both Wyatt and Derek return outside and step out under the dim yellow porch light.

"We checked the house," he says. "There's no one hiding in there."

"You checked everywhere?" I ask.

"Everywhere but upstairs," Wyatt says. "But you said you came down that way. So unless someone managed to walk right past you—"

"That's fine," I cut him off.

I already feel crazy as it is. I don't want him to think that I'm capable of walking right by an intruder without realizing it.

That's utter nonsense.

"The basement?" I ask.

Derek nods. "I pushed aside the bookshelf and even checked the secret passage where—"

I nod, not wanting him to finish his sentence.

The body.

I remember all too well.

"Anyway," he continues. "It doesn't lead to anywhere. It's a narrow passage that leads to a concrete room. Nothing else. And there was no one hiding in there."

I remember what the room looks like—or at least, part of the room.

But Derek's right—it's all concrete down there.

As far as I can remember, there was no other tunnel or doorway leading to anywhere else.

And he's confirming it now.

"The wind can sometimes shift the house," Wyatt says. "That, and weather changes. My house makes all sorts of weird noises this time of year."

Derek stares at him, probably wondering why he's going out of his way to make me feel like I'm not crazy, when in reality, I am.

"Like we said"—Derek's tone is a lot colder than Wyatt's—"your house is clear. Your alarm is active. No one set foot in there."

I've never been one to believe in ghosts or hauntings, but is it possible that the woman whose body was found is still lingering?

I keep my mouth shut.

I have the feeling that if I mention anything of the sort, Wyatt might *strongly* suggest I speak with Dr. Jackson.

Wyatt runs a hand through his hair, looking uncomfortable. Unlike Derek, he won't outright tell me there's nothing inside or that it's all in my head.

But I can see it all over his face.

He doesn't believe me.

CHAPTER 50

Lucas runs straight into Dr. Jackson's office, his Spider-Man backpack shifting from side to side with every stride.

If I weren't so preoccupied thinking about the sounds I heard last night, I'd be grinning from ear to ear. He may not be speaking yet, but he's making progress—he's showing signs of excitement and is more willing to communicate with nods and smiles.

We're getting somewhere.

I follow him inside and pay the office for Lucas's previous sessions using my recent blog money. I'm eternally grateful for their willingness to run me a tab. I've never heard of any business doing this—it must be a small-town thing. Either that, or proof of Dr. Jackson's good intentions. She's in this to help people.

Alice smiles sweetly at me when I tell her I'll be waiting in my car.

The parking lot is empty when I step back outside, and the trees, naked. The leaves have all fallen, most of them now crispy and brown rather than vivid reds and oranges.

A few stray leaves crunch under my boots as I return to my car. I wish I could forget about last night, but I can't.

I know I heard something.

Someone was in my house, and I'm not willing to ignore that because the police didn't find anything. I'm not delusional. I know what I heard.

I start my engine and recline my seat, phone in hand.

I'll catch you, whoever you are.

With a press of my thumb, my Hawk Security app flashes open. I scroll through the night's event clips and play them over, and over again.

There has to be something—a shadow or a sound that doesn't quite fit into the night. I play the clips at least four or five times each.

Nothing.

But . . . the timestamps.

They're all over the place. This makes sense, given that the camera only records when motion is detected.

One started recording at 11:54, and the next, at 12:09. Several more gaps are obvious throughout the night. I open my phone's call log to locate my outgoing call to 911.

1:48 a.m.

This means the sound I heard occurred somewhere between 1:40 and 1:47 a.m., seeing as I listened for a couple of minutes, and it took me several more to check on Lucas and Grayson.

There are four cameras in total—two at the front, and two at the back. One faces the front of the house, monitoring the lawn and driveway, whereas the second one is aimed downward toward the front door. The back cameras are positioned similarly.

If anyone had tried entering through the doors, the cameras would have caught them.

The side windows.

Would someone really manage to evade both the front and back cameras by sneaking up to the side of my house? And if that's the case, why wouldn't the alarm have gone off?

I spend most of Lucas's therapy session jumping from one theory to the next. But in the end, none of this makes any sense.

Sighing, I drop my phone onto my lap and rest my head back.

There are only two options:

Either someone is very much aware of my security system and is toying with me, or I really am having some psychological issues and am suffering from hallucinations.

What I really need is a solid night of sleep. Then, I can approach this with a clear head.

But how am I supposed to sleep knowing someone is coming in and out of my house? It isn't only about last night. It's about the notes, too.

I stare outside, watching a few leaves tumble across the pavement.

Think, Alice, think.

Right now, I refuse to believe I'm hallucinating. If I am—great. Then at least my kids are safe. But if I'm not, then we're in danger. So until I've thought of every possible explanation, I'm not willing to chalk this up to delusions.

Who would know about your security system?

It's not like I've told anyone.

But both Derek and Wyatt know. As well as Hawk Security. But Hawk Security is a professional business—no way would they want to ruin their reputation. Their whole purpose is to provide a sense of safety, and if they can't do that, they'll go bankrupt.

That leaves Derek and Wyatt.

Derek isn't exactly likable. And he does look at me funny half the time. Wyatt has been far too amazing with me. He's the one who suggested I get a security system in the first place.

My eyes widen at the red brick of Dr. Jackson's office, and I slowly sit upright.

Wyatt truly has been amazing. Almost too amazing.

And he even admitted to me that he would have access to my security information—the footage, everything. Something about Chief Madden approving the costs, since this is all a part of an ongoing investigation.

But what kind of police department pays for someone's personal security equipment? I thought it was weird at first but told myself that small towns are different. People are nicer. More willing to lend a helping hand.

Why didn't I see it before?

My mouth goes dry as I think back to all the footage James deleted from his camera monitoring app. I've been here before. I should have known better.

But I can't confront Wyatt. Because there's no way for me to prove anything, and if I come at him with accusations, it'll only give him ammunition to gaslight me some more.

I have a better idea.

Breathing fast, I Google the Thorn Lake police department's phone number and hit Call.

It rings twice before a woman answers at the other end, sounding bored out of her mind. "Thorn Lake Police Department, Officer Jones speaking."

I recognize her voice. Teresa, I believe it was. The young cop who recently graduated from the police academy.

"Hi, there," I say. "I'm looking to speak with Chief Madden."

She pauses, and a scraping sound follows. I picture her looking over her shoulder, phone squished between her chin and shoulder, to see whether Chief Madden is in the office.

"One moment," she says. "I'll transfer the call."

It rings several times before a clipped voice answers at the other end. "Chief Madden."

"Oh, um, hi there," I say.

Silence.

"My name's Emma," I said. "Emma Collins."

Still, she says nothing.

"I'm the new resident at Victor Huxley's old house," I continue. "There's currently an open investigation due to some notes found throughout my house."

"Yes," she says matter-of-factly.

She wants me to get to the point.

"I'm sorry to bother you," I say. "But I wanted to personally thank you for approving the costs for the security monitoring services and camera installation at my home due to my financial situation at the time," I say.

"I'm sorry?" she says.

It comes out sounding like a question.

I clear my throat. "Wy— Officer Daniels said you would be approving the cost of activating my Hawk Security system and installing the cameras at my home, to help with the investigation. And now that they're installed, I assumed the approval had gone through."

She scoffs on the other end of the line. "There must be some misunderstanding. We don't cover expenses for home security systems. Can you imagine how much that would cost our taxpayers? If someone feels unsafe in their home, it's their responsibility to take appropriate measures and to cover the costs themselves."

"Oh," I say. "I'm sorry. I must have misunderstood. There was so much going on when the system was installed. I'll call Hawk Security. W— Officer Daniels must have convinced them to defer my payments."

"More likely," she says.

She doesn't sound mean, exactly. It sounds like police work is something she's been doing her whole life. Like the kind of person who thinks only with their head and doesn't allow emotion to interfere with their work.

"Was there anything else, Ms. Collins?"

"N-no," I say. "That was it. Sorry again to have bothered you."

"Not a bother," she says. "I do hope your situation gets resolved soon."

I thank her, say bye, and hang up.

So he was lying to me.

This proves that I'm not crazy. I specifically remember him saying that Chief Madden would approve the request. I remember this so clearly because even Derek looked at him funny.

Maybe Wyatt isn't who I thought he was.

The whole thing feels like a stab in the back. He's been so kind to me throughout all of this. Why lie? Especially about something like that? To keep tabs on me? Does he have ties to James? James could be paying him off to watch over me.

And if that's the case, I'm worse off than I was before.

At least before, I could run to the police and *hope* a good one might help.

Now, I feel like they're against me.

A throbbing pain sets in my temples.

This is all too much.

I locate Hawk Security's number and hit Call.

"Hawk Security, how may I help you?"

"Hi," I say. "I'm calling regarding an account I have with you. I'd like to know what my balance owing is."

We go through a standard security check to ensure I'm the true account holder, and the young man at the other end of the line says, "No balance owing. You're up to date."

Up to date? I realize it hasn't even been a month yet, but shouldn't there be some installation fee?

"Oh," I say. "There was no installation fee?"

"Yes," he says. "Six hundred and ninety-two dollars. That includes the cameras and your first month as well. But it was already paid."

"By who?" I ask.

The sound of keyboard keys being stroked slips through the phone, followed by the pensive clicking of a tongue.

"Wyatt Daniels," he says.

Clenching my fist around my phone, I thank him and end the call.

He paid for my security system.

Why?

To watch you. To mess with you.

Although part of me feels like I should be thankful for this grand gesture of kindness, nobody forks up almost seven hundred dollars to help someone they barely know.

No one.

Wyatt is up to no good.

I thought he was on my side, but this proves that I can't trust him.

CHAPTER 51

BEFORE

Dear Chloe,

   I'm so sorry to have to do this again. I'll be disappearing for a while. James found out I'm in Colorado, and he'll soon find me if I don't leave.

   I can't tell you where I'm going, but I'll be safe. And I'll be in touch again as soon as I can, okay? Promise. I love you.

   —Your sis, Alice

CHAPTER 52

Tonight is a special night.

I can't remember the last time I shared a beautiful meal like this with my boys.

"This looks so good," Grayson says, eyeballing the takeout containers.

I'm still waiting for the inheritance money, but I received a deposit of nine hundred and some dollars from that one blog post the other day. Typically, I would never spend money like this for supper. But tonight, I wanted to celebrate my blog's success, so I ordered takeout from Thorn Lake's most popular diner, the Bistro.

Admittedly, tonight isn't only about celebrating. It's about forgetting all the chaos in our lives. Even if only for twenty minutes.

For the last several days, I've felt a distance from Lucas and Grayson, and I know that's because of me. My mind has been in survival mode for so long that I've stopped living in the moment, and I've stopped giving them the love and attention that they need and deserve.

I'm hoping tonight changes that.

I prepare our plates with roasted vegetables, buttered rice, and chicken breasts. Everything looks so decadent. I crack open a container of gravy, the smell causing saliva to pool in my mouth.

"You sure we aren't rich?" Grayson asks as I hand him his plate.

"Not rich," I say. At least, not *yet*. "I made a bit of money from work, so I want to celebrate with you guys."

I screech my chair back and sit down. Lucas is already shoving vegetables in his mouth, barely breathing between bites.

The Bistro is popular for a reason.

I take a bite of the rice and roll my eyes. Lucas seems to think it's funny. He lets out a soft giggle, and the sound is like an orchestra to my ears.

I smile back at him, wanting to freeze this moment.

"This is nice," I tell them.

Lucas nods, and in a single bite, eats half a buttered bun.

"Really good," Grayson says, his mouth half-full. "Thanks, Mom."

I smile at him. "You're welcome, honey. Oh, I almost forgot. I bought a new juice today at the grocery store. You guys want a glass?"

They both nod.

I push my chair back, get up, and make my way to the fridge, deliberately ignoring the fact that I grabbed this juice minutes after finding out about Wyatt lying to me.

Tonight, none of that matters. You can try to figure things out tomorrow.

I pull out the glass bottle labeled Pineapple Splash and set it on the kitchen counter.

Clink.

Just as I'm about to reach for glasses in the cupboard, I'm drawn toward the window in the foyer. There's no reason for it. It's subconscious. A bit like the feeling you get when you're in a public space, and your eyes immediately dart to someone else's. It's as if part of you senses that someone is watching you.

And just now, I sensed it.

At the end of my driveway is that man again.

He stands still, his face aimed toward my house.

I clench my jaw. I'm so furious I could smash the juice bottle and use a shard to threaten this man, even if it cuts my palm.

"What's wrong?" Grayson asks.

"Wait here," I order.

Without thinking, I pull a butcher knife out of our knife block. I don't intend to use it unless he attacks me.

"Mom?" Grayson asks.

His chair slides across the dining room tiles.

"Wait here!" I bark.

Still in my slippers, I storm out of the house, slamming the door behind me. I should be afraid, but I'm not. I'm pumped so full of adrenaline that I don't take the time to think anything through.

I don't know who this man is, but at this point, it doesn't matter. I'm so sick of being toyed with . . . being manipulated and treated like an injured mouse at the mercy of a tomcat.

I'm done with these games.

They're an attempt to frighten my boys and me, but I refuse to be afraid anymore. I don't deserve this. I don't deserve what James put me through, and more importantly, my sons don't deserve any of this, either.

This ends tonight.

My heart throbs loudly in my ears with every step I take. The man doesn't move. He stands there, almost like he's waiting for me.

"What the fuck do you want?" I shout across my driveway.

I must look unhinged, marching with my arms swinging dramatically. Every time my right hand comes up, my knife glints under the streetlights.

"I'm talking to you!" I shout.

Does he think standing there quietly is going to scare me? If anything, it's only making me angrier.

"You think this is fun?" I say. "You enjoying yourself?"

Saliva splashes out of my mouth as I shout at him.

I move closer and closer, and still, he doesn't move. I wish I could see his face, but it's hidden in the shadows of his oversized hat.

Why isn't he answering?

With sharp, bloodless knuckles, I raise my knife,

pointing its tip at the man's face. "You stay the fuck away from me and my family! Do you hear me?"

As if suddenly entering reality, the man's eyes widen at me. He lets out a little squeal, followed by a deep wail. It's an odd lament, which takes me so aback that I lower my knife.

Then, he drops to his knees, and two wrinkly hands come popping out of his long sleeves. He holds them up, seemingly begging for mercy, and laments some more.

A yappy dog barks in the distance, and my neighbor's porch lights turn on. In a panic, Stella—the woman who brought me the muffins I worried were poisoned—comes running out in a bathrobe, whipping the strap around her body. She shakes water out of her hair, and her golf ball–sized eyes turn toward me and the man on his knees.

Barefoot, she hurries down her steps and runs toward me, waving frantically over her head. What is she trying to tell me? What the hell is going on?

"What's going on?" she says, hurrying next to the man.

I tuck the knife behind my back, but not fast enough.

"Is that a *knife*?" she spits. "What the hell is wrong with you?"

The man cries some more, and Stella holds his head as he leans into her, sobbing against her knees.

"Y-you know this man?" I ask. "He's been stalking me. Watching my house!"

"He's my dad!" Stella shouts at me. She's so angry that her fists are balled against her robe. "He has dementia! He goes for evening walks all the time!"

I'm so embarrassed, I don't even know what to say.

She sucks in a quivering breath, and it seems to calm her. "He gets confused," she says, more calmly this time. "Especially with your house. Ever since you moved in, he talks about your boys as if they're his brothers from when he was young. He's only looking for his brothers. He's harmless."

"I— I'm so sorry," I say. "There's been a lot going on, and I've been receiving threatening notes. I— I—"

She sticks a flat palm up. She sucks in a deep breath, likely trying to compose herself before saying something she will regret, which is extremely kind of her, given what I just did to her father. "Look, I get it. I've seen the police here more than once. But I can promise you that my dad has nothing to do with it."

She helps him up, and for the first time, I see his face—dull, wrinkly skin, curly gray brows, a long, crooked nose, and a confused look in his glassy gray eyes that makes me feel even worse.

"I'm so sorry," I tell him.

His whole head is quaking. I can't tell whether it's due to fear or simply old age.

"Come on, Dad," Stella says.

She gives me a disappointed look, and all I want to do is click my fingers and disappear from existence. How could I have threatened a poor man with dementia?

You thought he was watching your house.

I should have come out more calmly than that. There was no need to come charging at someone with a knife.

It could have been someone working for James. You were only trying to protect yourself.

First, I point a gun at my own son. Now, I've threatened an innocent old man with a knife.

What's next?

CHAPTER 53

Grayson looks a bit happier than usual this morning. And it isn't only because it's Friday.

"Something going on?" I ask him.

The pep in his walk disappears. Every time I point out that he's in a good mood, he tries to hide it. Maybe he doesn't want to talk about whatever is going on.

"It's pizza day," he says.

I feel like I knew that somehow.

"And we're having some sort of lunch party," he continues. "Mrs. Pelowski has been talking about it all week but won't tell us what's going on. Someone thinks she's going to give away an Xbox."

I hold back a scoff. No teacher would give away an Xbox. First, it's too expensive, and second, that would be a sure way to upset parents who try to control their kids' screen time.

But I don't say anything.

It's nice to see him this happy, anyway. Even if he doesn't win an Xbox.

I walk them down the driveway and send them off before reaching into my pocket and checking my phone.

Still no word from Carla.

I texted her again last night, asking her to let me know whether she is okay. I scroll through my sent messages—there are six in total. The first three are me checking on Lucas, but the other half are me checking on her.

There are no read receipts, so there's no way for me

to know whether she's read them. An unpleasant ball of anxiety forms in my stomach. What if I did make things worse? I basically threatened to shoot her husband.

I can't show up there again. Not after that. He told me to stay off his property, which means if I go back, he'll consider me a trespasser, and for all I know, he has a shotgun in his house.

For a moment, I consider calling Wyatt. I know he already told me that he can't divulge any information about reports that don't involve me, but I just want to know that she's okay and not at the bottom of the lake.

Wyatt isn't on your side.

Chief Madden might be able to help.

Leave it alone. This isn't your business.

But I have a sickening feeling that something is wrong. Even if she had a bad case of the flu, it only takes two seconds to respond to a message. Why isn't she saying anything?

Years ago, I would have kept my nose out of this. But after everything I've been through, I know what some men are capable of. I can't stand by and do nothing. And I know we aren't friends, but that doesn't change anything. I see myself in Carla. I have to help.

Walking back toward my house, I type out one last message to her.

Sorry for all the texts. Just worried. Please let me know you're okay, or I will have to get the police involved.

Seconds later, my phone dings.

It's her.

There are still no read receipts, which means they aren't turned on. That also means that she's likely been ignoring my messages up until I mentioned the police.

I'm fine. Just really sick. No need to get dramatic. Will be back at school next Monday.

Well, that certainly sounds like Carla—at least the first impression I had of her. But what if it's her husband who wrote that?

Not that it matters.

She said she'll be back at school next Monday. Even if her husband is the one who responded, he wouldn't say she'll be back Monday if she's dead, or if he planned to kill her.

Unless she's been gone for days, and he's covering it up.

"Stop it, Alice," I tell myself aloud.

Great. Now I'm talking to myself. I should consider booking an appointment with Dr. Jackson. She might be able to prescribe me something for sleep because, at this rate, I'm getting four or five hours per night.

I'm about to enter the house when the sound of gravel spitting out from underneath tires echoes behind me.

Wyatt's police cruiser slowly rolls up my driveway.

I can barely see him through the windshield, but the passenger seat is empty.

Why is he showing up alone? And without calling?

He parks and steps out.

No ball cap today. His damp chestnut hair is slicked to one side, and his face, cleanly shaven. He doesn't smile, and instead, walks toward me with his shoulders drawn back and a scowl on his face.

What could he possibly want to talk about? Only the other day, I found myself fantasizing about what life *might* be like if I gave Wyatt a chance. But now, I see him for who he is—another liar, like James.

"Are you all right?" he asks.

I must be looking at him hatefully.

"Fine," I say.

He clears his throat, approaches me, and tucks his thumbs into the sides of his padded bulletproof vest. "Emma, I know you're going through a lot."

I hate it when he says that. James used to say it, too. *You're under a lot of stress. You aren't sleeping. You've been taking your meds, right?*

I'm so sick of the gaslighting, it's unreal.

"But you can't go around threatening people," he finishes.

One second, I'm staring at Wyatt's bright eyes, and the

next, I'm seeing that old man on his knees, his hands trembling above his head.

How would Wyatt even know about that? I highly doubt Stella contacted the police. She explained the situation and seemed to be understanding of mine, despite her anger.

"That was a misunderstanding," I tell him. "And how would you even know about that? Are you watching me?"

He pulls his face back, looking confused. "I'm sorry?"

"So you're watching me," I say, unable to suppress my anger this time. Especially since he's acting like he doesn't know what I'm talking about.

He manages to stay cool and places two hands on his hips before sighing. "Emma, I don't know what you're talking about. We received a call from Mr. McKenzie. He wanted to press charges for uttering threats, but I managed to talk him down."

Mr. McKenzie.

Shit.

I part my lips, but no sound escapes.

He straightens his posture and sticks his thumbs back into the sides of his vest. "Listen, Emma."

His tone is very police-like. No more sweet Wyatt. I guess I've pushed him to his limit.

"As a police officer, I'm here to warn you not to set foot on Mr. McKenzie's property again. And as a friend, I think you're under too much stress. If you want to talk, I'm here. But if not, then I really think you should book an appointment with Dr. Jackson."

I'm too stunned to say anything. For a moment, I consider lashing back by accusing him of being a liar and telling him that I know about the whole security system setup, and how the police department didn't cover the costs.

He did.

Why?

To keep tabs on me at all times?

Before I get the chance to say something I'll regret,

Wyatt turns around, gets into his car, and leaves.

CHAPTER 54

I'm so angry I could break something.

How dare Mr. McKenzie call the police. Especially since he's the one who should be behind bars. That bastard won't get away with this.

I pace back and forth in the kitchen a few times, muttering to myself.

And that's when I see it—the little slip of paper. It's tucked underneath one of the stool legs.

I stop moving and stare at it for what feels like minutes.

Pick it up, Alice.

I can tell it's a note. The ink is visible through the thin paper. What will it say this time? That I'm going to die? Maybe it's better if I don't read it.

No, I have to read it.

Dropping to one knee, I tilt the stool slightly and extract the note. When the leg hits the ground again, I'm reminded of the sound I heard the other night—the one that made me think someone had tripped over one of the stools.

Someone really was in your house. Someone left this note.

I look around, feeling watched, and slowly unfold the note.

STUPID BITCH.

I stare, wide eyed, my thumbs digging hard into the sides of the note. Who's doing this? And why? What the hell do they want from me? If they wanted to hurt me, they'd have done it already.

So why the games?

It could be James.

Why would James toy with me like this? I always imagined that if he ever found me, he'd blast his way in and try to kill me. Not take his time and torment me.

I reach for my phone, prepared to call the police.

No.

They won't help. And I can't trust Wyatt right now. What I need is to catch this person in the act.

Or move. Sell the house. Leave, and never look back.

But I can't do that. Not until I receive the inheritance money. Come to think of it, that would solve everything. I could put the house up for sale and get the hell out of here.

Whoever is doing this may follow you.

Not if they can't find me. I'll change my name again if I have to. I'm tired of living in fear every day.

Furious, I call Mr. Yonuk instead.

I'm surprised when he picks up. Since the day that I first spoke to him, that man has been overly busy. I've had to leave several voicemails before receiving a call back. "It's Al— Emma Collins."

He's completely aware of my name change, but it's important that I only use my new name moving forward. All it takes is one slipup.

"Ms. Collins," he says.

It sounds like he's about to say something else when I cut to the chase. "I need an update on the money. It's been over a month. I'm barely getting by. I—"

"Emma," he cuts me off.

I breathe out hard into the phone.

"I was just about to call you."

Sure you were.

"The funds are being deposited into your account tomorrow. Two and a half million dollars. Is your account still the one ending in 9227?"

"Y-yes," I say, feeling like a weight of a thousand pounds has been removed from my shoulders. "That's . . . that's great news. Thank you."

"It should hit your account at midnight tonight. If you run into any issues, please don't hesitate to call my office."

"Thank you, Mr. Yonuk."

"My pleasure. And Emma"—he pauses—"take good care of yourself, okay?"

I appreciate the concern. Mr. Yonuk knows everything—about James, about me using this inheritance as an escape, all of it.

"I am," I tell him, even though it feels like my world is falling apart.

He might be in on this.

I push this thought away.

Mr. Yonuk is a professional and has no reason to be an abettor.

When I'm done with the phone call, I hurry online and place an order for a bundle pack of three spy cameras. Someone is coming in and out of my house. I don't know how, but they're doing it. And the only way to prove it is by catching them in the act.

I crumple the note and throw it into one of the empty cupboards. It may be useful later, but right now, I don't need to keep looking at it. It's obvious someone hates me. Although part of me worries it's James, I get the feeling that it isn't.

This just isn't him.

He's forward and extremely impatient.

I can't see him lingering around Thorn Lake to make my life a living hell. These cameras will catch whoever is coming in here.

Once the order is placed, I rest my palms against my kitchen counter, bow my head, and suck in a painfully deep breath.

I want this to be over.

All of it.

Thorn Lake was supposed to be an escape—a fresh start. Instead, it's turned into a nightmare.

When I finally straighten myself again, I catch a

glimpse of my reflection in the microwave glass. My hair is knotted and straggly, and my eyes are sunken to the point of making me look severely anemic.

What if everyone is right? What if I'm the problem?

I sure look the part.

CHAPTER 55

I expected a little more enthusiasm from Grayson.

"Sure, whatever," he says.

"Sure?" I repeat. "We haven't eaten at a restaurant in . . . I don't know, years. I thought you'd be happy."

Now that the cameras have arrived and my funds are in the bank—two and a half freaking million dollars—I feel that deserves to be celebrated.

We have complete freedom.

Well, almost.

Tonight is about celebrating our financial freedom, but it's also about discussing leaving Thorn Lake. Once this house is sold, we can move wherever we want. Buy something a little more modest and live a comfortable life together. No more threats. No more memories of dead bodies in the basement.

I want to forget about this place and never look back.

For a split second, I think about Wyatt and how I might miss having him around. But then I remember that he isn't who he's been pretending to be. The Wyatt I thought I was getting to know doesn't exist.

"I said sure," Grayson says, attitude fusing with his tone.

When I sit next to him, he sighs and pauses the show he and Lucas are watching.

"What's going on?" I ask.

He stares at me, and I get the sense he doesn't want to talk about it. But then, to my surprise, he heaves. "I was supposed to have plans with Amelia, but her mom grounded her."

What did she do to deserve it? I want to ask.

Instead, I say, "I'm sorry to hear that. I hope she isn't in too much trouble."

"She shouldn't be in any trouble!" he says, his eyes widening passionately. "She didn't do *anything*!"

I'm not sure how to respond to that. I suppose most kids feel as though they don't deserve to be punished. But surely, Amelia did *something* to upset her mother. I can only hope it isn't something that warrants concern.

"How long is she grounded for?" I ask.

"Don't know." He shrugs, and then adds, "Her stup—" But he quickly corrects himself. "Her mom took her phone."

I appreciate the quick correction, as I wouldn't have tolerated that sort of speech coming out of his mouth. He may not understand the reasons behind Amelia's mother's discipline, but he should at least respect that she's her *mother*, and she knows what's best for her.

"Hopefully, this all blows over soon." I rest a hand on his lap. "How about we make the best of this weekend, and maybe you'll get to see her next weekend?"

Another sigh. "I was going to ask her out today."

Wow. He must really like this girl. Grayson has never shown much interest in girls. He's a good-looking kid, but he's always been more interested in sports, games, and music.

This means tonight's discussion isn't going to go very well. He was upset the first time we ran away. I can't even imagine how he'll respond this time around, now that a girl is involved.

Great.

"That's sweet," I tell him. "You must care about this girl."

He looks up at me with big puppy eyes. "I do. A lot."

This is bad.

How am I supposed to tell him I plan to put the house up for sale? He'll freak out. At the end of the day, it's my decision, but I want my kids to be happy. I don't want to put them through another move, register them in another school, and force them to make new friends all over again.

It isn't fair.

If I catch the person responsible for the notes, we won't have to move. If they can be reprimanded—and hopefully, jailed—then I'll know for certain that James isn't the one after us, and I'll be able to actually sleep at night.

As I stare at him, I make the decision to hold off on the conversation. Tonight, we can celebrate, and next week, I'll figure everything out.

***

The Bistro's ambiance lives up to its online reviews. Friendly staff, warm and charming atmosphere, and a level of fanciness I didn't quite expect for a small-town restaurant.

Despite its rustic decor, everything looks brand new. The gray chipped wood looks *intentionally* chipped rather than the product of years of wear.

A young male host with a dimpled smile leads us to a table, where he then hands us off to one of the waiters. The service is so good that it almost makes me uncomfortable. I can't remember the last time I felt this taken care of. It almost feels wrong. Like I don't deserve it.

The waiter, Aaron, starts us off with glasses of cold water and promises to return shortly to take our orders.

I go over the menu, pointing out things I think the kids might enjoy.

"Hey, Lucas, look at this." I tap on the laminated menu with a finger. "Chicken fingers. Your favorite."

He moves his face closer to his menu and licks his lips. I keep hoping he'll say something. Anything. But he doesn't.

I try not to get too disappointed in moments like these.

Dr. Jackson seems hopeful. She keeps reminding me that these things take time. We're talking months. Possibly years. I hope it doesn't take him years to start talking again. I can't even imagine how much of a dent that will put in his academics.

If he doesn't speak, that means he isn't asking for help when it's needed, or clarification when he doesn't understand something.

Grayson leans into his little brother and jokes about cutting up the chicken fingers to shape them into dinosaurs. Lucas responds with a frown, a look that I know translates to, *I'm seven, not four.*

I smile at the two of them, then run my fingers along the varnished tabletop, then the bench. For a split second, all of my gratitude vanishes as I imagine James barging in through the front door, demanding that the host point out our location.

Why do these thoughts keep popping into my head? I'm so sick of them. Everywhere I go, even when things are going well, my mind drifts toward dark thoughts I can't quell. They're completely unexpected, too, and seem to hit in moments of happiness especially.

It's almost as if James has imprinted himself on me. Now, no matter where I go, his ghost haunts me. All of the torment he put me through has left permanent pathways in my brain. I can never relax—at least, not completely. I'm constantly in survival mode.

And although I don't want to admit that I'm paranoid, I can't deny it, either. When the host led us to a table, I specifically requested another—one closer to the emergency exit.

I'm not certain this type of thinking will ever go away.

The young waiter next to me clears his throat. "Were you all ready to order?"

I blink hard, realizing I didn't even take the time to look at the menu. I apologize to the waiter and request additional time.

"Sorry," I tell Lucas and Grayson. "Did you boys pick

what you want?"

They both nod.

I'm about to start scanning the menu again when I hear a car door slam. Through the window next to our table, Carla walks with balled fists and her head bowed. She looks like a mess—her hair is pulled into a mussed bun that sits crookedly on the top of her head, and she's wearing a set of stained pink pajamas that are partially hidden underneath a winter jacket.

What is *she* doing here?

Did she follow me?

Oh, God . . . She must have. And I'm about to receive an earful about me threatening her husband.

CHAPTER 56

Carla nearly jumps out of her boots when I call her name. At first, she looks stunned, but that deer-in-the-headlights expression almost instantly warps to scrutiny.

Why is she looking at me like that?

Isn't she the one who followed me?

I wanted to confront her before she made a scene in front of my kids. I tighten my jacket, and a single snowflake sweeps through the air between us.

"Can I help you?" she says scornfully.

"Carla," I say. "I'm so sorry. About everything. I shouldn't have—"

"What? Threatened to shoot my husband? No, you shouldn't have."

Okay, she's pissed. And she has every right to be.

"I thought you were in trouble," I say. "But I was out of line. I'm sorry."

Her eyes flicker from side to side. "You made him really angry, you know."

Stay out of it, Alice.

But I can't.

"Did he hurt you?" I close the space between us. "Because of me?"

She scratches at her neck, and that's when I see it—a huge bruise that runs down her jawline. "N-no. Well, yes. But it wasn't that bad."

"Not that bad?" I say. I'm furious. It *is* that bad. Any form of violence is *that* bad.

"Look, I'm okay," she says. "I really was sick. And then me being home all the time—"

Got under his skin so badly that he took his anger out on you?

She looks as though she's lost at least ten pounds. Despite the bruise on her face, what's even more frightening is her ashen skin, her sunken eyes, and the way her cheeks seem to cave into her face. If they were any more sunken in, I'd see the shape of her teeth through her skin.

Maybe she's being honest about being sick. Whatever she caught really took its toll.

"You don't deserve this," I say.

She's looking at me as if she wants to slit my throat.

I get it.

It's hard to hear the truth because it makes you feel weak and pathetic for not leaving sooner.

But then, her eyes soften. "I appreciate the concern. I really do."

"If you need a place to stay, Carla—"

"I have kids," she says. "It's not that easy."

"I have kids, too. I get it."

I shouldn't have said that. But I have a sense that Carla is already aware of my past. Not in detail, of course, but she knows I've experienced abuse at the hands of a man.

"You received an inheritance property," she says, a hint of anger returning. "We can't all be so lucky."

She's not wrong. I was literally handed a ticket out of my own life. But that doesn't mean she can't escape, too.

"You and the kids are welcome to move in," I tell her. I'm not sure what's going through my mind. But this woman needs help, and if I do nothing and later find out she's been murdered by her husband, I'll never forgive myself. Worse, children are involved. "You'll be safe in my house. I have a security system in place, and I'm installing cameras inside the house this weekend. Trust me. If he tries anything, he'll be caught red-handed."

For a moment, it looks like she's about to burst into

tears, hug me, and accept my invitation. But out of nowhere, she says, "I don't need your pity, and I don't need your charity. Now, if you'll excuse me."

She brushes past me and beelines it for the pharmacy across from the Bistro.

So she wasn't following you. This was all a coincidence.

Unless, of course, that's what she *wants* me to believe. Maybe my act of kindness threw her off guard before she could lash out at me.

When I return inside the restaurant, Grayson watches me sit down. "Who was that?"

"Lucas's teacher," I tell him. "She's been sick. I just wanted to check in on her and say hi."

Lucas's big blue eyes search the parking lot. I can tell he misses her. I force a smile and put on my best happy face for the rest of the evening, even though I can't shake this awful feeling in the pit of my stomach.

I'm still thinking about Carla's reaction to my words when I go to bed. As she stood there, silent, I thought I had gotten through to her. That if she realized she wasn't alone, she'd accept a helping hand. She'd accept my offer for her and her children to move in with me.

I'm about to turn over on my pillow when my phone lights up the ceiling above me.

A text message.

From Carla.

I'm afraid to open it. What if she tells me to stay away from her? To never speak to her again?

To my surprise, her words are neither angry nor defensive.

> *Sorry about earlier. Going through a lot right now. Thank you for caring. I'll think about your offer <3*

Maybe I am getting through to her, after all.

CHAPTER 57

Weeks go by, and although I should be relieved that Carla is back to her position at school, I'm not. Despite her apologetic text the night of our discussion in the parking lot, we haven't spoken since.

What am I supposed to say?

Checking in. Wondering if you thought about my offer?

If she wants to accept my help, she will.

I can't chase after someone who isn't willing to help themselves.

I only hope this doesn't impact Lucas in any way. That she doesn't treat him any differently because of everything that's happened. But when he comes home from school every day, he seems fine. And Dr. Jackson says she's making even more progress. That he's started talking a little bit. A word here and there. I'm both relieved and hurt. I had hoped he would start talking to me. I'm his mother. Shouldn't he feel safest with me?

You haven't exactly been present.

How can I be?

I have yet to find the person responsible for leaving the notes. The strange part is that since I've installed the cameras, nothing has happened. No odd sounds at night. No cryptic notes hiding around the house. Although it's probably a coincidence. I expect something to happen any day now.

Previous notes were left approximately one week apart. It's only a matter of time before my tormentor strikes again.

Wyatt hasn't spoken to me, either.

Could he be behind the notes? Maybe he sensed I was on to him and decided to back off for a while.

Thursday night unfolds as it does every other week—a visit to Dr. Jackson's office, followed by a takeout supper at home. I've decided to make it a weekly treat to praise Lucas for his efforts in therapy.

After supper, I even manage to write another blog post—one about being willing to accept help when help is needed. I suppose I have Carla to thank for that idea.

I put Lucas to bed and kiss Grayson goodnight on the forehead, even though I now have to stand on my tippy-toes to do it. "Don't stay up past ten."

"I won't," he says, half-distracted by messages coming in through his phone. He's been on that thing all evening. It's obvious something is going on with his love interest.

I lie down in bed and try to meditate. It's a new bedtime routine of mine. When I actually manage to succeed, and there aren't a thousand thoughts cycling through my mind, it helps me sleep.

But it's a lot of work.

My phone suddenly rings and vibrates on my bedside table. The sound makes me jump. I reach for it, one eye half-open and the other squeezed shut.

What time is it?

When did I fall asleep?

And why is Wyatt calling? I haven't heard from him in days.

I answer, my voice gruff. "H-hello?"

"Emma. Get up. Now."

I'm wide awake now, a prickling sensation spreading throughout my body.

"Wh-what? What is it? What's wrong?"

"Get your gun, and get up. He's coming. He's coming up your driveway right now."

What? Who?

I jump out of bed and peer through my bedroom window.

A dark figure storms up my driveway, his long arms swinging on either side of him. He's wearing a ball cap, and his fists are balled so tightly that they look abnormally small.

My whole body starts quivering.

I'd know that walk anywhere.

It's James.

He found me, and he's coming to kill me.

CHAPTER 58

I can't see straight.

Everything seems surreal, like a dream. A nightmare. Is it? This could all be a delusion. Because I refuse to believe that I'm standing in front of my door, waiting for James to break into my house.

My lights are off.

He won't see me.

I'll shoot him, and this will all be over. But with how badly I'm shuddering, I'll probably miss. And then he'll grab me, and I'll be dead. My children will be motherless.

The police are on their way.

I still don't know how Wyatt knew to warn me, but that doesn't matter right now. All that matters is that I protect myself and my boys.

An explosive crack almost makes me pull the trigger.

Through the glass door, James is swinging something hard. A bat? A crowbar?

A deep crack splinters across the glass door. On his second hit, the glass shatters, and in comes a black-gloved hand. He sweeps from side to side, little shards of glass breaking away from the window frame, then sticks his whole arm in and unlocks the deadbolt.

Shoot him!

I'm so terrified that I'm frozen in place. In all my fantasies about standing up to James, this is never how it played out; I always imagined myself telling him he was a monster and then shooting him without hesitation.

But deep down, I don't have it in me to kill someone.

Even a person like James. If I wait long enough—hold him back—the police will arrive in time to arrest him. If I kill him, I could end up behind bars, and my kids will be sent into the foster system.

This isn't the way.

He grunts, and I'm trembling so badly that the barrel of my gun is now rapidly jumping up and down.

The door suddenly blasts open, bringing along with it a cold winter breeze that sinks into my bones. It makes my teeth clatter even more.

At the same time, a loud siren wails throughout my house, and the security hub starts flashing red.

His heavy boots stomp into the house, and something swooshes through the air.

Crack.

The touchscreen display goes black, and the siren stops. But there's another siren going off in the distance.

The back door.

James reaches for a light and flicks it on. The moment the house lights up, he stands quietly, taking everything in. What is that? Hatred? Envy? If I'm right, and his business hasn't taken off like he's been talking about for ages, then this is the kind of house he's always dreamed about owning.

The moment he sees me standing near the staircase with my wavering gun, his eyes bulge out in surprise.

He wasn't expecting this.

He'd planned on killing me in my sleep like the coward that he is.

I glance at the crowbar in his gloved fist. It's not like he needs a weapon to hurt me. His hands are plenty capable of that.

"Alice," he says, his tone tinged with amusement.

Why is he slowly walking toward me?

I stare at those dark eyes of his, feeling the size of a microbe.

"You aren't going to shoot me," he says.

I want to threaten him to stay back—tell him that if he

moves one more step, I'll shoot him in the heart. But I can't even talk.

There's so much adrenaline flowing through me that although I see him clearly, it doesn't feel real. Blood sloshes in my ears, causing his voice to sound like it's coming from behind a waterfall.

"Alice, honey, put the gun down."

I blink hard, and he takes another step.

The high-pitched alarm is still yelping throughout the house, but it's background noise at this point.

Why haven't the police arrived yet? Why is it taking so long? I want to yell at him to back off, but I don't even have the strength to do that. All of the anger I've felt these last couple of months—the rage brought on by self-reflection and the realization that I didn't deserve what he put me through—seems to dissipate in his presence.

I'm right back to being at his mercy.

Helpless.

Afraid.

He doesn't even look the way I remember, even though his physical appearance hasn't changed. I've spent so much time reliving everything he put me through that his memory somehow warped him into a literal monster.

But he's very much human.

"You aren't a killer, Alice. Put the gun down. I only came here to talk."

To talk? That explains the broken glass and your breaking into my house.

"I've changed," he says.

His crowbar says otherwise.

"Please, baby," he says. "I'm sorry about all of this." He drops his crowbar to the floor when he realizes I'm staring at it.

Clang.

"I acted out of anger," he says. "But seeing you now, I realize what a piece of shit I am." He bows his head and pinches the bridge of his nose. "I'll pay for the damage. I'm so sorry, Alice. I'm sorry."

He drops to his knees and cries into his palms.

Does he expect me to feel sorry for him?

To forgive him?

When I don't budge, he looks up at me through a crack in his fingers, and his demeanor darkens instantly.

"You have no fucking heart. You know that? I'm crying my eyes out, and you're aiming that gun at me. What the fuck is wrong with you?"

I steady my grip.

He gets up slowly, latching onto the kitchen island for support.

"I thought you loved me," he says. "I love you, with all my heart, and all I want is to give our family another chance. And here you are, threatening to kill me."

"I'm not threatening anything," I tell him, my own voice surprising me. "I'm protecting myself. From you. You abusive piece of shit."

His jaw muscles bulge, and a look of pure evil casts shadows across his features.

Without warning, he slaps a hand on the island counter, and I flinch so hard I almost fire a shot.

"You ungrateful bitch! After everything I've done. Carrying you financially. Taking care of you despite all your mental problems—"

"I don't have mental problems!" I snap back. "You do!" I jab my gun in the air at him. "You made me out to be some paranoid psychopath, when in reality, you're the psycho! You made me feel crazy for so many years. All you do is play games. But it's over, James. Do you hear me? It's over!"

He doesn't move, his hand still flat on the island. Instead, he watches me, then glances at the gun. One second, he's standing still, and the next, one of the stools topples over and he's jumping right at me.

CHAPTER 59

BEFORE: JAMES

I scrub the grime off my shiny Lexus wheels. With how much I paid for this thing, you'd think the car would be self-cleaning.

Fake it till you make it, baby.

I'll pay back that business loan. I know I will. Especially with how well things are going. I mean, it's only been a month with the new startup, but I have a good feeling about this one.

I think it's *the one.*

When I get off my knees and stand, I spot a woman looking my way. I smile at her, wondering what she looks like without that skirt of hers.

Probably even better on my bed.

I lick my lips, and she pulls a lock of hair behind her ear.

Yeah, you play shy, you little bitch. I bet you're real loud in bed.

I'm not an idiot. Ever since I got this car, women have been looking at me differently. Makes me realize how greedy women are. All they want is my money.

Which is why Alice left me. I know it.

Greedy cunt.

I wasn't making money fast enough for her, so she wanted to hook up with someone else.

I push the thought of her away. Every time I think about her, I want to smash a hole in the wall. It's one thing that she ran off, but to take my boys, and to fight for full custody?

She might think she's safe, wherever she is, but I'm still

looking. Every day, I'm looking. And I will find her.

Don't think about that whore. You have a woman flirting with you right now. Focus on getting her back to your house.

I draw my shoulders back, remembering who I am.

James Fucking Remington.

Soon-to-be CEO of a multimillion-dollar corporation.

I'm about to walk over to the woman and introduce myself when I get a notification on my phone.

Ding.

I get emails all the time from my new business partner, but this sound was different. Something I didn't recognize.

I fish my phone out of my pocket and stare at the screen.

Messenger? I thought I deleted that app ages ago. I don't even use it.

I stare at my phone in my palm.

Is this real?

The message across the screen has my heart pumping at what seems to be three hundred beats per minute.

The sender's name is obviously from some fake account: Anonymous9991.

But I don't care who the message is from.

What has my pulse throbbing in my neck is the message underneath:

> *Do you know this woman?*

Then there's an image, but I can't see it until I open the message. With trembling hands, I press on the notification to open the message.

Across the car wash lot, the woman who was watching me scoffs and walks away, her heels ticking.

Not that I care.

This is way more important.

I blink hard.

Am I imagining things?

For the last eight months, I've been trying to track her

down. I've been searching for her name on Facebook, hoping someone might have slipped up and tagged her in a picture.

But there's been nothing.

Absolute silence.

Until today.

That's Alice all right.

She looks like she's in a rush, walking with her head down and a baseball cap fitted snugly over her long, brown hair.

Next to her are Grayson and Lucas.

They both look taller now . . . and Grayson looks like he's aged several years. It's only been eight months. I squeeze my phone but immediately loosen my grip when I hear a faint *crack*.

"You fucking bitch," I mutter at my phone.

I'm shaking so badly that I can barely keep my thumbs over the letters.

> *Yes. I do. Where is she?*

No, that's too obvious. Whoever this person is, they can't know I'm desperate to find Alice. I need to act neutral.

I erase everything except for *Yes*.

Within seconds, three little dots start to trickle and throb on the screen.

> *1472 Thorn Lake Drive, Thorn Lake, Maine, USA*

It takes everything in me not to roar at the highest decibel. I want to dance like a maniac while breaking something.

I found you, you bitch . . . I fucking found you.

CHAPTER 60

The heavy weight of his body slams into me, rocking my head violently.

I crash into the staircase behind me, and at the same time, an ear-splitting *bang* fills the air. It's so loud that I think my house blew up from underneath me. A high-pitched ringing echoes in my ear as I blink hard, trying to understand what happened.

My elbows ache from the fall.

I push myself off the stairs, gun still in hand.

That's when I see it.

There's blood everywhere.

All over my hands, my wrists, and on my shirt.

I stare at James's still body on my dining room floor.

Is he . . . *dead*?

He groans, and I flinch. Eyes fluttering, he rolls onto his back and reaches for the gunshot wound in his abdomen. He raises his hand and inspects the blood, seemingly in disbelief.

Did he think I wouldn't shoot?

Wouldn't protect myself?

I walk toward him, my legs barely cooperating. I stand above him, though not close enough for him to grab one of my legs.

"A-Alice," he says, looking up at me.

I raise my gun, the muzzle aimed at his chest. My hands aren't shaking anymore. They're steadier than they've ever been.

He stares at me pleadingly with one trembling hand

sticking straight out. Of course he doesn't want to die. Nobody does. But he came after me. This is my home, and I have every right to defend myself.

You've already defended yourself. The cops can take it from here.

"A-Alice," he repeats, raising his head off the floor. "You don't have to—"

"You're wrong," I say. "I *do* have to. Because you'll never stop."

"Alice, please—"

"And my name isn't Alice anymore. It's Emma."

Bang.

His head falls back with a thud, though in comparison to the gunshot in the house, it sounds like a marble landing on a pillow.

He gazes vacantly at the ceiling, lips slightly parted.

Slowly, a pool of dark red expands underneath him.

The reality of my situation suddenly hits me.

My legs give out, and I drop to my knees. Everything seems fuzzy . . . unreal. I didn't *want* this. But at the same time, I did.

I suck in a quivering breath, feeling as though my entire house is closing in on me.

"Mom?" I hear from up the staircase.

I want to tell Grayson to go back to his room, but I can't speak. I peer over at James's dead body. Although I should be mortified by everything that has happened . . . by what I did . . . I'm not.

Strangely, I feel at peace.

"Mom?" His voice quavers.

A red and blue light sweeps throughout the kitchen, accompanied by the sound of car doors closing. Rapid footsteps draw in closer and closer until I glance up to see Wyatt and Derek bursting in with their guns in the air.

The moment Wyatt sees me, he raises a closed fist, ordering Derek to hold or stand down.

"Is he—" Wyatt starts.

"The kids . . . " I tell him. "I— I don't want—"

Derek nods and hurries up the staircase. "Hey, bud. Why don't you come with me for a second?"

Derek's heavy boots thud against the upstairs floor as he leads Grayson back into his room.

Wyatt hurries to me. "Emma, I'm so sorry."

I can't say anything. All I can do is look at James's ashen face. He's dead. Gone. He'll never hurt me again.

"Are you all right?" He reaches for my shoulder, but I pull away. It takes everything in me not to shove him away. This is probably his fault.

"How did you know?" I say, looking up at him.

"It's a long story," he says. "I'll explain everything. Paramedics are on their way."

"Am I going to jail now?" I ask.

His eyes shift to the gun in my hand.

"No," he says.

I'm taken aback by his answer.

"It was self-defense," he says. "I'll attest to that. And so will Derek."

Why is he doing this? I thought he was involved. Why would he help me?

With a look of sorrow, he lowers himself to one knee.

"I should have told you sooner," he says. "But I know who you are."

I'm too exhausted from all the adrenaline to react.

"You were being secretive, and with everything that started happening, well, I ran your name in the system to see if you had any past encounters with the law. Since we have an open investigation, I technically had every right to do this. I should have talked to you first. But then I asked you if you were safe, or if you were running from someone, and when you told me you were fine, I knew you were lying. It only made me want to dig deeper. So I made a few calls, and, well, I found your name change record.

I hold back a gasp. "That was supposed to be sealed by the courts."

He purses his lips. "That doesn't hide your information from law enforcement."

"But the cameras. You lied—"

"About Chief Madden approving the costs," he says. "Yeah, I did. I'm sorry. It was unprofessional of me to do that, but I knew you were low on funds, and I wanted you to feel safe. I wanted to protect you."

He reaches for my hand, but I pull away.

"Why?" I say. "You barely know me."

He nods like he agrees. "You're right. But there's something about you. I care about you. And Lucas. And Grayson."

"You're telling me you went out of your way to protect me because you *like* me?"

I'm not buying it.

It's one thing to have a crush on someone and want the best for them, but this was extreme. He paid hundreds of dollars for my security system.

"Yeah," he says. "Well, and—" He pauses, biting his lower lip.

There's a deep sadness in his eyes. Trauma. But I don't want to press him. Whatever happened scarred him.

He sighs. "My sister was beaten to a pulp by the man who was supposed to love her. She ran away, and he hunted her down. I didn't see the signs back then. I was too young. But looking back, I *should* have seen what was happening. And with you, well . . . I saw the signs, Emma. They were all there. I could tell you were running away from someone, and I didn't want history repeating itself."

I feel terrible. Why didn't he tell me this sooner?

"Is she—" I start.

"She's alive," he says. "She was in a coma for four months. We almost lost her, but she made it. She spent years in physical rehabilitation to regain function of her right arm, and it still doesn't work the way it used to."

He looks devastated. Even though it isn't his fault, there's no doubt he wishes he could have done something to prevent his sister's assault.

"I'm so sorry I lied to you," he says. "I wanted to help without bringing up your past and causing you to relive the trauma. I hoped he wouldn't find you, but to be safe, I kept my phone on at all times and the cameras set to motion alert."

He pauses and rubs his hands over his face.

"I know I was out of line. I'm so sorry, Emma."

"Why do you keep calling me that?" I ask. "If you know my real name is Alice?"

Our eyes lock.

"I was trying to be respectful of your name change. Do you want me to call you Alice?"

No, I don't.

I don't feel like Alice right now. I don't even know who I am anymore.

But before I can answer, more vehicles pull into the driveway. Wyatt gets up, goes to speak with someone, and returns.

He offers me a hand. "The paramedics want to have a look at you."

I turn to look at James's dead body. "What about—"

"We can't do anything about him. Unfortunately, this place is now a crime scene. I had to call in a medical examiner. He'll deal with the body."

"But I don't want my boys—"

Wyatt rests a hand on my shoulder. "Don't worry. Derek will get them out without them seeing a thing. We've done this before."

I nod and step out onto the front porch, blinding red and white lights spinning across my house and lawn.

I didn't expect things to end like this. With James lying dead in my kitchen. I suck in a deep breath, the cold air soothing my lungs.

Maybe this is exactly how everything was supposed to end.

CHAPTER 61

ONE WEEK LATER

I walk into our house, with Lucas and Grayson standing close behind me. It feels different. Almost as if this place is no longer our home.

The smell is completely different, too.

It isn't our smell.

This makes sense, given that after James's body was removed, I hired professional cleaning services to clean the house from top to bottom.

A hint of lemon and bleach lingers in the air.

"Do we have to stay here?" Grayson asks.

Although he didn't see James on the floor—Derek made sure of that with blindfolds—he knows what happened. This place will forever be where his mother killed his father.

"Only for a little while," I say. "Unless you want to keep living at the motel."

Lucas makes a sour face.

"I didn't think so," I say. I hesitate, not wanting to set foot inside just yet. "There's a real estate agent coming on Wednesday."

"Are we leaving Thorn Lake?" Grayson asks. "Moving into a different house?"

I haven't decided yet.

Although part of me wants to stay here now that we're safe, I can't help but wonder whether a fresh start would be ideal. After all, this town is small—everyone talks. Which means no one will ever look at me the same. All week, I've received odd gazes. Some sympathetic, others, disturbed.

Those who understand domestic abuse know I did what I had to do. Others, however, now view me as a killer.

Sighing, I step inside the house. "Let's cross that bridge when we get there."

Lucas and Grayson walk in slowly behind me.

Thankfully, neither one of them saw where James died. But I did. And I can't keep my eyes off the tiles. The cleaners did a wonderful job. There doesn't appear to be a single bloodstain soaked into the grout. No hint of a dead body having ever been here.

Suddenly, I picture James that night storming into the house with his heavy boots, and the pleading look on his face before it hardened into a venomous scowl.

"Mom?" Grayson asks.

I flinch, and an involuntary squeal escapes me. He reaches for me, his hand warm yet clammy on my arm.

"Are you okay?" he asks.

I look at him, and for the first time, I don't see James. He may look like him, but Grayson is nothing like his father. He has a huge heart. And despite the teenage attitude that surfaces from time to time, he's a good kid.

I wrap my arm around him and lean in for a hug. My head falls on his shoulder. I can't believe how much he's grown in the last six months. Last year, he was shorter than me.

"I will be," I say. "How are you doing? You okay?"

He shrugs. "I will be."

"And you, my little man?" I ask Lucas.

Instead of answering, he throws his arms around my waist, and the three of us stand there, hugging each other.

I close my eyes, appreciating the warmth of my children.

"We're going to be okay," I tell them.

Grayson sniffles, and I cup his neck, pulling him into a tighter hug. Then, Lucas starts to cry, and the next thing

I know, we're all on the floor, sobbing, holding onto each other.

We're free.

Finally free.

CHAPTER 62

"Emma," Wyatt says with a sweet smile on his face. He gets up from his chair like a gentleman.

It's nice to see him dressed like a normal guy for a change—no police uniform, no bulletproof vest. He's wearing a button-up flannel shirt, and next to his coffee and bagel is a black winter hat and shiny leather gloves.

"Can I get you anything?" he asks.

A plume of steam rises from the surface of his light-brown coffee. His bagel is perfectly toasted and slathered in rich cream cheese.

"I'll have what you're having," I say.

He waves at the woman behind the counter of Beans & Stuff and points at his food. She seems to understand him; she nods and starts moving around quickly.

"Please, have a seat," he says.

I sit across from him.

I still can't believe I agreed to have coffee with him. I expected to become a hermit after killing someone, but instead, all I want to do is move on. I'm not ready for a relationship, but I'm ready to start trying. To at least socialize and get back out into the world. Especially now that I know I can be myself without the risk of James looming over me.

He'll never hurt me again.

I sit down, and we talk about trivial things such as winter approaching, our plans for Christmas, and the unique decor in Beans & Stuff, which is an odd blend of vibrant eccentric paintings and earth-tone furniture.

"Cute place," I say.

He sips his coffee, and a bit of creamy brown sticks to his growing facial hair. The beard looks good on him.

The server brings me my coffee and bagel, and after a bite and a whole conversation about how they make the best bagels in town, Wyatt's gaze darkens. He taps his fingers several times on the table and says, "I wanted to apologize again for everything."

"Wyatt, you don't have to—"

"No, I do," he says. "I've had feelings for you since the day I met you. But that didn't make it right for me to do things behind your back, even if I thought I was protecting you."

I reach for his hand, and we lock eyes. "We can't change the past. Honestly, I want to forget about it all and start fresh."

When I realize I've been holding his hand for almost a minute, I pull away, feeling uncomfortable.

His cheeks look slightly pink.

"Thank you for everything you did," I say. "You probably saved our lives."

The alarm might have woken me up, but Wyatt's phone call ensured I was ready with my gun.

"I'm just glad you're okay," he says.

"I'm okay." I take a sip of my coffee, then set it down. "Can I ask you something?"

"Anything."

"Are we sure James was the one behind the notes?"

Wyatt ponders this for a moment. "Nothing is certain, but it adds up. I did some digging around town, and he had about a month's worth of records at the Lambert Motel. Which means he's been in town since a little after you moved here."

It makes me sick to think that James was watching me this whole time.

"But what about the security system?" I say. "How would he get around that? Get inside my house?"

Wyatt scratches at his short beard, thinking this over.

"I've been trying to figure that one out. But you told me he's always been into tech, right?"

I nod.

"I'm thinking he found a way to hack into it. It happens all the time. As for the cameras, well—if he was watching you the way I think he was, then he knew about the cameras. He would have approached from the sides of the house and entered through a window."

As ludicrous as that sounds, I wouldn't put it past James. He was an intelligent man. But what doesn't make sense to me is why he would sneak into my house for weeks, only to then storm up my driveway and break a window to get in.

Why not sneak in as he did all the times before?

"What is it?" Wyatt asks. "You look like you're thinking."

"I am," I say. I explain to him what I'm struggling with, and he sits back in his chair.

With a sigh, he says, "Humans are complex. Honestly, there's no telling what was going through his mind that night. He could have been drinking, and something inside of him snapped. A memory, a trigger—something. And he decided to stop playing games and to come finish things once and for all."

I shudder at the thought.

Wyatt is right.

I'll never know what was going through James's mind. But does it matter? As long as we're safe. And the notes have stopped, which only further validates the theory of James being behind it all.

I just—" Wyatt says, then goes quiet and gazes out through the frosted window next to us. "I shouldn't have doubted you. For a while, I thought you were starting to imagine things. You know, from your past trauma. The late-night police calls, and then no sign of breaking and entering."

He looks ashamed.

But it isn't his fault. Anyone in his position would have thought the same thing.

I force a smile. "It's the past. And this is what James does . . . *did*. He was good at making people feel crazy."

My words don't seem to do much to comfort him.

"Can I ask you something else?" I say.

"Of course."

"Why are you single?"

I don't mean for it to be so direct or rude. I'm about to apologize and rephrase my question when he laughs, revealing a beautiful set of white teeth. His laugh is adorable, too.

"That's a fair question. I'm thirty-five and haven't settled down." He pauses. "I was actually married for five years, and she cheated on me with my best friend."

"Oh, Wyatt, I'm sorry—"

He peels a hand away from his coffee mug. "No, no, it's okay. It's what pushed me to get myself a real job. And then everything that happened with my sister . . . Well, I joined the police force. I was in Chicago at the time, so I received a lot of domestic calls." He pauses, likely reliving those days. "After a while, it gets to you, you know? As much as I loved police work, I was tired of seeing how awful human beings can be to each other. The horrendous things people can do. So I moved here. I saw a picture of a house for sale online and decided I wanted a fresh start away from my ex, my supposed best friend—everyone."

"Any family?" I ask. "Parents?"

"A mom," he says. "Never met my dad, but I heard he was a real piece of work. My sister remembers him, unfortunately."

"I'm sorry," I say. "And I didn't mean to pry. I just . . . I noticed many women seem fond of you, yet you have no dating history in Thorn Lake."

There's that laugh again.

"Wasn't ready. I loved my wife, more than anything. A betrayal like that cuts deep, you know?"

I part my lips, but he continues, "And then you came along, and I don't know. For the first time, I wanted to get to know someone. I wanted to stop feeling sorry for myself, and well, I guess trying to protect you made me forget about my past. It gave me a purpose again. Reminded me of why I became a cop in the first place."

"Well," I say. "I'm glad you did."

A lopsided smile appears on his face. "Yeah, me too."

CHAPTER 63

ANONYMOUS

Alice Remington should have paid closer attention to the notes I left around her house. But no—instead, she decided to ignore them.

What did she think would happen?

If a dog growls at you long enough and you keep ignoring the warnings, it'll bite.

I tried to be nice.

I tried to scare her off, but she's too stubborn. No wonder her husband beat her.

And the longer she stuck around, the more I realized that I didn't only want her out of Thorn Lake, I wanted her out of this world. If she never existed—if she was *dead*—my life would be completely different right now.

I'd be happy.

Truly happy.

I stare at her fancy house through her cedar shrubs. Only last week, I stood here, watching. The funny part is that I almost made my move then but decided against it. I can't have the life I deserve if I'm behind bars.

So I got her ex to do my dirty work for me.

Finding him wasn't all that hard.

When you have connections, information can be easy to find. And as soon as I discovered her real name, well . . . finding the husband wasn't all that difficult.

But now he's dead.

Idiot.

I suppose that's on him, though. He was so fueled with rage over finding her after all this time that he didn't even bother to stake out the house, watch for patterns, learn her routine.

Nope.

That asshole broke through the front door in the middle of the night and went for the kill.

I'm not sure what was going through that thick skull of his when the alarm went off. Why didn't he run? Try to come back on a different night?

What am I saying?

I know why.

He was ready to kill her, the kids, and then himself. He didn't care about the alarm. I'm surprised Alice bought into him camping out at the Lambert Motel.

A few hundred bucks can get just about anyone to lie. That kid was what—nineteen, twenty years old? All I had to do was ask for the motel's logbook and tell him to look the other way. He didn't care. It was free money for him. Probably weed money. The guy reeked of it.

So now, Alice thinks she's safe inside that big house of hers.

She killed her ex-husband, for crying out loud. Why does she get to roam around freely while he's buried in the ground? Shouldn't she be rotting behind bars?

No, instead, pretty little Alice wins again.

She always wins.

But not this time.

I grit my teeth, watching her eldest son through the back window. I never liked that kid. He walks around the sofa, reaches for the remote like he does every night, and presses the power button.

Their oversized TV goes black, causing the whole room to darken.

Bedtime for the kiddos.

Emma—I mean, Alice. Damn, that habit is hard to break. I can't believe she had everyone fooled for so long.

Not that it matters anymore.

By morning, justice will be served.

I spot the shadow of her figure moving around from

window to window. She's getting the kids to bed and making sure the security system is active.

But I'm not an idiot like her ex; I won't be tripping off the alarm. I know how to get past it.

I tug at my jacket, trying to keep the cool winter air out. It might be cold now, but soon, I'll be the one living in that big, warm house.

Because it's mine, after all.

At least it will be—after I kill Alice Remington.

CHAPTER 64

Every time I fall asleep, I jolt awake, kicking violently at an invisible enemy in my room.

I hate this.

Ever since James broke into my house, I've struggled between not being able to fall asleep and night terrors that wake me in a cold sweat.

I've debated talking to Dr. Jackson over a session or two before we sell the house. It can't hurt, right?

I tap my phone's black screen, and it awakens, illuminating my room.

It's 1:03 a.m.

Have I even slept?

I'm about to roll onto my back when my bedroom door creaks open. A few weeks ago, I might have jumped three feet high at the sight of this. But now I know it's either Lucas or Grayson. They've been struggling to sleep, too.

It opens wider, and in comes a figure with rounded shoulders and disarranged hair.

My heart almost climbs out of my throat.

It isn't Lucas or Grayson.

Who the hell is sneaking into my room? And why?

I'm frozen in place, watching the figure's slow movements. The intruder bends their knees, the upper half of their body swaying from side to side.

This person is looking right at me, almost as if trying to confirm that I'm me, and not one of my sons or someone else. I snap my eyes shut, peering through the cracks of my eyelids the way I used to do when my biological dad got angry and I wanted to pretend I was sleeping.

Despite the fuzziness caused by my eyelashes, a glint reflects off what looks to be one of my kitchen knives.

Oh my God.

My heart pounds so hard it's a wonder it doesn't cause my blanket to jounce.

I don't have my gun, either. It was taken after I shot James—something about it being part of the crime scene and Wyatt needing to confiscate it for the investigation. He promised he'd return it as soon as possible, but I have yet to receive it.

Which means I'm defenseless.

The figure approaches one slow step at a time.

Whoever they are, they think I'm asleep, and they're trying to sneak up on me. My mom always taught me that a woman's power is in her legs, and that always stuck with me.

If this intruder is a man, I don't stand a chance against him physically. Not unless I give one hell of a kick.

"Stupid bitch," the figure mumbles.

The voice is gravelly, and it's difficult to make out whether it belongs to a man or a woman. Not that it matters. Because seconds later, they raise the knife over their head, prepared to strike down.

At that exact instant, I raise my knees and kick out as hard as I can, smashing my heels right into the intruder's stomach.

A deep *oomph* escapes their lungs—the sound someone might make while vomiting. The hit was a success, and they go flying back farther than I expected, landing against the wall.

Something cracks—either my dresser or the wood of my door—and the knife falls to the floor.

Clank.

I pounce out of bed and run straight for the light. If I'm about to fight for my life, I need to see who I'm up against.

The second my room lights up, I can't believe my eyes.

"Carla?" I blurt.

CHAPTER 65

Carla McKenzie curls over, clutching onto her stomach. I may have broken a rib, or two, or more, but I don't care.

What the hell is she doing in my house?

I locate the knife next to my bed and snatch it up, my entire body shaking uncontrollably.

"You . . . you stupid bitch," she repeats, her hateful gaze rolling up at me.

She looks sick. Beyond sick, even, with her pallid face and rough, thinning hair. Even her eyes appear to have lost their blue.

"What the hell is this?" I say.

I point my knife at her. I'm more shocked than angry because I don't understand. Why would she want to hurt me? Before she can answer, I call the police. In my other clammy hand, I hold on tightly to the knife, its tip aimed at Carla. Within five seconds, I blurt out my address and tell the 911 operator to send the police due to an intruder.

Carla watches me carefully as I place my phone down on the end of my bed.

"You took everything . . . " she says, fighting to breathe, "everything from me."

"What are you *talking* about?" I say.

I should be yelling or threatening to kill her after she came at me with a knife like that, but I don't have any anger in me. I want answers.

"This house," she says, glowering at me with so much animosity I'm afraid she might get up and attempt a second strike. "It was supposed to be mine."

"This house? I don't understand. Are you related to my uncle?"

She clutches her abdomen and seals her eyes shut, little wrinkles forming above her cheeks. "What? No . . . You idiot. We were having an affair."

The knife slips from my grip, but I latch my fingers around it just in time.

"What?" I blurt. "You and my uncle? Isn't he, like, forty years older—"

"Age doesn't matter!" she spits. "He promised me everything. And somehow, you were the one on the will."

"I don't get it," I say. "He was a recluse. How would you even have met him?"

She scoffs and throws her head back into the wall behind her. "My God, Emma. Do I have to explain everything to you?"

"Kind of, yeah," I say. "You came in here trying to kill me."

"Well, maybe if you'd listened to my notes, I wouldn't have had to!"

"*You* wrote those?"

Okay. Now I'm angry. I take a step toward her, the knife feeling awfully heavy in my fist right now.

"Yeah," she says. "I was trying to be nice. Scare you off a bit. But you just wouldn't leave."

She claws her fingernails into my hardwood floor and bares her teeth at me.

"You're delusional," I say. "Even if you were having an affair with my uncle—I was the one in the will. Did you really think me leaving and selling the house would entitle *you* to it?"

"It was supposed to be mine!" Her voice comes out shrill, and with how psychotic she looks right now, I'm surprised she isn't trying to rip out her own hair. "Who do you think took care of the house after he died?"

It did smell awfully good when I first moved in—*too good*, for a house that had been vacant for several months. There wasn't a speck of dust anywhere, either.

"I tried to forgive you," she says, heaving. "But then your boy had to go and take my little girl from me, too."

What the hell is she talking about now?

"Oh, don't pretend you don't know," she says. "Grayson can't keep his hands off Amelia. It's only a matter of time before he takes her virginity, too! My sweet little girl. Your son should be keeping his filthy hands off her!"

Amelia is her *daughter*?

It all makes sense now. Grayson said some kid at school accused Amelia's mom of being a pill popper. I would never have imagined that her mother was Carla. I mean, she's an elementary school teacher. Don't they vet their teachers before hiring them? Besides, Grayson said the pill-popping accusations came on because of a bout of depression.

What I'm looking at right now isn't depression.

It's psychosis.

And then seeing Carla at Dr. Jackson's . . . she looked caught off guard when I spoke to her. Like she was hiding something. She said she was there to book an appointment for her daughter. But now I get it. It was for her, and likely for a prescription. Because a while after that, I ran into her on her way to the pharmacy.

Her husband outright told me she was sick. I didn't believe him. I thought he was gaslighting her. But now I see it.

Carla is deeply ill.

"I thought we were the same," I say. "I thought—"

"That my husband beats me?" She scoffs. "Please, Pete is harmless. I mean, he's a grump, and a pain in my ass, but he'd never put his hands on me. I'd kill him if he ever tried."

"But the bruise—" I start. "And the marks on your arms."

Her eyes go dark for a moment. Maybe I crossed a line by bringing up her scars. But then, she forces a huge smile and wiggles a finger at the fading speckles of purple and yellow on her face. "Shouldn't mix booze with medication."

"You're telling me you fell?" I say, my eyelids flat. It seems too easy to be true.

"Maybe if my dumbass husband picked up after himself, I wouldn't have tripped on his toolbox!" she shouts.

Her anger is very real, which tells me she isn't lying.

I can't believe what I'm hearing. This whole time, I thought her husband was beating her. I'm about to ask her about the scars on her wrist when she says, "Pete didn't do these." She stares at them, lost in thought. I imagine she's reliving the day she received them. "My mom had more mental illnesses than she could count and refused to get help."

I'm not sure whether to apologize or remain quiet. But now I understand why Carla turned out the way she did. Her mother probably put her through years of torment.

"You know, everything was fine before you came here," she says, hatred glimmering in her eyes. "I was going to get Victor's house—"

"You were never going to get his house!" I snap back.

She looks at me as if I spat in her face, then slams a fist against the floor. "He told me he would give me everything!"

"Well, he didn't!" I shout back. "Did he?"

And then I remember something—everyone in town liked to talk about how eerie my uncle was. Even the pizza boy tried to peer inside, wanting a glimpse into the house of a disturbed man. He was accused of all sorts of horrendous things.

"Did you make those accusations against my uncle?" I ask. "Did you leave those notes around town?"

A malevolent smile pulls at the corners of her lips. "Of course I did. The bastard deserved it."

"I thought you loved him," I say.

She scoffs. "I never said that. I said we were having an affair. I picked up a few shifts with ZoomShop and started delivering groceries for him. He was old—like, gross, old. Which meant he'd die soon. All I had to do was get him to fall for me. And you know what? I did nothing wrong. The man was disturbed. He spent some nights sleeping in that godawful basement of his because he couldn't stand the sound of a car driving by."

"But he didn't skin rabbits or hurt anyone," I say.

"Course not," she says. "He was too soft for that. But I started leaving little romantic notes in his grocery bags, and eventually, he opened the door for me. The sex was okay. I mean, a bit weird, if you ask me. But I put in over a year of work to get that man to fall for me . . . And for what? For you to get handed a free house?" She slams her fist again, fury reemerging.

"Once the affair started," she continues, "I stopped bringing him groceries. It felt demeaning at that point. I'd cook for him, clean for him, do all of it. Then he suggested someone else do the cleaning, and he hired that pretty little bitch."

I swallow back a gasp.

The body.

"M-Marta?" I say.

She leans her head against the wall again, her hair flattening against her skull, and lets out an unpleasant laugh that causes her double chin to jiggle a bit. "Oh, don't act surprised, *Alice*. I caught Victor watching her every now and then through the basement door. He thought she was beautiful. And why wouldn't he? She *was* beautiful. But she was a threat."

It takes everything in me to stay upright.

Is Carla really responsible for killing that poor young woman?

She tried to kill you. She's unhinged.

"So you killed her," I say.

"Yup."

She has no remorse. What the hell is wrong with her?

"Hid her body in the well tunnel for weeks. You know, that shit starts to stink real bad after a while. And Victor, well, he wasn't dying fast enough. A little bit of rat poison goes a long way. All I had to do was move that bitch's body after Victor died. I suppose I could have left it in the well tunnel, but it was ruining my appetite every time I traveled through there."

I stare at her, unable to speak.

"What? Are you confused?" She taps her temple hard and lets out another laugh. "You were probably trying to figure out how someone kept breaking into your house without tripping the alarm. Maybe if you'd looked around a bit more, you'd have found the hatch in the basement. It leads out to the old well in your backyard. You know—the one behind the hedges and out of sight from your precious cameras."

"Victor was a weird man, but that tunnel did wonders for our affair. It's how I got into his house without anyone knowing what was going on. For him, it was an emergency exit. You know, in case he had to escape from his creepy ass basement."

My mouth is so dry I can barely swallow.

I can't believe it was her all along.

She lets out a frustrated grunt and starts smashing her head into the wall behind her. "Idiot! Idiot!"

I can't tell whether she's insulting herself, me, or someone else.

"It wasn't that hard a job, was it?" she says, now smiling big at me. "I mean, all he had to do was come in here and kill you, and I would have never had to get my hands dirty!"

"What—" I start, but then it clicks, and I think I'm going to vomit. "You contacted James."

She's now rolling her head from side to side with a serene smile on her face and her eyelids closed. This woman is clearly on some heavy medication.

"You know, you really should be blaming your boyfriend for this."

"My boyfriend? I don't have—"

She flicks her wrist at me. "The cop. Wyatt, or whatever."

"What does *he* have to do with this?"

"He had a report printed on his desk. All about you. Your past, which you erased when you had your name changed."

This comes as no surprise to me—I'm already aware of Wyatt extracting my record for investigative purposes. But how does Carla know about it?

"It was too easy," she says. "And you know how men are. They'll do just about anything for sex."

What the hell is she talking about? Was I right about Wyatt when I didn't trust him? Was he in on this?

She lets out a cackle, then rolls her head until her neck cracks.

"I mean, I wanted Derek to do it himself, but he said he didn't want to risk his career, or some bullshit."

Derek? Has Carla been sleeping with Derek?

"I kept trying to convince him," she continues. "Told him I saw bruises on Lucas's arm at school, and that I had a bad feeling about you. The bruise thing really got to him." She makes an exaggerated sad face that you'd see in a cartoon. "And that's when he spilled. Said he'd seen your record and knew your real name. A few drinks in him, and I got the info I needed. The rest, well, Facebook can do wonders in tracking family members—even those pesky exes you try so hard to run away from."

I tighten my grip around my knife, even though I have no intention of using it. The police will be here any minute, and Carla will get what she deserves.

"There's one thing I don't understand," I tell her.

She rolls her eyes and laughs. "I'm not surprised."

"I always thought movies and books had it wrong when some psycho reveals everything in the end. You know? They just spill, down to the very last detail, about everything. And I always wondered—why? Why the hell would they confess to everything like that?"

Her smile fades, and a sour look contorts her features.

This time, I'm the one smiling. "I get it now. It's because the bad guy . . . that's *you*"—I twirl my knife a few times, then aim its tip back at her—"is always a fucking narcissist. They have to share with *someone* how much of a *mastermind* they are. Otherwise, what's the point? I mean, someone has to hear it, right? Someone needs to witness their brilliance."

She grimaces, and I get the feeling she's about to jump at me and wrap her hands around my throat. But I'm the one holding the knife. She'd be stupid to do that.

"Here's the thing, Carla," I say. "You aren't a mastermind. You're twisted, and you're sick, and you need severe mental help. And even then, intensive therapy probably wouldn't help you."

She lets out a roar and claws the air, about to get up, when I shout so loudly I feel veins bulge from my neck. "Stay the fuck down!"

I suck in a breath, regaining composure. "As I was saying, I get it. I understand, finally. You want recognition." Still holding the knife, I clap, though it barely makes a sound. "Well, good job, Carla. You tormented me and my family for weeks. Are you *happy*? Do you feel like a *mastermind*?"

She smirks, and I'm tempted to backhand her across the face.

"Well, I've got news for you," I tell her. "You aren't a mastermind. You're a fucking idiot."

Her scowl returns.

"You just confessed to everything. Seriously? I mean, why would you do that? For a short-lived moment of glory?"

"Oh, please," she says. "No one's going to believe a word you say. And after the way you threatened my husband, which is on police record, by the way—well, let's just say you're the one who looks unhinged. Besides, you invited me to live with you, remember? That's why I'm here. You're also the one holding your own kitchen knife."

Yeah, the knife *she* took, which I'll have on video, thanks to my spy cameras.

I must look unimpressed.

As if reading my mind, she snorts and says, "And if

you think your spy cameras are going to save you, think again. You told me all about them in the parking lot, remember? I admit that saved my ass. I wouldn't have known otherwise—" She pauses as if thinking over her luck. "And you can find just about anything online these days."

She looks so proud of herself. It's enough to make me want to slice my knife across her face and give her a permanent smile.

"What are you talking about?" I ask.

"Wi-Fi jammer, hidden camera detector. You know. Basic stuff."

That's not *basic*.

She reaches into her pocket and drops my three tiny spy cameras on the floor next to my feet. "Your micro SD cards are floating with the fish now. And your Internet is down, so there's no cloud footage."

She really *did* think everything through.

Her lips curl up at one corner.

She isn't wrong to think she'll come out innocent in all of this. I suppose she could twist the story, and after everything that's happened, the police would have a very difficult time proving who's telling the truth. Worse, Derek is supposedly sleeping with her. He'll back her up and crush me in a heartbeat.

But there's one advantage I have that she doesn't know about. If she did, she wouldn't be laughing so hard, amused by her own wicked ways.

Her laughter makes me want to hurt her. Especially after everything she's put me through. And to now learn that the body was *her* doing? That *she's* the murderer? She killed an innocent woman over *greed*.

It's all too much.

I grit my teeth, suddenly reminded that my son doesn't talk anymore, thanks to her.

But my focus is drawn to a faint red and blue glow flashing against my bedroom wall. It gets brighter and brighter as the police pull into my driveway.

But Carla still thinks she's ahead of me.

She thinks she's going to talk her way out of this and pin everything on me.

She's wrong.

It takes everything in me not to punch her across the face before Wyatt and Derek come in—and there's someone I don't want to see right now.

Derek.

He'll likely be the first to defend Carla.

He can try. He's going down with her.

Slowly, I unball my fist.

Carla isn't worth my energy. The legal system can take care of her. Besides, what kind of example would I be to my son if I used violence against a mentally ill woman?

"Did you catch all that?" I say, picking up my phone.

I never ended the call with the 911 operator.

Carla's eyes widen, then dart from side to side.

At the same time, Grayson opens the door and wiggles his cell phone. "I got it, too, Mom."

CHAPTER 66

TWO WEEKS LATER

I breathe in the scent of gingerbread cookies and sip on my morning coffee.

"They almost ready?" Grayson asks.

Lucas perks up from a pile of Legos he's working on.

I remind Grayson that the cookies are for commercial purposes only right now. My real estate agent told me that the smell of freshly baked cookies has been proven to help with the sale of a house.

Something about making the atmosphere feel homey.

I'm not sure how anyone could consider this house homey. Two people have now been murdered here. My real estate agent was very candid with me, which I appreciated. She explained that the house's property value has decreased significantly due to the murders.

I don't care about the value.

All that matters to me is getting out.

Carla's in jail, currently awaiting trial. She's pleading not guilty by reason of insanity, but I don't think she'll get away with it. She put *way* too much thought into everything she did.

Derek's been suspended for an indeterminate amount of time for divulging confidential information to a civilian. At first, I was angry with him. But it turns out he never meant any harm. He had genuine feelings for Carla, and she told him she planned on leaving her husband to be with him. He also thought I was abusive toward my children.

Turns out the day I saw Derek at Carla's place, he was

there consoling her after an emotional breakdown. It had nothing to do with her husband, who was on his way home from visiting his ill mother in the South.

The well tunnel has been sealed. I hired contractors to fill it with concrete. I still can't believe Victor went to such extremes to stay hidden from the world. What makes me even more angry is that Carla took advantage of him. She manipulated him into believing she had feelings for him. And for what? His money.

I stare at the antique bronze key on my counter. Wyatt handed it to me the night of Carla's arrest. Apparently, it was used to unlock a gate in the well tunnel. I considered throwing it away, given that the tunnel is now decommissioned, but oddly, I *want* to keep it.

It's a reminder of the horrors I went through and how I *survived*. Because not every woman gets out like I did. I'm one of the lucky ones, and I never want to forget that.

"Not even one?" Grayson asks.

Lucas is standing next to him, a puppy-dog look in his eyes.

I roll my eyes playfully. "Fine. One."

Medora, my real estate agent, will be here any minute. After handing the boys a cookie, I hurry them out of the house and into the car.

As Medora pulls in, I walk up to her shiny BMW, and she lowers her tinted window.

"Emma," she says with a grin.

She tells me to return in about an hour to give her adequate time for the viewing. It's plenty of time to take the boys to Beans & Stuff and treat them to a hot cocoa and a muffin.

We're greeted with a smile when we enter, which makes me feel at ease. Most citizens of Thorn Lake haven't been able to stop staring at us. Word spreads fast, and now everyone knows what happened inside of the Huxley mansion, and that I killed my ex-husband.

I haven't bothered trying to explain my story to anyone. After everything that's happened, I don't have the energy.

If they want to judge me, so be it. I'll be out of here soon enough.

We order our food and sit down at a cute wooden table with a purple ogre ornament at the center. Lucas seems entranced by it. He leans forward, rests his chin on his forearms, and pokes the ogre's plastic eyeball.

I slurp a glob of whipped cream off my hot cocoa. "What do you guys think about Florida?"

Grayson's mug stops midair, right before he takes a sip. "Florida? Why so far away?"

I shrug. "A big change. The heat. And I want to be close to Grandma and Grandpa and Aunt Chloe.

Grayson's eyes soften. I can tell he wants to be close to family, but he's struggling with the idea of leaving Amelia behind.

"I know it's hard," I say. "Leaving people we love."

I think back to my family and to my best friend, Reese. The idea of reaching out terrifies me. We stopped talking years ago, and although I didn't understand why she stopped reaching out—now I do.

It was all James.

I still don't know what he said to push her away, but I intend to find out.

"Family is important," I add.

He nods slowly. "I know. Just sucks."

"I know," I tell him. "But everything will be better now. You'll see. And you'll both make new friends in Florida."

Lucas smiles up at me, whipped cream clinging to the tip of his button nose. I can't help but laugh.

"I was thinking Coconut Creek," I say. "I like the sound of it. Coconut Creek. You know? And the population is a lot higher than here, but it's not a big city by any means. We'll have access to everything we need there. And it's only thirty minutes away from Grandma and Grandpa in Fort Lauderdale."

I considered moving back to Fort Lauderdale, where I grew up. But there are too many memories there. It's where I met James.

"Will there be someone there who can help Lucas?" Grayson asks.

My throat swells.

"There's plenty of psychologists there," I say. "I already looked into it."

I was so busy trying to figure out what was going on that I never really stopped to consider how much of an impact Lucas's mutism was having on Grayson.

He misses his little brother.

"Soon," I say, reaching across the table to tickle Lucas, "we won't be able to shut him up."

Lucas giggles, and I want to reach across the table and hug him as tightly as I can. I can't remember the last time he laughed like that.

He really is getting better.

I set my hot chocolate down and rest my arms on the table, watching them intently. "We'll be okay. I know it."

Grayson doesn't look as sad as he did only seconds ago. There's a hopefulness in his eyes that fills me with joy. "I know, Mom."

Despite the curious eyes watching us inside Beans & Stuff, I get off my chair and open my arms. "Come here. Both of you."

Lucas is the first to jump up. Grayson, despite being a typical embarrassed teenager, gets up and wraps his arms around me. I hold them both and breathe in the scent of Lucas's freshly washed hair.

"We'll be okay," I repeat, and for the first time in as long as I can remember, I believe myself.

EPILOGUE

ONE YEAR LATER

"Come on, Aunt Chloe is waiting," I say, sweeping the air as if this will somehow get Grayson and Lucas to move faster.

"I'm coming," Grayson says lamely.

He waddles past me, his heavy steps filling the entire house. I can't believe how much he's grown in the last year. He's fifteen now, but he looks *eighteen*.

Lucas hurries down the stairs wearing his new Batman hoodie that I bought him for his birthday.

I still can't believe this is happening.

We hurry outside, where my sister Chloe is waiting for us in her minivan. She smiles at the boys, then waves at me with a theatrical grin stretching her face. All that's missing to make this image complete would be her excitedly shaking two balled fists on either side of her face.

The second I open the door, she does exactly that, and I burst out laughing.

"What?" she squeals. "This is so exciting!"

I let out a long, unsteady breath.

"You nervous?" she asks, her big honey-brown eyes wider than I've ever seen them.

"Yeah, a bit," I admit.

She pats my lap. "Don't be. Mom and Dad will be there in fifteen minutes, and you said Reese is coming?"

"That's right," I say.

I'm so grateful that Reese is back in my life. We've been talking again for almost a year now, and it's as if we're right back to the way we used to be—before James.

I told her everything.

The abuse.

The inheritance.

The body.

Me killing James.

She was *happy* about it. She told me he got what he deserved and that I could finally be free.

After telling her everything, she confessed that she received very hostile letters from *me*.

"Obviously, that wasn't me," I told her.

"I know that *now*," she said. "But you were changing, Alice."

I'm still struggling with my name. Part of me wants to change it back to Alice Winslow, but the other part of me wants to leave it as is.

I don't feel like *Alice* anymore. The whole thing is muddling my brain. My parents will never come around to calling me Emma, and even Reese is struggling with it. My sister said she'll try but that old habits die hard. Worse, I don't feel like Emma, either.

Chloe follows her GPS to the address I gave her.

When we pull up to the decrepit redbrick building, I feel like crying and dancing at the same time.

This is really happening.

I reach into my purse for the envelope my real estate lawyer gave me and open it up.

A large metal key slips out and falls into my palm.

My mom and dad are already waiting at the front door, my father rubbing my mom's shoulder as if trying to get her to calm down.

She's as excited as I am.

Lucas and Grayson run out and hug my parents. My dad ruffles Lucas's hair and says, "How you doing, kiddo?"

Lucas smiles up at him. "Good."

Even though he started talking a few months ago, his voice makes me pause. Every time he speaks, I want to cherish the moment.

Reese comes jogging down the sidewalk in a pair of white sneakers and a light sports jacket. She waves at me, and I wave back.

"This is the place?" My dad asks.

"It is," I say.

I'm so excited my teeth are clattering.

It feels much better to be shaking due to excitement than fear.

The contractors arrive on time. Two men step out of a pickup truck and walk to the bed.

"Emma Collins?" one of them asks.

I nod.

"You want it over that sign right there?" The driver points up above the building's doors. He's got a salt-and-pepper beard to his navel and looks like he's been doing this for far too long.

"Yes, please," I say.

"Well," he says. "We cut it according to the measurements we took. Let's hope it fits."

He forces a smile that isn't all that reassuring. I'm not sure whether he's trying to be funny or whether he's made measurement mistakes in the past.

We all step aside as the men get to work, drilling screws while standing at the tops of ladders.

When they're finished, the ladders are removed and stored back in their truck.

I rest a hand over my chest, staring up at the sign above the glass doors.

Wilson House.

A safe house for battered women, in honor of the police officer who saved my life.

I reached out to her again—Emma Wilson—and she was so touched that she booked two weeks' vacation to come down to Coconut Creek to help in any way that I need.

I've also reached out to a martial arts instructor, who graciously agreed to volunteer some hours to teach self-defense classes, and a lawyer, who generously offered her time to guide women through the entire process of a name change, as well as all other legal matters involved during a separation from an abusive partner. Emma Wilson also had a hand in this—she has so many contacts willing to help.

While there are several hundred shelters throughout the country, there won't be one like this.

It used to be an apartment building with a hundred and fifty units. Each unit will be renovated to include five beds.

My goal is to provide a space where we won't have to refuse entry to anyone.

Because that's a huge problem right now. I know—I've been there. Shelters are at full capacity, and women have nowhere to go.

"I'm so proud of you," Reese says.

She wraps an arm around my shoulder and rests her head against mine. My throat swells painfully.

"This will save lives," she says.

"Reese, stop it," I say, no longer able to hold back tears.

She pulls me in for a big hug, and it all comes out.

Then, everyone joins in, and we stand on the sidewalk, group-hugging in the middle of the afternoon.

I'm wiping away my tears and trying to shake off the emotion when my phone vibrates in my pocket.

It's Wyatt.

I stick a finger up, asking everyone to hold their thoughts for a minute. Chloe waggles her eyebrows at me, and I give her my *don't even* look.

"Hey," I answer.

"Hey," Wyatt says. "Am I on time?"

I smile against the phone. "Yeah, they just installed it."

"Can I see?" he asks.

I press on FaceTime, and he appears on my screen. He's on duty with his police uniform, and he looks as ruggedly handsome as ever.

We've been talking almost daily since I moved to Florida, and he's visited at least ten times.

While we aren't exactly dating—I've asked Wyatt

for time, and he's been extremely respectful of my boundaries—we have slept together, and the experience was out of this world.

I turn my screen to the new sign.

"Whoa," he says. "That looks incredible. I'm so proud of you."

I twirl my phone back around so I can see him.

"See you Saturday?" he asks.

I smirk. "Yeah, see you Saturday."

Chloe is still waggling her eyebrows in the distance. After I hang up, she says, "Are you two dating yet?"

I blush. "Not yet, but I'm thinking of making it official this weekend. He's coming down for two weeks. He's been hinting at applying for a job here, but he hasn't really said it. I think he's scared to upset me or to push me away."

"You're saying he might *move* here?" Reese asks.

My mom squeals and claps like a fourteen-year-old girl.

I roll my eyes at everyone and demand that we drop the subject.

"Did you tell them yet?" Chloe asks.

"Tell them what?" I ask.

"You know—" Her eyes go abnormally large. "Tomorrow."

Suddenly, my anxiety is back, and I'm emotional again. "Oh, no . . . I didn't."

I hate getting emotional like this.

My mom's jaw drops open, and she looks at me, then at Chloe, to decipher our code language. "What? What is it?"

Chloe beams and speaks for me. "Local news is coming by tomorrow. They want to do a story on Alice. Apparently, there are already several people who want to help with funding to keep this place up and running. It's going to make national headlines."

"I don't know about national," I say.

"Um, really?" Chloe says. She swipes her open palms through the air as if spreading out an invisible banner.

"Battered woman survives husband's murder attempt and launches a battered women's shelter with her own money."

I smack her on the shoulder.

Well, when she puts it like *that*. The most amazing part is that my blog is becoming more and more popular, which means I'll continue to have a steady income to support this place.

When she finally stops laughing, she wraps an arm around my neck and pulls me in the way Reese did only seconds ago. "Seriously. You did good, Alice."

She stiffens awkwardly, her cheek against mine. "Have you decided yet?"

I look sideways at her. "What?"

"If you want us to keep trying to call you Emma? I mean, I will, if that's what you want—"

"Actually, I have decided," I say. "Just now."

"Oh?" Reese lets out.

"I changed my name to Emma to run away," I say. "To shed my old self to become someone else. Someone capable of escaping James. But that's over. I'm not running anymore. I fought back, and I'm going to keep fighting for every other woman out there."

Chloe is staring at me with sisterly pride. "So . . . "

"Alice," I say. "My name is Alice."

Visit **www.shadeowens.com** for more works by Shade Owens.

Printed in Great Britain
by Amazon

42626660R00212